SPEED TRAP

By Joey Ledford

This book is dedicated to my wonderful wife Beki, my first and best reader, whose advice and encouragement made it possible.

Table of Contents

Prologue

July 1959

Near Astoria, Georgia

The air boiling in through the open windows of her 1953 Studebaker felt like the discharge from a furnace turned up high, but Carly Sue Jennings didn't care. She had never felt so alive. She had finally escaped and was on her way to a new life.

It was close to midnight on the deserted, two-lane highway somewhere in south Georgia. There was a mixture of scents in the air that a New York woman like Carly had never experienced. Part of it was the smell of the coast somewhere off to the east – a rank, swamp-like stink. But there was also the pleasant aroma of the loblolly pines that lined this lonely road and the distinctive scent of the hot asphalt of the road itself. Fireflies blinked in the woods and a new moon was sneaking up beyond the tree line on the horizon. Hank Williams was crooning on her AM radio.

It had been a long hard day of driving and Carly was hot and tired, and her foot was heavy on the gas. It got even heavier in the long straightaways that seemed to be the rule along the coastal plains of south Georgia.

With no warning, Carly Sue had left her husband up in Albany for several good reasons. One, she was tired of being physically and verbally abused and treated like an unloved possession. And two, she suspected she was pregnant and didn't want to bring a child into a world where a drunken father was beating her mother whenever he got angry, drunk or bored. She had stolen the proceeds from his just-cashed paycheck and the keys to the Studebaker and was bound for Florida.

Carly, just 23, hadn't shown much gut or gumption up until now, but she knew in her heart it was time to move on. She figured she could get a job as a hotel maid in some beachside motel, or maybe even sling some hash in a Florida diner. She could cook and clean. A high school graduate, those were about the only skills she had brought out of her life and her two-year failed marriage.

Like most people riding into Hyde County, Georgia, on U.S. 55, Carly Sue's mind was on anything but her speedometer. So when she saw the blue lights of the law in her rear view mirror, she let go with a loud swear word that she had once promised her mother she'd never repeat.

SPEED TRAP

The big burr-headed cop who pulled off the road behind her left his headlights on so he could keep a wary eye on his prey. He didn't often work speed at night, but when he did, he enjoyed it. It was his world, and he ruled it supremely. He pulled his 6-foot-3, 240 pound frame out of the squad car, tapped his holster to make sure his piece was in its place, and also felt the reassuringly comfortable rub of his trusty billy club on his left leg. He loved his job because nobody else had this kind of power and control. When he had a motorist pulled over, he felt like God Almighty himself.

Carly Sue rolled down the window, produced her license and registration on demand, and immediately began pleading for mercy. She didn't mean to be speeding, but even if she was, she was driving safe, she declared. Besides, she hadn't seen another car in at least five minutes.

The cop rolled his eyes at that comment, but he had to admit he liked what he saw behind the Studebaker's wheel. She had long brown hair and was slim. He liked slim girls.

"You was speeding, Miss Jennings and frankly, we don't give a whit's damn around here how safe you think you was driving. You are guilty, and I need $35."

Carly was shocked at the bold demand for money up front. Almost all her cash was stowed in a false compartment in her suitcase in the trunk. She pulled her wallet from her purse and saw she had just $21 and change.

"This is all I have," she lied.

"Really?" asked the cop, whose face curled into a sneer. "I'm going to have to ask you to get out of your car and come back to the squad car."

Carly Sue had a pretty good sense of when she was in a bad way because of her life experiences to that point. This was not good at all.

"Why would I have to do that?" she asked, her fear rising to terror as she saw hate and devilish intent in the officer's dark eyes.

"Are you resisting arrest?" he asked.

"No, but why would you arrest me?"

"You are, as I see it, about $14 short."

She was about to offer to get the rest of the money, but before she could say a word, the cop had opened her door, pulled her out of the car and roughly began walking her back to the police cruiser. He reached inside his window and turned off his headlights and flashing blue dome, which she considered quite strange.

Then he walked her to the side of the car away from the highway and ordered her to lay her face on the squad car's hot hood. She complied, and the cop proceeded to fondle her, first her breasts, then between her legs. She screamed, and he responded by reaching up and thumping her head – hard – against the hood. Carly Sue was stunned, and was now gasping for breath. So much so that she could no longer scream.

Now the cop opened the back door of his squad car and moved her towards it. She thought about bolting and running for the woods, but she knew he was bigger, faster and stronger and he knew this country. She didn't.

He pushed her into the car, head first, and before she could do anything else, he had reached between her legs, hiked up her skirt, and ripped off her panties. She somehow regained the ability to scream, and did, loudly. But in the dark Georgia night, there was no one to hear it.

He pulled a handkerchief from his pocket and it became a gag. He put handcuffs on her flailing hands, with which she had begun to try to defend herself.

There in the backseat of the squalid squad car, which reeked of sweat and puke and beer, the cop raped Carly Sue Jennings. All she could do was whimper and shake with fright. She found herself thinking that she might as well have just stayed home in Albany and taken the same medicine from her miserable husband.

It didn't take him long to finish the deed, and he promptly pulled her back out of the squad car, feet first this time. He removed the gag, and then the handcuffs, and looked at her with a strained smile on his face. He handed Carly her ripped panties.

"I guess that was worth $14," he said. "I've had worse. Many times.

"You get on out of here, honey. I'd strongly recommend you don't come back here ever again."

In pain, bleeding and sobbing, Carly Sue returned to her car. Within seconds, the cop had made his getaway. She never saw his name on any identity badge. Nor had she even read the identifying words on the squad car.

Carly quickly considered her options. It was not like she could report this crime to the police – the police had committed it. To her knowledge, not a single car had passed and none were in sight now. Carly didn't even know exactly where she was, but she knew she didn't want to be there any longer.

Carly started the Studebaker and quickly decided to do nothing but continue her trip. After all, she was already pregnant. And being raped was nothing new. This time, though, the rapist hadn't been her husband. It had been a police officer, someone people expected to trust, to serve and to protect, not to rob and rape.

Tears still flowing down her face, Carly drove away. She watched her speedometer far too much for the remainder of her journey across the state line into Florida.

Carly didn't know it, but she had just driven through Astoria, Georgia. Speed Trap, USA.

Chapter One

Three days later

Georgia State Trooper First Class Calvin Bocock was confused, so he asked the dispatcher to repeat herself after she had passed along his assignment for the day shift.

"You want me to do what?" he barked into his radio microphone, a decided departure from State Patrol protocol. He was curtly informed he had heard it right the first time.

"You are to join Units 35 and 64 and guard the billboard on Highway 55 outside Astoria," replied Dispatcher Angela Davis, who managed to pass along the ridiculous order without a hint of emotion in her voice.

"Guard it from what, termites?" asked Bocock.

There was a long delay before Davis responded, with a coded instruction to call GSP headquarters in Atlanta and speak to the shift commander. Bocock sighed as he realized his sharp tongue had gotten him in trouble yet again.

He pulled off U.S. 12 at a white clapboard diner called Lil's Place. The cigarette-smoking waitress pointed to a pay phone near the restrooms and soon Bocock was talking with Maj. Samuel Westbrook, a 30-year veteran nearing retirement.

"Bocock, I know this sounds like bullshit, but these orders come from on high," said Westbrook. "Like the highest place they could come from, the governor's office.

"Don't say anything, just listen to me. The governor has had it up to here with the boys running the show down in Astoria and Hyde County. He's declared war on them."

"With a damn billboard?" asked Bocock. "Is he tryin' to sell them something?"

Westbrook was getting impatient. "Get in your damn squad car and get on down to Astoria. Pickens and Sloan are already there and they were briefed at length yesterday. They can explain. You were added on at the last minute."

"I understand, Major," said Bocock. "I guess it became clear it takes three Georgia state troopers to guard a damn billboard."

Bocock got another tongue lashing about his wisecracking nature, and even though he had been ordered to double-time it the 38 miles on down to Astoria, he decided billboard duty could wait long enough for him to answer nature's call and order a cup of black coffee for the road.

"This is clearly why I chose a career in law enforcement," he said to no one but himself as he pulled back onto the highway.

SPEED TRAP

Bocock was 26 years old, two years out of the Georgia Police Academy. He was a good trooper and knew it, and despite his proclivity to shoot off his mouth on occasion, he had generally good performance reviews. A native of Dahlonega in the north Georgia mountains, Bocock was single, sandy haired and attractive to the young ladies who often commented about how good he looked in uniform. He was six feet tall and weighed 179 pounds, and even though his mother bugged him regularly about girlfriends, he never seemed to get attached to anyone. Perhaps it was a fear of loss stemming from the war.

His dad was a World War II veteran with a Silver Star and was also a peace officer. In fact, he was police chief in Dahlonega. His mom had been a typical tend the home fires housewife, raising Cal and his two brothers and one sister. Cal had followed in his father's footsteps, enlisting in the Marines and serving in Korea. He had earned a Purple Heart though he dismissed the shrapnel hit he suffered in a firefight as a mere flesh wound. In truth, he had risked his life to save four wounded Marines, and only two of them made it home. One who didn't had been his best friend.

What Bocock liked most about being a state trooper was the relative freedom and lack of supervision. Most troopers rode alone, and most days were spent patrolling Georgia's many miles of two-lane highways, writing tickets, responding to wrecks, assisting local police, but also occasionally getting involved in some real police work when crime erupted, as it did on occasion in the rural, sandy flatlands of coastal Georgia.

Bocock emerged from his open road daydream when he saw the object of the day's assigned duties looming over the right side of bustling U.S. 55, a major north-south route between the Northeast and Florida.

Trooper Oscar Sloan was already in place, looking bored and angry. Passing autos slowed to read the billboard, some blowing their horns, earning a steely glare from the stoic trooper. When Bocock digested the contents of the message on the big wooden banner, he laughed out loud.

"BEWARE!" it began in bold black type that took about one third of the entire billboard, which was about the width of the police cruiser sitting below its standards. "You are in Hyde County and are approaching Astoria, Georgia. Don't get fleeced in a CLIP JOINT. Don't get caught in a SPEED TRAP."

At the bottom was the cursive signature of Georgia's colorful, populist governor, Buford L. Dunlap.

Sloan, a 10-year veteran of the patrol, nodded at Bocock as he climbed out of his squad car. Even though it was still only 8 a.m., it was clear it was going to be an especially steamy July day in south Georgia. "Welcome, Cal. Ready for some serious guard duty?"

Before Bocock could reply, Wayne Pickens, the second trooper, popped out of the woods where he had apparently just taken a bathroom break. "Hi, Cal. What took you? Now that you're here, I'd better get to the other one."

"The other one?" Bocock cried. "You mean there are two of these God-forsaken things?"

"Why yeah, Cal," Pickens drawled matter of factly. "This one warns the southbound tourists. The one on the other side of town warns the northbounders."

"Of course," said Bocock. "We obviously need maximum coverage."

Gov. Buford Dunlap chomped on his cigar, red-faced and fuming as he read yet another letter of complaint, this one from Atlantic City, New Jersey. It was letters like these, hundreds of phone calls, and an increasing number of newspaper stories that had incited his wrath. And if you knew Buford Dunlap, the last thing you wanted was to incite his wrath.

"Governor," wrote the motorist, "I know you guys are out in the backwater and hurting for money, but must you pull over every single tourist who passes through your pitiful state? It cost me $35 to obtain safe passage from this hamlet you call Astoria, all because I was supposedly a measly 3 mph over your punitive speed limit."

Dunlap penned a quick note to his secretary, Bonnie Triplett, to send the surly traveler the standard Hyde County apology letter. This was why Dunlap had taken the unusual step of ordering up the two warning billboards. Despite the considerable powers of the Georgia governor, who sits under an impressive and historic gold-plated dome in the Capitol Building in Atlanta, there was not much he could do to keep the two-bit crooks in Astoria from bilking nearly every tourist passing through on their way to and from the sunny beaches of Florida.

It wasn't just constant speed traps being run by officers who hid in the bushes and brambles along U.S. 55 and another byway, State Route 42. There was also a notorious stop light in downtown Astoria that had a way of changing from green to red with no yellow in between right before an out-of-state motorist passed underneath.

There was also the issue of at least three so-called "clip joints" in Hyde County beyond Astoria's city limits. The subject of complaints from several states, these little concrete holes of hell looked like tourist gift shops from the road. And they did offer a wealth of tacky junk, ranging from plastic toy alligators to cloth bags containing sea shells, sand dollars and starfish; beaded belts supposedly made by real Georgia Indians and an assortment of velvet paintings. There were also cold Co-Colas, as the merchants called them, boiled peanuts, crackers and snack cakes.

But the real reason for the joints was a harmless looking game of chance called "Razzle Dazzle." Tourist dads and unsuspecting truckers were lured into the game with offers of free rolls of the dice. That first roll always left the player a dollar or two ahead of nothing, so naturally the inclination was to keep on rolling, especially when the huckster with the bad teeth and big promises made it clear there was a prize of $1,750 or more ready to be taken.

It helped that the "dealer" always played the role of ignorant country bumpkin, while the Northern tourist who had arrived in a big boxy Buick with a healthy bankroll for the beach usually carried an air of superiority.

Players earned points and the goal was ten. It was easy to get nine or so, but the tenth was literally impossible to earn. The sly dealer had a points conversion chart that seemed legit, but the bottom line was that the only possible winner at Razzle Dazzle was the man who held the chart and owned the dice.

Tourist after tourist lost hundreds of dollars playing the game.

Dunlap grimaced every time a letter of complaint crossed his desk. The billboard tactic was almost a last resort, but it wasn't the final salvo in the battle. He had decided he was going to see if the billboards did any good before waiting to play his final cards.

####

Fewer than 4,000 souls resided in Hyde County, with about half of them located in or near Astoria. It was close enough to the coast that some residents scrapped out a rough living on shrimp boats or along the docks where the seafood was processed. There was a textile mill as in most Southern towns of the era, but wages were low and the work was tiring and repetitive. Some major landowners raised cotton, but some had begun to move to peanuts or soybeans. Some people kept a cow or two or several pigs. There was also a sawmill and a logging company that harvested the shortleaf and slash pines that dominated the flat, sandy forests.

In town, there was a bank, two schools for the white children and one for blacks, integration still on the horizon. There was a dry goods store, a hardware, a grocery store, a hotel, a movie theatre and the county courthouse, a smallish brick building with a spire that made it look a bit more like a church than a government center. And there were churches, of course, Astoria being located near the buckle of the Bible Belt. There were three of them, one for Baptists, a second for Primitive Baptists and a third for Methodists. There were smaller community churches dotting the backroads outside town.

Making a living had always been hard in Astoria and Hyde County. People being the way they are, they tended to take advantage of the resources the environment left them. The best resources available were U.S. 55 and State Route 42 and the never-ending string of vacationing Yankee tourists. One widely quoted report claimed one million cars a year streamed through Astoria on their way north or south. It became the Hyde County way of life to be able to milk a living out of that steady traffic flow. Folks got darn good at it. Some might call it creative. Others would not be as charitable.

According to local legend, even Astoria's name had its origins in a grand scam. In the 1830s, it became known that John Jacob Astor, a merchant, investor and fur trader who was America's first known millionaire, was scouring the country looking for ways to invest his burgeoning fortune. One of the town's founding fathers came up with the innovative idea of writing Astor and offering to name the town after him in exchange for money, investment or other favors.

Excited about the prospect of the great man answering the call to form an outpost near the Georgia coast, the new settlement became known as Astoria. Apparently, Astor never even bothered to answer the letter. The name, however, stuck anyway. Maybe the Southerners got the last laugh about the deal that was never struck a century later when Astoria's powerful perfected the art of gathering money from Northerners like Astor with thick wallets.

Ledford, Joey

Chapter Two

Six months before the billboards

Patrolman Wesley Crane of the Astoria Police Department told anyone who asked that he loved his job. Why wouldn't he? In addition to his hourly wage, which by itself was pretty average for small town Georgia cops, Crane and his fellow patrolmen had a special benefit that few officers enjoyed.

He got a cut from every ticket he wrote. And Crane wrote a lot of tickets.

"I'm so bad I whup my own ass twice a week," Crane liked to tell his drinking buddies at Bart Taggart's beer joint, where he was generous enough to buy a round on occasion. He made enough money to easily make the payment on his family's trailer and buy Dorothy, his wife, a piece of costume jewelry on occasion. His 12-year-old son, Bobby, rode a J.C. Higgins bicycle his proud dad had personally selected at the Sears and Roebuck store down in Savannah.

17

"It's not a bad life at all for a country cop," he often told himself as he fought his way through the Monday morning hangover to go assume his position out on U.S. 55.

There was more than one good staging area, but Crane's favorite was about a half mile south of the bridge spanning the Altamaha River. The county road boys had paved a great little ambush spot, mostly shielded from the road by pines and thick underbrush. Crane would sit in his black and white V8 Chevy catty-cornered to 55. He would aim his radar gun back over his right shoulder where he had a good view of oncoming traffic. It never took many shots to hit his next victim because the two-lane road was ramrod straight and the miles between New Jersey and Miami were so long and so boring that virtually everyone had the hammer down.

"That road's as long as a country woman's clothesline," Crane liked to say.

This morning's first duck on the pond was a red 1956 Ford Fairlane. Crane grinned when he knew his first shot of the day had scored – 71 mph in the 50 mph zone.

The big Biscayne's well-tuned engine growled as Crane hit the gas and emerged onto 55, its siren screaming, its blue light flashing. The G-forces pushed Crane back in his seat, the car's power becoming his own. As was usually the case, the Fairlane's driver quickly realized his fate and pulled over a quarter-mile beyond the bridge in an all too convenient wide strip of right of way.

Thomas England was on his way to Fort Lauderdale with his wife Carolyn and two kids, Brad, 10, and Sandy, 4. Carolyn was ranting at her husband as Crane approached the driver's side window. The two kids were wide-eyed as they stared at the towering patrolman and his formidable looking sidearm.

"I told you to slow down, Thomas!" said the stocky Carolyn as her husband began a slow burn. Sandy promptly burst into tears.

"What's the problem, officer?" asked England, a line Crane had probably heard a thousand times.

"Sir, you was exceeding our speed limit. Please hand me your driver's license and your registration."

"Uh, I can't imagine I was too far over the limit," stammered England, as he dug into his back pants pocket for a battered brown billfold. Crane was happy to see the billfold contained lots of cash.

"Sir, the cemetery's full of folks smarter'n me, but I am pretty good at operatin' and readin' a radar gun," Crane said with a practiced drawl. "You was going 71 and our posted speed limit here right outside of town is 50."

"Fifty?" argued England as his wife focused her glare on the bickering men. "I didn't see a sign."

"You should pay more attention to the road, sir," replied Crane. "There was a speed limit sign right after you passed that little fruit stand." The officer's line was a bit tongue-in-cheek because he knew full well that the sign was pretty much obscured by a live oak that towered over the roadway.

"Well, I sure didn't see it," England said, surrendering the piece of paper that declared him a legal driver in New Jersey as well as the Fairlane's registration.

"Thank you, sir, I'll be right back. If you want to save yourself some time, you can have $35 in cash awaitin' on me when I get back."

"Thirty-five dollars? For a speeding ticket?"

"Yes sir, that's what the Hyde County rates are," said Crane, who added, menacingly, "I could do an inspection and make sure your lights and brakes and other matters are law-worthy. That would up your bill a bit, I believe, since most of you Northern folks are kinda careless with your automobile maintenance." He added extra drawl on "Northern," which clearly communicated his distaste for all things Yankee.

"No, that's OK. You go write the ticket. I'll have the money," the red-faced tourist said.

Crane had his pre-ticket shit-eating grin on his face as he returned to the squad car. Sometimes, if a motorist acted as reckless as a hen on a hot rock or did too much mouthing off, he'd call Carole on dispatch and have her call the motorist's home state to find out if there was any outstanding warrants or holds on the license. They'd been warned not to do that too much, though, because it was a sure-fired way to fire up the Yankees about the Astoria speed trap, and that resulted in newspaper stories and political pressure from Atlanta. Crane tried to save his call-ins for sure bet felony arrests or to punish drivers who had really pissed him off. Because, as you might expect, it took Carole a while to check somebody out since she talked slow and didn't think much faster most days.

Crane pulled out his well-worn ticket book and broke out two new pieces of carbon paper. There needed to be three copies of each ticket, and he had to press heavily enough that the third copy was readable because that one was his. No ticket, no $5, and $5 was a mighty nice payoff for 10 or 15 minutes worth of police work.

He was a bit regretful that speeding was all he could pin on England because that wallet and that bright new Fairlane made it clear that he was so rich he probably bought a new car every time the old one got dirty.

The ticket was written post-haste and Crane returned to England's window for his payoff.

The Jersey man had a crisp new twenty, a ten and a five waiting, just as Crane had planned. He didn't even tell him the bit about how he could come back and fight the ticket in Astoria

Municipal Court a month from Thursday because he knew well England didn't want to see him or this stretch of road ever again.

"Thank you, sir," he said, flashing a five-dollar smile that included a gold-plated incisor. "It's nice doin' business with ya."

Crane knew from experience that the wife would be tearing poor old England a new one and the kids would have lots of questions. The Fairlane wasn't even running yet and Crane had already done a U-turn (technically illegal but allowable for a peace officer) and was on his way back to his ambush spot to repeat the ritual. This was going to be great day, nice and cool but not cold, a perfect south Georgia January morning.

"Thomas, that was a lot of money," Carolyn nagged as her husband turned the ignition to resume their long trip. "That is coming out of what you would be spending on cocktails once we get to the beach."

"The hell," her husband replied. "What just happened may easily result in my consuming even more alcohol than I would have previously."

"The children!" she said, aghast at her husband's crude language.

"Yep, there they are, right in the backseat where they belong."

On cue, Brad piped up. "Dad, did you come close to going to jail there?" he asked. "That guy had a big gun. Would he have used it on you?"

"You know, Brad, in a hick town like this one, I might have gone to jail had I not had some cash money handy," Thomas said candidly, and accurately as well. "And that hayseed probably wouldn't have shot me, but he likely had a big old billy club that he might have slapped me around with had I not paid him off."

Brad's eyes popped and his mouth flew open. "Gosh, dad! That's scary!"

"Yes it is, son. Yes it is. It's been scary down here ever since the War Between the States."

Chapter Three

North of Astoria on the left side of State Route 42 stood a stark, concrete block building with a wooden sign hanging over the door. "Melvin's," it said, which prompted some curious tourists to ask, "Melvin's what?"

That would elicit a gap-toothed grin from the 63 year old proprietor of Melvin's, Melvin Guthrie. Guthrie, who had a pot belly and skin that appeared to have never experienced sunshine, had been in business for nearly 30 years.

During that time, Melvin's establishment only had seen one paint job, that one during a particularly prosperous 1952 when Guthrie was a little worried that Tom Stokes' place a couple of miles south was snaking off some of his business due to Stokes' impressive new neon sign.

Guthrie loved his job and played his role quite well. And despite his gee golly gosh country boy ways, he was quite worldly and rarely found himself in a situation where he was not going to pocket a profit. He never admitted to anyone how much money he made. Most of the time he was cajoled to talk about his business, it was to bemoan his expenses and the fact that not enough people stopped. To hear Melvin say it, he just barely got by.

An hour or two after Wesley Crane had his encounter with the England family south of town, a couple from York, Pennsylvania pulled into Melvin's. Vernon and Darlene Crabtree were driving a blue Studebaker, its distinctive round hood ornament looking a bit like a stubby nose to match the car's eye-like headlights.

Darlene was thirsty and was pleased to see Melvin had a cold drink cooler. The open metal box was filled to the brim with cold soft drinks, ice and water. Darlene found herself a Nehi Orange and was also happy to see bags of pecans for sale, one of which she carried with her to the cash register.

As Melvin was ringing up the merchandise, he looked at Vernon and grinned. "You know this purchase qualifies you for a free roll of Dazzle," he said.

"What's Dazzle?" asked Crabtree, who was an ironworker by trade.

"Razzle Dazzle is the ultimate fun game," said Melvin, who might have been a public relations practitioner in a different era. "It is sweeping the nation. I can't believe you haven't heard about it. Heck, I can't believe you don't know anyone who has won."

"Won what?" said Vernon, his curiosity adequately piqued.

"Why, money of course. Lots of it," said Melvin. "I give away big jackpots all the time."

"Gambling is legal in Georgia?" asked Vernon, who secretly dreamed of traveling to Vegas to play the slots.

"Sure it is! Special local ordinance."

"Well, how does this work?"

Melvin launched into a detailed explanation of the game designed to confuse a certified public accountant. It involved the throwing of eight dice and the scoring of points on each roll based on that total's location on a paper conversion chart.

"Normally, the first roll costs $1, but since you have made a qualified purchase, you can roll once for free," Melvin said, handing Vernon a cup containing eight well-worn, faded white dice. "A roll of eight or 64 is an automatic winner, and I think the jackpot today is more than $400."

Vernon looked at Darlene, who shrugged her shoulders. Now seeing himself as a big-time Vegas high-roller, he took the cup from Melvin.

"Well, I guess one roll wouldn't hurt," he said.

Vernon shook the cup, blew into it, then rolled the dice into a faded green velvet-lined box that Melvin had caused to materialize from under the counter.

Calculating far faster than Vernon could, Melvin said, "Wow, forty-seven! That's worth eight points."

"That's good, huh?" grunted Vernon.

"Why that's great!" Melvin chirped, ignoring the fact that he had cheated – in Vernon's favor. "With eight points, you only need two more to take that jackpot with you down to the beach. Why I bet you could upgrade to a suite at the Fontainebleau with all this money."

Vernon had a vague recollection that the Fontainebleau was a big hotel in Miami, but Miami was the furthest thing from his mind at this point. He was seeing only green.

His first roll, which "only cost you a dollar," got him no closer to ten. But eight is so close, right?

The second roll cost $2. Each roll doubled in price. After several rolls, Vernon got suspicious of Melvin's quick counts and insisted he count himself, and then check the total on the chart. But the last two points remained amazingly elusive.

At one point six rolls in, Vernon rolled a 16, which got him to nine points and made him absolutely sure that victory was at hand.

But as gamblers who know Razzle Dazzle know so well, there isn't any way to win without beating some astronomical odds. It was Darlene who finally grabbed Vernon's sweaty hand after his tenth roll.

"Vernon, that's enough!" she said.

It was like he was awakened from a deep sleep. Emotion rolled across his face and his hands began to shake. Melvin, meanwhile, did his absolute best to look sympathetic. He wasn't really very good at that.

"Well, sir," you owe the house $1,024," he said. "I'm really surprised because I thought you had me there once or twice. Just one mark off."

Vernon, stupefied by his debt, thought about bolting and running for the Studebaker, but he suddenly noticed that Kelley, Melvin's burly 28 year old son, had appeared in the doorway, a Little League baseball bat in his hand. Clearly, Kelley's job was to ensure that marks like Vernon paid their debts.

Realizing his only two choices were paying up or meeting the business end of that baseball bat, Vernon wearily pulled out his wallet. He had bought a few dollars of gas up around Augusta, leaving him with only $968 in his wallet. That was several weeks pay, far more than he needed for the couple's vacation, but Vernon believed in being prepared. However, this time, he wasn't prepared enough.

"This is all I got," he said after a long and laborious count, looking nervously at Kelley, who was stretching a bit and looking ready to load up.

"Now this is highly irregular," said Melvin, when in truth it happened nearly every day. "Our customers are pretty responsible people and they pay their debts in full. So I wonder what we're going to work out here."

Melvin scratched his bald head, paused for a minute, and then, like King Solomon, whose wise ruling with an infant child claimed by two women saved the baby from being chopped in two, he issued his decree.

"It looks to me like you have a fairly decent gold watch on your wrist," he said. "Even though I doubt it is worth anywhere close to the $56 you still owe me, I'm going to accept it as payment and let you be on your way."

Grateful he was not going to be beaten, Vernon unstrapped the buckle of his rectangular Bulova, which, as Mel noted, was not worth nearly that much, even though it was almost new, and handed it to the grinning huckster.

The Pennsylvania couple backed towards the door, Darlene still clutching her Nehi.

"Oh ma'am," added Melvin with a sweet smile, "That will be 5 cents deposit for that bottle."

With as much dignity as she could muster, Darlene downed the last few ounces of Nehi, turned and put the bottle into the rack by the door.

"That'll be fine," grinned Melvin. "We'll waive that charge if you leave the bottle with us."

Back in the car, Vernon quickly pointed the Studebaker south, only to realize within a mile that with no money in his pocket, there would be no Florida vacation. In fact, when the last of that Georgia gasoline had worked its way through the carburetor, the couple would be stranded on the road with no way to get home.

Vernon pulled over and did something that Darlene had not seen him do in more than 30 years of marriage. He burst into tears and began to cry. Darlene thought about comforting him, but realized she just didn't have it in her. Instead, she reached across the Studebaker's big seat and slapped him right on his red nose.

"You stupid son of a bitch!" she cried, her pity quickly transforming to righteous anger. "You know I've been waiting on this trip to Florida for 20 years and you blow all our money throwing dice? What you have done is so stupid it's like wiping your butt before you go poop!"

Stung by the slap and further sobered by her words, all Vernon could do was wail a little bit louder.

Nearly 30 minutes has passed before he had composed himself enough to turn the car north and start on the sad and silent drive home. Of course, without his watch, he didn't know how long it had been.

Hopefully, he thought, he'd be able to get his brother to wire him some money so they could get there.

When they passed Melvin's, the gambling man was standing out front. He saw the Studebaker, raised his hand and waved like only rural Southerners could.

"Y'all come back now, hear?" he shouted before bursting into a roar of evil laughter.

SPEED TRAP

Chapter Four

In the very heart of Astoria was the mechanism that came to symbolize the corruption of the place. It seemed no different than any other traffic signal in the United States – unless you happened to have out of state license plates and had the misfortune to roll into the intersection of U.S. 55 and Main Street at the wrong time.

What would happen to you then would definitely cause you to do a double take. Motorists were astounded to see it happen, and it happened multiple times most days. Locals would see it during their errands about town and would merely snicker and occasionally pause to watch the ensuing mini-drama.

The light would turn from green to red in an instant – the very instant your Ford or Chevy was passing through the intersection. The other direction's traffic flow would remain unaffected, meaning the tomfoolery associated with the Astoria red light would only lead to moving violations, not collisions.

How it worked was ingenious, if you can consider anything associated with fraud ingenious. The Astoria Police Department had permanent possession of a second-floor room in the Astoria

Hotel. The windows of Room No. 16 provided a panoramic view of oncoming traffic, primarily to allow the operators, who had binoculars, to catch a glimpse of the license plate, which was on the front and back of most cars. It was a matter of friend or foe. If the Ford, Chevy or Cadillac approaching the intersection belonged to a local with a Georgia tag, the light performed just as hundreds of thousands of others around the country and the car either passed through the light without incident or proceeded after the light turned green.

But it was a different story if the tag was from out of state. That prompted the operator to pick up his switch, which was connected via wiring directly to the light. As the vehicle approached the intersection – when it was clearly too late to slam on the brakes – the operator flipped a switch.

As if by magic, green became red, without benefit of the customary warning yellow. Many times, the motorist had no idea what had happened, but most often, he or she was immediately irate, because in those days, most people were law-abiding and did not like the thought of running a red light.

As the violation occurred, the operator, usually Theo Sullivan, called "Sully" for short, a friend of the town's police chief, would radio a description of the car to a waiting police unit. That would repeat the scenario experienced by motorists caught in the speed trap: a traffic stop, the writing of a ticket, and the on-the-spot collection of $35. Sully was paid under the table an amount unrelated to how many lights he changed, but the ticketing officer got a cut just like Crane and his colleagues got from working the speed trap.

On this particular January morning, the ninth mark of the shift proved to be a problem. Astoria Officer Colin Smith, whose girth and buzz-cut dark-hair were remarkably similar to Crane's, found himself unable to collect from the driver of a 1954 Chevy BelAir.

Amos Canton of Baltimore, Maryland, the driver of the BelAir, wasn't the typical southbound tourist. Canton was a close-to-the-edge drifter who was ready for a change and hoped to find a laborer's job in Florida where he wouldn't have to freeze his ass off every day. It was just like the luck that Canton felt he always had that this red light blitzed out and this country cop was working to get his last dollar.

And even if he succeeded, it wouldn't add up to 35.

Smith was getting angry because time he spent trying to collect was time he could not spend stopping the next car.

"Bud, it seems to me you got two choices. You can give me $35, or you can accompany me to the city jail."

"You're really going to take me to jail because I can't come up with $35?" asked Canton. "What about a citation that I can mail in after I get a job and raise the money? That's what happened to me in Baltimore when I got a speeding ticket."

"Dorothy, you ain't in Kansas anymore," replied the geographically-challenged Smith with a hateful glare. "Have you got $30?"

Amazed at the question, Canton paused, and then told the truth. "I have about $16, which I figured would get me to Florida. I have a friend there who knows where I can get work."

Smith wasn't interested in a half-price ticket. "OK bub, out of the car."

"You're kidding me, right?"

"Do I look like I'm kidding? I don't kid around with assholes."

Canton thought about getting out of the car and taking Smith down, but the fact that the officer had his right hand on his sidearm ended that illusion. He got out of the car and obeyed Smith's orders to put his face down on the BelAir's trunk and spread his legs for a search.

Smith discovered that his mark had pretty much told the truth – he found $16.35 on him, along with a handwritten letter from a man in Ocala, Florida. Sure enough, it appeared to be from a friend and told of a construction company that was hiring laborers.

The officer roughly tapped the back of Canton's head with a billy club, and after taking the ignition keys from the BelAir, ordered Canton to stay put as he returned to his squad car.

"Sully, shut 'her down," he said into the radio.

"Dispatch, over," he said.

Carole Friedlander, the city police department's dispatcher and woman of many talents, came on the radio. "What is it, Colin?"

"I have a freeloader here at Decker and 55. Send a driver to get this Chevy BelAir and I'm bringing one in."

He looked back at Canton. "Roll out the red carpet."

Sully was directed to fetch the BelAir and drive it to the city's impound lot. He walked down the steps by the Greyhound bus station and hiked down to where Smith and the now-handcuffed Canton were waiting by the Maryland man's turquoise and white four-door sedan.

"Sully, I thought I told you to avoid singles," Smith muttered under his breath. "These damn singles don't have the money to pay and this is costing us time and money."

"I'm sorry, Colin. It gets busy up there and sometimes I can't see through the windshields."

"You're as windy as a sackful of farts," Smith said as he handed the lackey the keys. He unceremoniously stuffed Canton into his patrol car and headed off to the station, less than a mile away.

Intake was remarkably efficient at the Astoria City Jail, not surprising considering the lockup was accustomed to accepting several new customers every day. Friedlander asked Canton some questions, closely examined his driver's license, and then asked him if he could call someone to wire him $20.

Canton expressed surprise that the ticket was now $20 considering Smith had demanded $35. Friedlander replied that it looked like he had already partially paid.

"You are taking all my money?" cried Canton. "How am I going to get to Florida?"

"I guess that's your problem, hon," said the dispatcher, who was sucking on a Camel. "So who can you call?"

"I don't have any family and I don't have any friends who are going to just up and send me $20," said Canton. "Can I serve overnight and pay it off that way?"

"This ain't no luxury hotel," said the woman, grimacing and snarling at the same time. "Are you sure you can't call your dad, or uncle, or grandmother, or President Eisenhower?" That was a regular line, and Friedlander always laughed at her own jokes.

"I got nobody," said Canton. "My ex-wife is as broke as I am."

Friedlander sighed and called out, "Popsi!" Canton thought she was referring to the soft drink and considered it a strange time to get thirsty.

But then a big man appeared over Friedlander's shoulder. "He's all yours, Popsi," said the dispatcher.

Buck "Popsi" Colanaise, who wore no uniform nor a badge, shoved Canton away from the intake window and down a narrow hall. He steered the protesting man into a small concrete block room, about 10 by 10 feet square. He closed the door and leered at

Canton. The room seemed even smaller after the olive-skinned man, who was about 6-feet-3 and weighed at least 250 pounds, knocked Canton to the floor and loomed over him.

"I'm going to give you one more chance to remember somebody to call," snarled Popsi. "You need to go deep now because you won't like what I'm going to do to you."

Canton was shaking with fright. He honestly had no one in the world he could count on to wire him $20, or even $5 for that matter. He quickly dismissed a strange notion that suddenly came to him that it might be a good idea to make some more friends.

Popsi pulled Canton to his feet, and the handcuffed mark noticed for the first time that his adversary wore a pair of imposing brass knuckles. Seconds later, he felt their impact for the first time. It would not be the last.

Screaming, Canton pleaded for mercy, but Popsi clearly enjoyed this part of his job. "You sumbitch, you had your chance. Now you're going to pay up in blood."

####

When Canton awoke the next morning, he was so sore he could hardly open his eyes. Then he realized he could open only one of them – the right one was swollen shut. He was in a cell about half the size of Popsi's reception room. There was no furniture other than a filthy toilet and he was lying on a cold concrete floor.

In about an hour, a uniformed officer appeared, and Canton assumed he was about to be served some breakfast. Instead, the officer asked him again for someone he could call on his behalf. "I got nobody," Canton sobbed.

"Well, get off your ass," said Officer Curly Walton, who, like the famous TV and movie stooge, was bald. Canton was ushered back into the same hall, and down the opposite direction. The two went out the back door of the police station into an alley and Canton was pushed into an unmarked Oldsmobile.

The officer started the car and proceeded to pull away from the station, out of town, into a wooded rural area.

"Don't kill me, man, I'll ... I'll do any kind of work to pay my debt!"

Walton burst into laughter. "You ain't worth killing! Calm your ass down!"

Around a curve, Canton was amazed to see his car, though he immediately noticed it was missing its chrome hubcaps. Walton stopped the car, pulled Canton out of the back seat, removed his handcuffs, and handed him the keys to the BelAir.

"We are at the county line," said Walton, who pointed north. "That's your way out of here, and I recommend you get on down the road and don't come back."

Relieved, the battered and defeated Canton climbed into his car, started it, and headed in the recommended direction. "Thank God," he said, still shaking.

He found his driver's license sitting beside him, along with his empty wallet. It was only then he looked at the gas gauge. Less than a quarter tank remained. He knew it had been nearly full when he ran the red light.

"Bastards!" he screamed, proceeding to push the BelAir as far from Astoria as his remaining gas supply would allow.

Chapter Five

Astoria and Hyde County abounded in creativity, so it was inevitable that other kinds of extremely private enterprise would develop and thrive.

Consider Flo's, nestled in a wooded area along State Route 42. It was so well hidden it would really sneak up on motorists, much as the stealthy police cars would along the two main roads.

Unmarked by any kind of sign, Flo's was once a restaurant and motel. The restaurant, like most buildings in the county, has been built with simple concrete blocks and offered two front windows, both stained cloudy with age and with shades always drawn, not offering a view inside.

The old motel consisted of six pine wood cottages, still marked with faded and rusting metal numerals. Cottage one was down a dirt trail and was barely visible from the main road. Two through four were closer to the old restaurant and five and six were off the other side, down a similar trail, this one having been graveled because the rain tended to wash it out.

Considering there was no signage or other clues that indicated the place wasn't what it appeared to be and had been since the beginning of the automotive age, weary and hungry travelers would occasionally stop. On this evening in late January, Bill and Doris Maples of Derry, Maine, and their two children, Ruth and Robert, rolled into the parking lot. Bill Maples was still simmering about the speeding ticket he'd gotten south of town and was determined not to spend any more money in Astoria.

But he figured (wrongly, it turned out) that the five miles he'd driven had gotten him into the next county, which he hoped was a bit more hospitable and civilized than the sneering cop who'd relieved the prosperous accountant of $35. Dinner was overdue and the family was tired and hungry. The goal was a home-cooked meal and, if the price and quality was right, an overnight stay in one of the little cabins he'd noticed behind the main building.

The family trooped into the "restaurant," which still looked the part on the inside, being that there were four tables surrounded by old, but sturdy looking wooden chairs. There was a bar of sorts, but Maples immediately noticed it lacked the usual accoutrements or equipment one usually associated with restaurants. There was nothing to speak of on the walls, except for a ten year old calendar behind the bar and a rather bizarre seascape painting on another wall. There was no silverware, plates or soda fountain, no sounds nor scent of food, and so far, no staff.

"This place is a bit queer," offered Doris. Robert, 13, didn't process his mom's comment. "I really want a big hamburger," he said.

Finally, the door behind the bar opened and a middle-aged, red-haired woman emerged. She had clearly been a beauty in her prime, and was still quite attractive. Her hair was eye-catching and her eyes were dark with mascara and big false eyelashes, but what was more striking was her outfit.

Doris gasped immediately. Flo Riley was wearing a bright pink negligee. It had a plunging neckline that offered a clear view of ample cleavage. She wore fishnet stockings and high-heeled black shoes. Young Robert's eyes popped. Bill was speechless, and it was the grinning Flo that finally broke the awkward silence.

"What y'all looking for tonight?" she said, flashing a huge smile.

"Well," Maples stammered, "we had dinner in mind."

Flo giggled. "We don't have anything like that," she replied.

"What do you have?" asked Robert, which brought a kick from his mother under the table.

"Well sweetie, everything we have is $35," said Flo.

Maples was struck by the pricetag, since he'd dug the same amount out of his wallet about an hour ago when Colin Smith had demanded it at the speed trap. Is everything in this damned place $35?, he thought.

"So this isn't a restaurant?" the blonde-haired Doris smartly surmised.

"No, honey. I suspect you folks ought to load back up and get on up the road," Flo said sweetly. "There's a diner about 12 miles down the road from here. They got a decent meat and three."

Bill didn't even ask about the cabins. He knew too well what was going on in those.

"OK, thanks!" he mustered, pulling himself to his feet and motioning for the family to do the same. Six year old Ruth was not happy. "I haven't had my hot dog!" she wailed.

Doris grabbed her hand and followed her husband toward the door. She had to push Robert, who had stopped in his tracks and was staring a hole through the first lady of the night he had ever seen. He clearly liked what he saw, and Doris ended his trance with a look that could easily be fatal.

The family got into their cavernous Plymouth Suburban station wagon and resumed the quest for roadside food and lodging. It was a story Doris told her friends for years.

"Let me tell you about the time that damn Bill took the whole family to a cathouse," it would begin. It always had a rapt audience.

####

At any given time, Flo would have two to as many as five girls in her employ. Most were referred to her by her ex-husband down in Savannah who always managed to recruit a never-ending supply of girls eager for work in the whorehouses on the riverfront. If a girl had too many run-ins with the law or rough and drunken sailors or just wanted a more-laid back environment, Moe Riley would tell them about Flo and make sure they had the $3 Greyhound bus fare to ride up to Astoria. Occasionally, a girl would like it and stay awhile. Most of them moved on fairly quickly, figuring out that Astoria was a backwater with too many bribes and other costs getting in the way of what could be a decent income for a pretty girl, or even a not-so-pretty girl with the necessary skills.

Flo could be motherly with the girls she liked, but she could ride herd on those more interested in drinking or doing drugs or working tricks on the side rather than in the shabby little cabins. Occasionally, she allowed a girl to actually live in a cabin, but usually they were a workplace and the girl established a separate residence. That was a deal breaker for some, especially those intent on sending some money back home.

She'd taken a special liking to a 19-year-old from Savannah who called herself Fancy Fontaine. Fancy was a dark-haired looker with piercing green eyes and long lovely legs. Fancy was smart, too, and the way she could flirt with the men and then make them so happy they'd pay more than she would ask made Flo consider Fancy her special girl, the kind of girl that would have been her daughter if she'd ever had one.

Fancy was allowed to live in Cottage No. 1, which not only signaled her location, but also her status at Flo's. Fancy had been there only three months, but already had more regular customers than any other girl Flo could remember. Almost as many, Flo thought, as she'd had herself back in her prime.

Fancy was the only daughter of a Savannah millworker. Norma Fontaine was herself an only child, and Fancy was the product of a one-night stand. When she was younger, Norma was nearly as attractive as Fancy, and had no shortage of male millworkers anxious to spend some of their Friday payday plying her with beer and affection.

But none of the relationships ever worked out for Norma, particularly after Fancy came along. Norma's focus became being a good mother for Fancy, and for the most part she was, making sure she got good marks in school and always wore clean, if not new clothes. As Fancy began to mature, Norma worked to separate her extremely attractive daughter from the riverfront riff raff that began to court her. Secretly, the last thing Norma wanted was for Fancy to be married and move away, leaving her alone and miserable.

But then the mill closed, and Norma could not find steady work. She did some cleaning and laundry for some of Savannah's wealthy matrons, but nothing that consistently kept the rent paid and food on the table.

Then Norma's health began a steady decline. She always knew in her heart that the unfiltered Pall Malls she smoked weren't good for her, and it became apparent once she developed a persistent cough. When the cough became painful and began to produce blood, Norma knew the end was near.

Terrified that Fancy would end up destitute on the streets, Norma concocted a plan for Fancy's future. It wasn't the best of plans, but it was all Norma could think of. Ironically, it was the direct opposite of her early strategy to keep Fancy away from leering, lustful men.

With as much money as Norma could save, she bought a fine party dress for Fancy. This was a revealing – and some might say sexy -- gown, designed to show her attributes, her fine figure and long, willowy legs. She also bought Fancy a couple of nightgowns far better and more provocative than any she had ever owned.

Norma then proceeded to school Fancy on her future occupation. "Fancy, you are attractive and men already love you," Norma told her daughter. "You know that – you see how men look at you. You will learn to give them what they want in exchange for money -- money that can keep you off the street."

Fancy had always done what her mother said. She didn't question Norma's plan. In fact, she applied herself to be the best she could be. At first, she didn't like it at all. But soon she realized she could make more money than she and her mother had ever seen.

"One does what one has to do," she told herself. "It's just a job, nothing more, nothing less."

Norma died in her bed one night while Fancy was out earning her keep. A tearful Fancy had enough money saved to pay for a decent burial.

It was three days after Norma's funeral when Fancy met Moe Riley. Moe, a pimp with a heart, had seen Fancy on the street and realized quickly that Savannah's rollicking riverfront was bit too rough for a girl as young and attractive as Fancy. He immediately realized that Fancy needed Flo as much as Flo needed Fancy. So he wished his new acquaintance well and put her on the afternoon bus to Astoria.

Flo and Fancy hit it off immediately. Flo just hoped she could keep Fancy around because there was already a steady stream of cars bound for Cottage No. 1. Fancy made enough to keep the powers that be at bay, because, as with everything else in Astoria and Hyde County, they shared the wealth.

Fancy liked Flo, who reminded her of her mother in the way she talked and her good looks. And Cottage No. 1 was the nicest place Fancy'd ever lived, by far. There was a lot to say for having your own place, and even though she didn't particularly like her work, it was the fate God had dealt her, the career her mom had chosen for her. It had fed her, clothed her, and now it was housing her as well. And in her mind, it had also filled the hole in her heart that was left by losing her mother. Unless something really bad happened, Fancy figured she'd just stay in Astoria awhile and save all the money she could.

Chapter Six

Earl Griffin was known as Boss. It had been that way as long as most folks could remember.

Griffin was 65 and set in his ways. He was mean as a copperhead to anyone who crossed him, but he could display a genteel, old-style Southern charm when he wanted to, say in the presence of a pretty woman or another man he wanted to impress. Boss didn't have to impress other men very often, though. If they knew anything about life in Astoria and Hyde County, they were already either impressed or possibly terrified.

Simply, Boss ran everything. Most things had run so long that he didn't have much to do except oversee. Overseeing generally meant looking at the bottom line to make sure nothing was going wrong.

The police department collections stemming from the speed trap, the traffic signal and other selected fees and assessments were as automatic as sunrise and sunset. Either Carole Friedlander or Popsi Colanise was responsible for making weekly cash payments to Boss' office in the courthouse. Boss didn't like checks or paper. His was a cash enterprise.

Popsi or one of the cops would go by Mel's and the other clip joints every week. Melvin Guthrie and the other proprietors knew it was not a good idea to keep the Boss' couriers waiting or to do anything to raise questions or suspicions. Likewise, the same duo, usually Popsi since it wasn't too smart for cops to be around scaring the customers, checked in regularly at Flo Riley's and the black cathouse on McAdoo Street.

There were other sources of revenue, of course. Boss trafficked in moonshine whiskey as well as the legal stuff, despite the fact that Hyde County, though not Astoria itself, was on the books as dry. A shipment of guns would come in via the coast on occasion, and naturally Boss had a hand in that. Drugs were starting to hit the coast in a big way, and anything that would raise revenue and be controlled was in Boss' best interest. And there was also a unique situation at a gas station owned by Luther Bickle, Boss' lifelong friend. Bickle's boys had a talent for finding something wrong with tourists' cars – maybe a fan belt or a radiator hose or sometimes some major like a transmission or a fuel pump.

Almost never was anything actually wrong. And usually, the original part was washed all clean and sometimes even painted to look like new. Old mangled components were used to show the mark what had been wrong with their Chrysler or Ford, and after inflated collections, the weary travelers were sent on their way. Since Luther was so grateful that Boss and his cops would look the other way when people complained, there was always a healthy cut for Boss. In exchange, Luther was always available when Boss needed something, and Luther had a lot of boys who did his bidding without asking any questions.

Needless to say, Boss was awash in money. Nobody really knew where all it ended up, but every year it seemed he owned more land. He was by far the biggest landowner in Hyde County, and many said he owned more land than anyone in south Georgia. He didn't like to talk about such things and would frustrate any comments about his holdings with a vicious scowl. Boss didn't mind being well known in Astoria, but he'd just as soon nobody in Macon or Atlanta knew his name.

Boss was married to Cecilia "CeCe" Mason, daughter of a World War I veteran from near Savannah. CeCe had been a teacher at Astoria High School, but became principal after six years on the job and defacto school superintendent one year after that. Griffins always ran things, and the school was no exception. CeCe was famous for the brand of corporal punishment she condoned in the high school. Kids might get a paddling for misspelling a word. She was driven to excel and that was tough when so many kids were dirt poor and just plain dumb.

Earl and CeCe had one daughter, Patsy, who had been Miss Hyde County, the fairest of the fair, and a contestant in the Miss

Georgia Beauty Pageant. Those things had always been rigged by those up in Atlanta, so Patsy didn't win, much to Boss' disgust. She briefly attended college, but quit to marry Marvin Justus, a sharp but temper-prone attorney. Few people knew, but Justus was a key player in Boss' smooth as silk operation. His slick performance was a big reason the operation was as smooth and silky as it was.

Boss had been born and raised in Astoria, the son of Clint and Mabel Griffin. Clint Griffin was a cotton farmer, and his holdings had been a plantation back when folks like the elder Griffin owned slaves. Clint Griffin was also a power in local politics and taught young Earl how easy it was in those days to be a local boss. In Clint's day, most of south Georgia was run by local strongmen. Now, those days were waning. Only Boss and a nearby high sheriff and a lone county commissioner in a county mainly composed of the Okefenokee Swamp were left. Such thoughts made Boss sad and sent him to his liquor bottle. The old ways were best and this new liberation of the blacks and women and God knows what else would ruin this country, Boss often said.

Boss' first real job growing up had been to run a group of hands Clint Griffin kept to tend to his cotton fields. The six boys were all the sons or grandsons of former slaves, and the way life had evolved in Hyde County, they practically still were. In theory, the boys were sharecroppers or indentured servants, but they really weren't much more than slaves of the Griffin family.

Boss preferred being inside out of the hot south Georgia sun, so when one of the boys stirred up trouble, it really ticked him off. If one of the hands happened to get drunk on moonshine and not show up in the fields to work the next morning, there was hell to pay.

Legend has it that Boss got after one such boy with a whip one hot August morning and by the time Clint pulled him away, the boy was dead. Some said his body ended up in the Altamaha River and, him being black and all and not worth much to anybody except Clint Griffin, they say nothing ever came of it.

Boss went to the University of Georgia and graduated, but refused his daddy's desires he go to law school. He'd had enough of book learning in Athens. He wanted to come back to Astoria and go to work. He did meet CeCe in Athens, though, and two years after he graduated, he made her his wife.

Boss served a couple of terms as county commissioner, but he quickly realized the job was a pain in the ass. People were always coming in wanting something and Boss didn't want to be accountable to anyone. He quickly learned how much easier it was to pick the guys to run for the offices, run the elections, and plain old just run the county. In more than two decades, none of Boss' candidates had ever lost an election. And none of them ever refused him anything he wanted or needed.

A time or two over the years, somebody had gotten high and mighty with him. Once the Baptist preacher had seen himself as the new political powerbroker and decided to run for commissioner. After a couple of high spirited speeches that were witnessed by Popsi and reported back to Boss, his church mysteriously burned to the ground. The preacher then had a couple of prayer meetings with some of Boss' boys who advised him to move out of town. After a second meeting that some say had been a bit violent, he wisely decided to take that advice.

And Boss rebuilt the church, better than new, for the new preacher, who just happened to be Boss' nephew, fresh out of seminary.

Boss was indeed rich, powerful, feared and respected. But there were some strange things about his personality and the way he lived.

The Griffins lived in a modest one-story wood frame ranch house in Astoria just a mile or so from the courthouse. It was hard to believe that the richest man in the county, as well as the most powerful, chose to live so simply. CeCe did have nice furniture and the home was tastefully decorated, but there were quirks that were a testimony to her husband's unique personality.

For example, there were no windows in the couple's bedroom. At one time, there had been two, but Boss paid someone to come and take them out and seal them up. It was like he was afraid someone would attack him when he was the most vulnerable. To say he valued his privacy was an understatement.

A short, squat balding man, Boss always wore cheap dark suits. His dress shirts were old and faded and stained by chewing tobacco and cigar smoke. His shoes were always black, always scuffed and worn, rarely polished.

Boss loved to drink and in fact drank bourbon or scotch every day. At times, nagged by CeCe, he would cut down, but he never stopped. He was home before 4 p.m. every day, and the rumor around town was that he needed to be home because he was getting pretty drunk by then.

And then there were the pills. He told some people they were his heart pills, but to people like Luther Bickle, that didn't make much sense because they seemed to make Boss act differently. Sometimes they seemed to calm him down. Other times they would agitate him or make him burst into unexplained bouts of loud, boisterous laughter.

Earl "Boss" Griffin was one strange man. He did not look, or act the part of a south Georgia colonial dictator. Perhaps that is the reason that he presented such a challenge to Gov. Buford L. Dunlap.

Chapter Seven

The governor of Georgia was a notorious insomniac. And his bouts of insomnia could be cured by only two things – copious amounts of scotch whiskey or the surefire belief he had solved the problem that was keeping him awake in the first place. On this steamy June evening, he had failed to find either cure. So when Loretta, the 30-something nude buxom brunette with huge hair who was currently sharing his bed, groaned after he turned on the light, Buford Dunlap got out of bed to contemplate a solution to his latest problem.

His latest sleeplessness was prompted by a public advisory and press release from the United States Automobile Association. Dunlap searched his brain, but he was pretty goddamn sure he'd never even heard of this "exclusive auto club" until today. Apparently, without his knowledge, which he found surprising since his knowledge was infinitely more far reaching than the average Southern politician of his age, this was an especially popular enclave of thousands of American motorists. Dunlap had no idea why anyone would join such a club.

"Hell, you just get in your car and go," he said when his chief of staff had brought the bad news to his desk earlier in the day. "Why in the Sam Hell would you need a club to tell you when, how or where to get in your car and go?"

He forced his fevered brain to focus as he downed his first double scotch on the rocks. He looked again at the piece of paper he had initially crumpled in anger when Floyd Perkins had put it in his hand and insisted he read it.

"The United States Automobile Association announced today it has issued a traveler's alert to avoid a stretch of federal highway in South Georgia near the Atlantic Coast," it read.

"Large numbers of travelers are reporting that they are being subjected to overly aggressive traffic enforcement in Hyde County, Georgia, an area north of Savannah. This unfair and subjective use of police force aggression appears to be focused near the small town of Astoria.

"Travelers are advised to avoid this area. Motorists are being subjected to abnormal numbers of traffic stops and speed is not always the issue. Travelers are questioning the ethics of speed limit enforcement in the area as well as overzealous enforcement of red light running. In addition, there are serious questions about the bilking of travelers who stop in the area for rest room or food breaks. It has been reported that motorists are being induced to participate in illegal dice games that inevitably result in the losses of significant amounts of money.

"The USAA will continue to monitor the situation and will report on any new developments. For now, and until future advisories are issued, travelers are advised to track west of the Georgia coast and avoid U.S. 55 in all north or southbound travel."

Dunlap crumpled the field of paper a second time and threw it in the general direction of his open bathroom door.

The problem with politics, he thought for the thousandth time, is not getting votes or kissing babies or ass or dealing with the tiny little egos in the Legislature with all their esoteric wants and needs. The problem with politics is goddamn little maggots like Earl Griffin who run their little kingdoms and do what they will with precious things like the reputation of the State of Georgia!

Nobody bound for Florida from the Northeast can avoid Georgia, he knew. It is damn near impossible, and nobody in their right mind is going to drive hundreds of miles out of the way when Florida is the golden destination. The problem was that there's not a goddamn thing for tourists to do or spend their money on along the roadways off the coast. Dunlap knew it because he knew his state top to bottom. If the tourists track westerly from the coast, they won't stop for souvenirs or alligator farms, Georgia beaches or pecan stores. Hell, in some stretches, they'll have trouble even finding gas!

Dunlap needed to keep U.S. 55 wide open and free flowing. Tourists needed to get the word that they would be welcome in Georgia. We can get their money without doing it in a crooked and illegal way, he declared to himself with a heavy draw on heaven's nectar. And as a regularly used alternative, he needed State Route 42 to also be heavily traveled. Not only was much of Georgia's tourist attracting infrastructure along these routes, but also the interests of a large number of influential Georgia taxpayers who regularly and generously contributed to the cause most important to Buford Dunlap: Buford Dunlap.

His thoughts then turned to one Earl Griffin, who was rapidly becoming Public Enemy No. 1. He'd only met the little snake oil salesman a couple of times and found him utterly repulsive. For one, he had a slimy, unfirm handshake and didn't look a man in the eye when pressing flesh. Any man worth his salt in politics knows that when a man can't pump a palm and can't pass a wink, he isn't much of a man. He recalled the tight little cheap black suit Griffin was wearing at the county commissioner's convention when they'd first met, as well as the sweat on his brow. Hell, Griffin had been sweatin' like a whore in church!

Even then, Dunlap had known Griffin was running Hyde County and had been for years – that's why he had made a point to remember him. He'd basically inherited the throne from his dad. What was this bald bastard up to? Why did he look like a pauper when he apparently was taking every dollar from every

Yankee from Maryland to Maine who had the misfortune to have to stop in his insignificant little county? From the looks of him, he was tossing all his money in the ocean rather than living it up.

Focus, Buford, focus, the governor told himself as he poured his second double scotch. His mind wandered to the marvelous piece of womanhood in his bed, but then he pulled his attention to the problem at hand, not the opportunity in bed. "I need an idea!" he said aloud, as Loretta briefly stirred, but then settled back into sexy slumber.

Everyone thought Georgia governors were bastions of power. In reality, the local rule system had led to the state having an amazing 159 counties – the most in the nation -- each of which had evolved into a virtual fiefdom. Over the years, little by little, one-by-one, the local gods had either died off or had been tossed from their thrones. Griffin the Insignificant was one of the last vestiges of this system of local empowerment. And like all the others, Dunlap vowed that this tiny little king would die!

Dunlap realized he didn't have too many choices. He could call the bastard in and read him the riot act. Intimidation by rank and title was an important chapter in the Georgia rule book. He quickly decided he'd do that first and foremost. Griffin was a puny little punk – surely he'd listen to reason and be scared as hell when Dunlap made it clear who was running this state, in which Astoria was just a putrid knot on a mighty log.

Another possibility was to call in the feds. No, that wasn't an option, he immediately realized. This was Georgia's problem and the feds were nothing but trouble. Dunlap was a well-known segregationist, though truth be known he was quite friendly to black folks and gave a lot of 'em state jobs. But you know, a man has to do what he has to do to get elected, and to get elected in Georgia, you have to make it clear that Negroes have to know their place, Dunlap thought, repeating a common mantra. This issue alone made federal intervention in his Hyde County problem impossible. The feds were already beginning to push for integration. Dunlap and the all-white money that put him in the Gold Dome wanted separate, but equal accommodations for blacks. It was the Southern way of life and it would continue, by hell or high water.

A third option was going directly to the public. Dunlap mentally decided to hold back on that for now. If he couldn't intimidate Griffin into cleaning up his act, he had an idea or two about taking this problem to the traveling public -- in a much more direct way that this United States Automobile Association had. God, the more he thought about that bunch, he realized they sound like a bunch of goddamn communists!

OK, this seems like a plan, he thought as he drew deeply on his third double scotch. He grabbed a piece of official Georgia governor's office stationery and scribbled the following:

"Get on the phone to Earl Griffin in Astoria and demand he get his ass to Atlanta posthaste. I want to talk to him."

He put that in his outbox, which his handlers would be checking in his personal residence at 7 a.m. He had Plan A, and he had Plan B. And even though he really hadn't thought too much about it yet, he was even starting to formulate a Plan C.

That little cocksucker won't know what's hit him when I'm through with him, thought the Governor of Georgia, who chuckled with delight as he realized he was almost ready to go to sleep, but not quite.

Then, his politically expedient mind turned to Loretta and he decided to wake her up for a zesty what fer. Oh gee, golly mercy me, Dunlap thought. It's great being me!

Chapter Eight

James Robert Crane, known as Jim Bob to his friends, Bobby to his parents and Big Time Trouble to his classroom teacher at Astoria Elementary, was as happy as a Georgia country boy could be. School was out for the summer and nothing was more fun than the hot, lazy days of a south Georgia summer.

That meant endless hours of riding his bike on the many miles of streets, roads and pig trails around Astoria. It meant playing Army and Cowboys and Indians with his two best buds, Zeke Wiggins and Sarah "Sassy" Smith. It was true that Sassy was a girl and not many 12-year-old boys counted girls among their friends, but Sassy was super cool. She was actually faster than Zeke and maybe as strong. Although Jim Bob wouldn't insult Zeke -- at least to his face -- by saying so, she was probably smarter, too. Jim Bob wouldn't admit this to anyone, but he thought she was also pretty.

The Three Musketeers, as they called themselves, had lots in common. All three lived in the Astoria Trailer Court, a hodgepodge of mobile homes. Sassy lived just two trailers from

Jim Bob and his folks, and Zeke lived at the end of the next row of trailers, probably a football field away.

They were in the same class at Astoria Elementary, and all three loved to make fun of their teacher, Clara Belle Carson, who they had probably pissed off for the last time since school was out and sixth grade promised yet another teacher. All three despised principal Cecelia Griffin, probably the meanest woman in the world who should be hung, shot and then killed for all the bad times she caused the kids at Astoria Elementary.

They were also all kids of cops, which made them a special breed. Their dads worked for the Astoria Police Department and that was really cool because sometimes they would let them ride in their squad cars and sometimes even turn on the sirens. That was the best thing in the world, especially when other kids saw and heard what they were doing.

Jim Bob was very proud of his daddy, Officer Wesley Crane, and the fact that he protected the citizens of Astoria from all those wild-ass tourists who tore through town like they were driving jet planes. Jim Bob was old enough to ride his prized J.C. Higgins bicycle along the shoulder of U.S. 55 and sometimes he would ride by while his dad was giving some lawless Florida beach bum a well-deserved speeding ticket. Those folks would run a kid down for no reason, so it was great that the officers were out enforcing the law and protecting them from harm. Sassy's dad, Officer Colin Smith and Zeke's pop, Tony Wiggins, were all top-notch cops. When the three were together grilling hamburgers and drinking a brew, they almost looked like brothers, being that they were all big guys with crew cuts. Every now and then, Jim Bob would go up behind his dad to ask him a question and realize he was talking to Officer Smith instead. The Musketeers always got a laugh out of that.

It being the first full day of summer, Jim Bob rolled by Sassy's house, knocked on the door of their trailer and was greeted by a real oddity -- a cold breeze.

"Sassy, what's going on?" he asked as his blonde-haired friend opened the aluminum door. "How'd you get it cold in there?"

"Come in, Jim Bob. Quick, don't let all the air out," she replied. "Daddy got us air conditioning!"

Jim Bob had heard about such a thing, but he'd only experienced it in businesses, like in the Bijou Theatre downtown or the Pic and Pay Grocery. It had never dawned on him that you could actually have air conditioning in your home.

Sassy pointed to the unit mounted in the kitchen window and Jim Bob immediately heard its motor's low roar. It had cooled the trailer's kitchen and adjacent 12-foot wide living room to a most comfortable temperature. In fact, Jim Bob actually felt chill bumps appearing on his bare arms and legs.

"It doesn't really make the back bedroom cool, but it's great to be in here watching TV," she chirped. "I would say let's watch the Lone Ranger, but why don't we get Zeke and go bike riding?"

"That's what I wanted to do!" replied Jim Bob. Having the flexible mind of a kid, he'd already forgotten the marvel of home air conditioning and was ready to get outside and start on this summer.

Sassy and Jim Bob tromped down the trailer's metal steps and jumped on their bikes, Sassy's a blue and white Schwinn with plastic tassels streaming down from the handle bars. They pedaled down the concrete driveway of the park, waving at one neighbor woman en route to the park's community mailbox and then a second who was lugging a load of dirty clothes to the park's coin-operated laundrymat.

The park housed a wide range of Astorians. There were some folks who worked for the town, a teacher or two and the school custodian, and also some people who ran neighborhood businesses, possibly even a clip joint or two. The kids didn't know it, but there was even a trailer on the third row which housed three of Flo Riley's working girls who lacked Fancy Fontaine's status of actually living in a cottage at Flo's.

The park was an amalgamation of American country life. The trailers, ranging from less than 30 feet long to newer models of 48 feet or more, were lined up in parallel queues, each sitting about 15 feet apart. In the summertime, since very few residents enjoyed the luxury the Smiths had with air conditioning and closed windows, and trailer walls being paper thin, everybody had a good idea what their neighbors were doing because voices and other sounds tended to carry.

So everybody pretty much knew when somebody had had too much to drink, everybody knew when domestic troubles were brewing and everybody knew when violence broke out. The Musketeers knew better than most, since usually one of their dads went to make the peace. Not surprisingly, nobody broke it up when it involved their dads. Jim Bob was embarrassed on those occasions when his dad and his mother, Dorothy, had loud arguments that every once in a while resulted in his mom taking a punch from her husband. Jim Bob would cringe in his bedroom with his head under his pillow and ride it out, because that's just what kids did.

Zeke popped out of his family's trailer when his friends approached since he had heard them coming. His Green Panther, another Schwinn, was quickly rolling alongside Jim Bob's and Sassy's rides.

"Let's go under the bridge!" Zeke suggested, and the others agreed. It was their favorite place in all of Astoria.

They rode out to the trailer park's entrance, and turned right on 55 and rode about a mile to the Altamaha River bridge. They veered off the wide shoulder on the right side of the road onto a dirt strip worn through the already high summer grasses. The path, coincidentally just wide enough for a single bicycle, plunged down a slope towards the river.

The area shaded by the bridge offered a big concrete post great for sitting and dangling your feet into space. Far below was the river itself. They could look down upon what they called The Pit, the deepest and slowest part of the lazy river. Some said The Pit was a hundred or more feet deep – Jim Bob didn't know and didn't want to find out.

The older kids sometimes swam there, launching themselves way out over the water by holding onto a tire tied to a big live oak with a long piece of steel cable. Swinging down off the steep bank, the drop to the cooling water below was probably 10 feet or more.

The three friends had vowed that this would be the summer they would finally get permission to join the older kids in the deepest part of The Pit. All three of their dads had thus far strictly forbade this practice, fearing that the trio might not be able to make the long swim back to the bank from the middle of The Pit. There was also concern about alligators, which occasionally decided that The Pit should be part of their territory.

A dirt road ran alongside the river below the area shaded by the bridge. It also linked off from 55 and gave the land owner access to rich fields of bottomland where cattle usually grazed. The only problem was in times of heavy rain, the cows had to be brought to higher ground because the Altamaha would flood the bottom lands, endangering the livestock.

It was a great view from under the bridge, and the Musketeers felt it was their own special place that no one else frequented. It was here the three tried their first cigarette (stolen from Zeke's dad). All three hacked violently and declared they hated it and swore they'd never smoke again. It was also here that the three shared the great secrets that best friends shared.

The only obvious one they hadn't shared was that Zeke, a freckled-faced red-head who took after his mother, and Jim Bob, whose dark hair and features favored his father, would eventually be rivals for Sassy's affections.

But that was literally miles down the road. For now, none of the three would admit to anything other than being the best of friends ready for the best times this new summer could offer.

Little did they know that events were converging among the adults in their world this steamy summer that would change their lives forever. Since life in Astoria almost never changed, this was certain to be a summer they would never forget.

Chapter Nine

Earl Griffin felt like a caged lion. He had been backed into a corner, and he didn't like that one bit. He liked space and Gov. Buford Dunlap didn't want to offer him an inch.

CeCe had just cooked him his favorite breakfast and he was starting to eat it with zest. Fried eggs, over easy, grits, a pile of bacon and a couple of slabs of country ham were hard to beat. When CeCe's back was turned as she pulled her freshly baked biscuits from the oven, he sweetened his hot coffee with a healthy dash of bourbon.

"If you don't want to go, Earl, why are you going?" asked his wife, who was settling into her summer vacation with school no longer in session.

"That asshole Dunlap is holding something over my head," replied Boss, grimacing at his own mention of the tiny little man in Atlanta.

"What could he possibly hold over your head, honey? You've told me before you're beholden to no man, not even the governor."

"My people tell me he has the power to revoke my boys' radar permit," said Griffin. "That would really cut into my … uh, our revenue."

"I never heard of such a thing," said CeCe. "Our police department needs Atlanta's permission to run radar?"

"Well, I hadn't either, but the chief says there is such a thing in state law. He thinks that if the governor pulled the permit, the state patrol could come and take all our radar guns." Just the thought of that prompted Boss to take a big draw from his coffee.

"So what are you going to do?" asked his wife, still a fairly attractive woman for her age.

"I don't know yet," said Griffin. "And I don't like that at all. I guess I have to hear what the little weasel has to say."

He heard Popsi pull into his driveway. They were going up to Atlanta in the best car the county owned, a two-year-old Lincoln Continental.

"I gotta go, CeCe. I'll see you tonight or tomorrow."

Griffin made sure his flask was secure in his breast pocket, and also checked for his pill bottle in his pants. He was dreading the meeting with the governor like the plague, but he was also girding his loins for a fight. The bastard was threatening his livelihood, his whole county's way of life. That shit won't cut it, not at all.

He greeted Popsi, who was dressed like a cheap country undertaker, at the door. "Let's get up there," Boss growled. It was a seven hour drive to Atlanta, so there would be plenty of time to mentally rehearse his lines on the way.

####

Griffin hated Atlanta. The hustle and bustle of the place turned his stomach. Popsi blundered into heavy traffic on Ponce de Leon Avenue near where the Atlanta Crackers were about to play the Birmingham Barons. Griffin fumed as the Lincoln finally worked its way to Peachtree Street and headed down toward the Capitol.

"Where should I park, Boss?" asked Popsi, who had circled the Capitol and was obviously ready for this trip to end. Griffin eyed a row of parking spaces along Capitol Avenue marked, "Governor's Staff Only."

"One of those will do fine, Colanise," said Boss. He was the only person in Astoria who refused to call the burly enforcer Popsi, considering the nickname absurd silliness.

"Whatever you say, Boss," Popsi said, pulling the big car to the curb alongside the gold-domed home of state government.

The two men entered the building, which had been relatively deserted since the Legislature had gone home in the spring. They were directed down the main corridor to the big glass window which announced "Office of The Governor."

Popsi advised the secretary, Miss Bonnie Triplett, of their arrival. She smirked and directed the men to a row of wooden chairs.

There they sat for 45 minutes. Griffin was incensed as Popsi, weary from the long drive through Georgia, enjoyed a nice nap.

Finally, the secretary put down the phone and looked over at the two men. "The governor will see you now," she said.

Griffin elbowed Popsi, who rubbed his eyes, stood and stretched. The two ambled into the wood-paneled office, the lair of Buford Dunlap, the Peach State's chief executive.

Dunlap was smoking a big cigar, his suit coat nowhere to be seen, his red tie loosened. Sitting in front of him and gazing back at the newcomers was Floyd Perkins, the governor's fresh-faced, 30-something chief of staff.

"Griffin, have a seat," said the governor, who did not offer to stand or shake hands. Floyd, why don't you take Griffin's puppet out and show him the Co-Cola machine? This will be just us, man to man."

Popsi, showing little respect for the office, snarled at Dunlap's insult, but stood and allowed Perkins to direct him back out into the outer office. As he passed, he offered a look down at Griffin, and Boss gave him a tight-lipped nod.

Now Dunlap stood and walked around his fine mahogany desk and towered over Griffin, peering onto his now reddening bald head.

"Just what in Sam Hell are you peckerwoods doing down there in Astoria?" he began, his voice rising. "Do you have any idea what you are doing? Do you know how many letters I get from people your lap dog minions are fleecing out of pocket money? Do you have any clue how many newspapers are writing about this goddamn speed trap you are running? And now, something called the goddamn United States Automobile Association says you have the nation's number one speed trap. Number one! In a shithole like Astoria! Your damn little police force is busier than a cat trying to bury a turd on a frozen pond!"

Griffin appeared shaken for a moment, but quickly gathered himself. He stood and looked the governor in the eye.

"I will never apologize for protecting the citizens of Astoria and Hyde County!" he fumed. "I don't know how often you get down our way, but our roads are straight and long and these godforsaken Yankee tourists have no respect for the law! They storm up and down our roads at breakneck speeds, endangering our school children and cleaning women! Our police force does a marvelous job and follows the law to the letter!"

"To the letter, huh? How about that crooked-ass traffic light in town that doesn't even have a yella?"

"We, uh, had some mechanical trouble with that red light for a time, but we got it corrected," said Griffin, easing back into his former persona as a government bureaucrat. "Some of those tickets were remanded once we realized there could have been some problems."

"You are so full of shit your eyes are brown!" raged the governor of Georgia. "I've had people from your county tell me you keep a hotel room over the light so you can time when it changes and pull folks over!"

"That's a fucking lie!"

"It is God's honest truth," said the governor. "And what about these maggoty little clip joints and dice games you people are running down there? I guess those are experiencing mechanical difficulties too?"

"There is no illegal gambling in Hyde County," said Griffin. "Free enterprise being what it is, ever now and then some of the boys have card games and maybe ever now and then a tourist might be around and pull up a chair for a hand or two, but that's all I know about."

"Griffin, you're about as useless as an ashtray on a motorcycle! You been down there with a shit shovel raking up tourist dollars for years. I goddamn guarantee you got more money than God Almighty His Own Self! What I don't get is why you don't buy yourself a decent suit with it?"

"I didn't come up here to get insulted," replied Griffin, who sounded a bit hurt at the personal attack.

"You damn right you came up here to get insulted. You came up here to get fuckin' abused, that's what. I am sick and tired of you ruining the reputation of my fine state."

"YOUR state!" Griffin shouted. "You tiny little man, this ain't your state! You are a fuckin' tinhorn, a bullshitter, a ... a cunt sucker!"

Dunlap chuckled. "Yeah, I won't deny that one, Griffin. You ought to try it sometime. It might loosen you up a little."

"You know what I meant," Griffin said, realizing he badly needed a drink. "You are a cock sucker!"

Dunlap's smirk disappeared and steam seemed to start coming from his ears.

"You are talkin' to the governor of Georgia!" he screamed.

"I am talking to a two-bit whore. I am talking to the littlest man east of the Mississippi. I'm talking to a tinhorn axe-handling boar hog!"

Dunlap closed the short distance between the two in a flash and tackled the older man, sending a coffee table sprawling. Griffin, surprised by the governor's attack, managed to knee Dunlap in the groin as the two rolled over the carpeted floor, exchanging rabbit punches and kicks. The noise of the crashing table and the breaking of a glass ash tray and some sort of ceremonial do dad brought a rush of men into the room. Two state troopers permanently assigned to the governor's office struggled to separate the two men as Colanise and Perkins rushed in on their heels. The governor's secretary, her mouth agape and her eyes as big as full moons, looked on in shock.

Dunlap quickly gathered himself, stood and motioned to Miss Triplett to return to her post. The two troopers nervously kept vigil between the two combatants as Griffin licked a bloody lip.

"Griffin," said the governor, his composure nearly restored. "Your county is lousy, rotten, corrupt, nasty and no good. You had better consider this a serious warning that you had better clean up your act or you will find the entire resources of the state of Georgia on your doorstep, on your ass and in your face! I will take every dollar you own and I will put your ass under the prison in Reidsville. You better mark my words because this will be your last warning!"

The governor noticed that Griffin had ripped a sleeve in his suit coat during their struggle. "Look at that, Mister Boss," the governor said with a snarl and then a laugh as he pointed to the rip. "I guess you'll have to get you a new suit now."

"Dunlap, you are a sleazy bag of wind," replied Boss, a bit surprised that he was not seriously hurt in the scuffle with the younger man and didn't even seem out of breath. "I told you once, and I'm telling you again that all we do in Astoria is enforce the law. We don't want, or need any state tinhorns to mess in our business. If you come down there, you need to realize you're in my back yard. Anybody that trespasses in my backyard needs to realize there are serious consequences."

"I will remind you that lawmen are in our presence, Griffin," said the governor. "Are you threatening me?"

"I do not threaten, though you certainly threatened me. All I will say is that I am a man of my word."

"Your word is bullshit. Get the hell out of my office, Griffin. Get the hell out of Atlanta. Your stench makes me sick."

Griffin looked Dunlap in the eye. "Fuck you, governor!"

He turned his head, nodded at Colanise and walked out of the office. "Well, that was a royal waste of time," he said to no one in particular.

Back out on the street, Griffin fumed yet again as he saw a parking ticket tucked under the Lincoln's windshield wipers.

"Assholes!" he said, grabbing the brown card and ripping it into shreds.

Missing the irony of the moment, he threw the remnants of the ticket onto the curb and climbed into the cavernous back seat of the Lincoln.

"Colanise, take me up to the Imperial Hotel. It's too late to drive back today, and besides, I need a drink."

Chapter Ten

Popsi enjoyed the evening far more than Boss. He was quite surprised and pleased when Boss invited him to have a drink with him at the bar of the Imperial Hotel. He had never actually socialized with Boss before. Maybe I'm coming up in the world, he thought.

And Popsi was not at all upset when Griffin told him after two stiff shots that he'd had enough and didn't want him hung over and going to sleep on the drive south in the morning.

So like the good soldier that he was, he followed his Boss' directives and went upstairs and went to bed. Popsi hadn't been in a nice hotel in years and slept like a fat, happy baby.

Griffin, meanwhile, stayed in the bar until last call at 2 a.m. He recognized no one and no one paid any attention to the Boss of Hyde County. He spoke to no one except the bartender, who noticed his swollen lip and ripped coat jacket but thought nothing of it. Businessmen got rolled in Downtown Atlanta all the time, and he figured that was what had happened to this rough-looking, worried fellow. Atlanta can be a tough place, especially in the summertime when everybody, including the working girls and the pimps, are on the street. He had no idea this man had had a fistfight with Gov. Buford Dunlap.

Boss thought long and hard about what he was going to do next, and had his plan set in his head a while before the bartender cut him off.

After a generous tip, the bartender agreed to fill Griffin's pocket flask for the road. Boss again thanked his lucky stars that he didn't have to pay for booze back home. It was yet another fringe benefit, this one for being the ringleader of the county's bootleg liquor trade.

####

During the long drive from Atlanta to Astoria, Griffin gave Popsi some marching orders. This was standard operating procedure – Boss typically issued his commands through his top-ranked underlings, rarely talking to any of the real people in Astoria, unless it was in church or on the street, and that was just small talk about how everyone was doing. It was the way business was done, and it had worked for a long time.

"Colanise, when we get back, I want you to go down to APD and let them all know we're shutting completely down for now," said Griffin.

Boss noticed from the way his man's head moved that Colanise was surprised at the directive. Griffin didn't usually explain himself, but Colanise had been with him a long time – hell, he had hired the muscular Greek off a shrimp boat not too long after his daddy died.

"It's this way," Boss began slowly. "That bastard Dunlap may have some things he can do to us. His man threatened before we came down that they could revoke our radar permits and have the troopers confiscate our guns, and that would put a real crimp in our style. I figure that we just shut down for a while, and he quits getting complaints, he'll figure I was intimidated and just leave us alone."

Popsi nodded, but he didn't like what he was hearing. Boss had always been tough. Boss had always been ruthless. This dick roughs him up a little bit and Boss backs down? Is he getting old and soft?

"What about the joints?" Popsi finally asked.

"Them too," said Griffin. "Some of them have been running wide open lately and they are a lot harder to explain away than speeding tickets."

"How about the light?" Popsi said.

"That, too," Griffin said. "Dunlap was on to it. He's got somebody who's talking to him because he knew way too much. Do some sniffing around and see if you can figure out who. If we can get to the bottom of it, some asshole is going to pay."

Popsi liked that a whole lot better. That was the Boss he knew and respected. "Will do, Boss."

"What about the houses?" said Popsi, meaning Flo's and the cathouse on the black side of town.

"Leave them alone," said Griffin. "I can't imagine them having unsatisfied customers who would complain to the Governor's Office. Besides, tourists don't usually stop at Flo's anyhow. It's mainly local folk that go there."

The time in the hotel bar had made Popsi feel a little more comfortable than he usually did with Boss, so he decided to share an idea or two.

"Boss, folks is going to be pissed about shutting down," he said.

"Colanise, that's part of your job. Make sure they get unpissed. We have been very successful doing things my way for a long time and this is still my way. This guy is a fucking politician, and to beat him, I have to play some politics of my own."

"Boss, we could do a job on him up in Atlanta," offered Popsi bravely.

"You want me to tell you to burn down the fucking Governor's Mansion? Fire some shots through his office window? Are you crazy?"

"That's what we do at home," said Popsi.

"That's what we do at home because we run the place," said Griffin. "He runs Atlanta. He's got a fucking police force just like I do, but his police force does very little except guard him. You and Bickle's boys do good work, but you do it on our turf, not on his."

"OK, Boss. You're right."

Despite his yes man response, Popsi really liked the idea of burning the Governor's Mansion. That would teach the sumbitch he can't fuck with Boss, he thought. But his thoughts moved on to the work he'd have to do once they got back to Astoria.

####

Wesley Crane was royally pissed. He could not believe operations had been suspended. School was out up north and U.S. 55 was bumper to bumper with easy marks. No tickets, no easy money. That was money out of his pocket and that sucked big time. Without tickets to write or traffic signal duty to do, there just wasn't much for one of Astoria's finest to do.

So Crane convened a session at Bart Taggart's, inviting his fellow officers and trailer park neighbors Tony Wiggins and Colin Smith to join him. Bart typically would give the boys the first couple of rounds on the house but then would gently remind them they drank a shitload of liquor and beer and the freebies lasted only so long.

Usually, that was no problem with Wes Crane, but today he was thinking about all the money he wasn't getting paid for writing tickets. But he knew not to take it out on Bart, so he proceeded to bitch to Tony and Colin.

"What happened to make Boss shut things down?" he asked after his third shot of bourbon.

"Confederate Memorial Day?" offered Tony, which got him an elbow in the ribs and a guffaw from Colin Smith.

"I heard Popsi took two days away and Carol Friedlander said he checked out the Lincoln from the motor pool," said Smith. "Maybe that's got something to do with it."

Crane scratched his head, processing that new information. "Popsi's never done that before, unless…."

"Unless Boss wanted him to take him someplace," interjected Tony.

"Well, the liquor's flowing good so there wouldn't be nothing with that. Guns or dope maybe?"

"C'mon Wes, you know Boss never touches anything, never sees nobody," said Tony, who motioned for Bart to bring him another double scotch.

"Well, he saw somebody. And Popsi didn't come back with the car until yesterday afternoon," said Colin.

"So they was out overnight," Smith surmised. "Think Boss was checking out some land upstate, or maybe down in Florida?"

Crane shook his head. "Boss is private as hell with his personal stuff. He wouldn't take Popsi to do anything like that. He'd take his son in law or nephew or go alone."

Wiggins laughed. They's one thing we know. Boss didn't go huntin' or fishin.' He's never done nothin' like that."

"Think he'd go see a woman?" Smith offered, prompting his two fellow officers to laugh out loud.

"CeCe would take a butcher knife and cut off his privates!" laughed Crane. "That'd go over like a fart at a funeral!"

The three friends laughed, and Bart came over and poured three more.

"Now I'm just thinking out loud here," said Crane. "Who in the whole wide world might have the power to get Boss to shut down?"

"The President?" said Smith.

"The General's got more important shit to worry about than the doings in Astoria," said Wiggins. "He's watching the Russians, keeping his finger tuned up for pulling the nuclear trigger."

"The FBI?" asked Smith.

Wes Crain scratched his buzzcut once again as he pondered the question. "That's an interesting thought, but don't we have to do something across state lines? What do we do across state lines?"

"We don't do nothing, but the people we stop do," said Wiggins. "They cross 'em."

"That's not no interstate criminal enterprise," said Crane. "All we do is right here in Astoria, and ..."

But then Crane stopped in mid-sentence.

"Boss got called in by the governor, I bet," he said. "I bet the governor threatened him with prison or something."

"Boss ain't scared of Dunlap!" cried Wiggins. "I heard him make fun of him after he got elected."

"Give me another, better theory," said Crane.

Neither could, even after another drink.

Then Crane had another much better idea.

"Carol Friedlander said Boss didn't shut down the cathouses," he said. "Why don't we ride over to Flo's for a little roll. I heard she's got a real amazin' looker in one of them outhouses I'd like to know a little better."

Wiggins and Smith looked at each other. Wes always had the most interesting ideas.

"We ain't never gone over there on patrol time," said Smith.

"Cause we's usually writing tickets, numbnuts," said Crane. "Do we usually go drinking at Bart's on patrol time?"

"Well, I guess not."

"OK then, it's decided," said Crane. "Let's ride over to Flo's. I want to party until my doot falls off."

Ledford, Joey

Chapter Eleven

Popsi Colanise wasn't an educated man, but he was savvy and smart. One might call Popsi "street smart," but nobody in Astoria would think of such a phrase because the only thing smart on its streets was that wonky red light. And frankly, smart would be the last adjective any of its hundreds of victims would use to describe it.

It was the red light that had Popsi's attention this day because Boss had ordered him to find out who had divulged its unique secrets to Gov. Buford Dunlap. Boss and the boys at the Astoria Police Department had gone to considerable trouble to devise a near perfect revenue-enhancer, and its existence, as well as how it operated, were known by only a select few.

Popsi started his investigation at the APD offices, where he typically spent a lot of time working in "the collections department." That is what Carole Friedlander called it, and that was another of her jokes that insiders had heard hundreds of times.

Carole liked to talk, but she liked her job more and that made her trustworthy. She knew the light's secrets, but she would never have told anyone about it, not even her ex-husband, Rex. Popsi immediately eliminated Carole from his list of suspects, every person with inside knowledge of the red light's operations. That list, provided by Carole herself, included all of the patrol officers, most of whom had worked the light for years.

Popsi knew that Wes Crane, Colin Smith, Tony Wiggins and even the jailer, Curly Walton, were beyond reproach. Who would tattletale on a device that paid them a cut for every single ticket? Compounding that was the fact any of them would be criminally liable were it ever publicly disclosed that the light was illegitimate. No, Popsi quickly decided, the cops were good.

He thought briefly about Biff Carlyle, who owned and operated the Astoria Hotel, home of the magic switch. Popsi dismissed him in a flash. Biff's most reliable revenue came from the constant rental of Room 16. No, Biff would not bite the hand that fed him.

A chat between shifts with Colin Smith, however, gave Popsi the clues he needed.

"Colin, you work the light more than anybody, right?" asked Popsi.

"At least three days a week," said Smith. "Wes gives me a break one day, and Tony on another, and on those, I work speed."

"Who is in the room?" asked Popsi.

"Most of the time, it's Sully," said Colin. "Occasionally, Slim works the switch."

Popsi scratched his chin and nodded. Slim Bickle was the oldest son of Luther Bickle, who ran a clip joint as well as the town's only garage, which specialized in bilking tourists with phony repairs. It had been Luther himself who studied the workings of the traffic light and invented the remote switch.

Popsi knew Slim well. He often joined Colanise for some of his more colorful after-hours assignments. Popsi would trust Slim with his life – and actually had on a couple of occasions. Slim would not betray the secret of his daddy's unique creation.

"So Colin, what do you know about Sully?" asked Popsi, finally focusing on his target. He'd met Theo "Sully" Sullivan a couple of times, but did not know him well. Popsi wasn't necessarily known as a people person, so it wasn't his style to make small talk with small timers like Sully.

"His wheel is still turning, but the hamster's dead," Smith deadpanned.

Popsi had lived in Astoria for many years, but he still struggled with some of the locals' more colorful expressions. "Say again?" asked Popsi.

"Sully's eat up with the dumb ass," said Smith. "He sometimes gives me townspeople when he knows to get out-of-staters. Sometimes, he's late on the switch and gives them green.

Then, sometimes he's Quick Draw McGraw and they have time to stop.

"He's also terrible to give me singles," said Smith, meaning lone travelers less likely to carry enough cash to pay the ticket. "I think you end up with a lot of them."

"Yes, they give me a lot of extra work," said Popsi, who might as well have been talking about audits and not assaults.

"How did he get the job?" he added.

"I think he's a friend of Carl's."

Popsi nodded again. That explained a lot. Carl Griffin was Astoria's police chief. Boss' second cousin, Griffin had not been blessed with much of the family smarts. He drank too much and could often be found participating in card games at Melvin Guthrie's clip joint. Popsi had made numerous mental notes that it was seriously stupid for Astoria's police chief to be playing cards at the town's No. 1 clip joint. But again, it wasn't Popsi's role in life to tell Boss his police chief cousin was a serious loser.

Popsi thanked Smith and rolled over to Bickle's. He talked briefly to Luther, who went into the auto shop to get a couple of things for Popsi. He put them into his pocket and walked out.

From there, Popsi drove to Mel's. Sure enough, in the back room, he found Melvin Guthrie playing blackjack with Carl Griffin and Theo Sullivan. There was a scent in the room that Popsi recognized as marijuana, and he noticed a spent joint in an ash tray.

"Sullivan, I have business with you," said Popsi.

Sully gave a nervous look toward Griffin, who shrugged his shoulders. The chief had learned a long time ago that he didn't want to know too much about Popsi's activities.

"I ain't done nothing, Popsi. I promise."

"We need to talk. Come with me."

Sweat was pouring off Sully's face as the two drove to the APD offices. Friedlander smiled and nodded as she saw Popsi guide Sullivan to his office in the collections department.

"I have reason to believe you have talked about the operation of the red light," began Popsi as Sullivan sat slump shouldered on a wooden chair.

"No, no … you got that all wrong, I ain't talked to nobody."

Popsi reached into his pocket and pulled out a simple radiator hose clamp he'd gotten from Bickle. He grabbed Sullivan's right hand and slipped the clamp over his index finger like a groom giving his bride a wedding ring at the altar.

"What are you doing?" cried Sully. Popsi pulled handcuffs from his pocket and secured Sully's left hand to the chairback. He pulled a screwdriver from his pocket and tightened the clamp on Sully's finger, causing a scream of pain.

"This is the finger you use to push the switch, right?" asked Popsi. "This finger has made you pretty good money, has it not?"

"Not nearly as much as Colin and the officers," whined Sully. "I don't get a cut."

"You may get a cut today," smiled Popsi. "It may not be the kind of cut you want."

Popsi continued his interrogation. A failure to answer or evasion by Sullivan resulted in the clamp being tightened. Soon, the finger was bleeding, its tip was growing pale, and Sullivan was screaming for mercy.

"You say you have not told anyone about the light, but I just do not believe you," said Popsi. "He tightened the clamp one more time and there was a perceptible crack as Sully's finger bone shattered.

"FUCK!" screamed Sullivan. "OK, OK. Stop! I think I remember something!

"I was at Bart Taggart's and I might have told a girl," said Sullivan.

"What girl?" asked Popsi.

"Linda… Linda Bishop. That cheerleader girl who goes to school in Atlanta."

"Uh huh," said Popsi. "What school in Atlanta?"

"Maybe Georgia Tech!"

"And why did you tell this school girl one of our most important secrets?"

"Why do you think? I wanted to fuck her!"

"Interesting," said Popsi. "I think, my friend, you have only fucked yourself."

SPEED TRAP

####

Sully Sullivan never got to work the traffic light room again. And, unfortunately, he lost that finger. Once Doc Bennett saw it, he told Sully there was nothing much he could do but snip it off and cauterize the wound. He cautioned Sullivan that he should be a lot more careful when working with clamps.

Popsi did a bit more legwork and with the help of a friend discovered that Linda Bishop had a very close friend in Atlanta. Her best friend and former fellow cheerleader at Astoria High School was only too proud to tell Carole Friedlander that Linda was dating none other than the governor's chief of staff, Mr. Floyd Perkins.

####

Popsi met with Boss the next morning in his office. He laid it all out in step by step fashion, and Boss, as he had expected, grew madder than a soaked cat.

He asked about Sullivan's condition and seemed satisfied. "I take it you made it clear he was no longer employed, right?" Popsi nodded.

"You made it clear that if we ever hear he has disclosed anything about Astoria, the red light, the police department, anything, that he will lose far more than a finger?" Popsi nodded again.

"Make sure everyone knows the Bishop girl is an informant and is off limits. Keep an eye on her parents, and her house and step it up anytime she comes home. I want to know anytime she asks anybody about anything in this town."

"Yes, Boss."

"You did good work as always, Colanise," said Boss, who reached into his wallet and handed him a $50 bill, prompting a slight smile from Popsi. "I'll deal with my idiot cousin myself."

Chapter Twelve

As it turned out, Linda Bishop was coming home to visit her folks that very Friday. Linda was a rising junior at Georgia Tech, one of a very few coeds at that august institution.

A shapely blonde with long, curly locks, Linda had been head cheerleader at Astoria High her senior year and had also been elected "Most Likely to Succeed." Since then, her life was going right to plan since her most fortunate meeting of one Floyd Perkins at a swanky Buckhead party back in May.

Floyd was not only going to make something of himself, but at the young age of 31, he already had. Linda swooned that night when Floyd told her that not only did he work for the governor, but he was the governor's number one guy.

Needless to say, at that point, Linda was determined that Floyd would be hers. And ever since Linda had been a little girl, she had been very good at getting what she wanted.

She was looking forward to telling her folks about Floyd because she knew they'd be proud. Her father, Clon Bishop, managed the Pic and Pay grocery store and Mary Bishop, like most women, was a stay at home mom and housekeeper. Linda's trip from Atlanta to Astoria was long and grueling, and she was happy to see she was getting close to home when she passed the nearly hidden speed limit sign near the fruit stand on 55.

Suddenly, a police car appeared in the rear view mirror of her Volkswagen beetle. Its lights and siren were flashing, and Linda was confused. She had known since she was 16 that very few folks with Georgia tags got pulled over in Hyde County.

She pulled to the side of the road, nervously adjusted her hair and waited for the officer to come to her door.

Tony Wiggins paused as he approached the rear of the Volkswagen. He pulled his billy club from his belt and smashed Linda's left tail light, then quickly returned the weapon to his belt. Linda was startled and confused.

"Miss, can I see your license and registration?" Tony's eyes popped when he saw the pretty coed in her somewhat revealing yellow sundress.

"What did I do, officer, and what did you do to my car?" asked Linda.

"Ma'am, I didn't do anything. But you appear to have a broken tail light and that will be a citation."

"A broken tail light? If it is broken, you must have broken it. Why did you stop me? I live here. My daddy runs the Pic and Pay in town."

"Missy, if you are going to be argumentative, I will have to ask you to get out of the car."

Linda fumed, but complied. She was shocked when the officer quickly slapped a handcuff on her left hand and snapped the other onto the rear view mirror on the driver's door.

"What are you doing? I demand to be taken home."

"That's not a bad idea, sweetheart," leered Smith. "I'm going to have to search you. You are one of them Atlanta college kids and you might have drugs or a concealed weapon."

"This is ridiculous! What are you ..."

Smith pushed Linda against her car, face first. His crotch pressed against her rounded posterior and he immediately put his hands around her and onto her firm breasts. Linda screamed, and Smith responded by bumping her head, a bit roughly, against the car.

"Young lady, you will quietly submit to this search or you will see the inside of the Astoria City Jail."

Linda whimpered, but remained silent as the officer grabbed both of her breasts and squeezed. His fingers searched for, and found, both of her hardening nipples. Then he lowered his hands and caressed both cheeks of Linda's ample behind.

Then, his right hand went under her dress, between her legs and rubbed her crotch.

"Well, I see you don't have any weapons on you, but you are otherwise well equipped," laughed the officer.

"Now let me tell you something, sweet cakes. We can make it very rough for you and your parents, that Pic and Pay daddy of yours and your lovin' momma. You need to keep your mouth shut when you are around your ritzy Atlanta friends. We don't need any of their interference down here."

Suddenly, Linda understood exactly what was going on. And she was suddenly very peeved at one Floyd Perkins.

"Now you get back in your little Nazi wagon here and you go on home. If I was you, I'd keep that pretty little mouth closed about anything that goes on down here, including this little traffic stop today. Loose lips sink ships." Then he paused.

"Though I bet yours could give a helluva blow job," chortled the officer, who then removed the handcuffs.

"I'm going to give you a verbal warning on that tail light," he added. "But you ought to go over to Bickle's and get it fixed while you're home."

"What is your name, officer?" said Linda, who had noticed he was not wearing a name tag.

"Sweetheart, I'm Officer Friendly," he laughed. "And if I stop you again, we'll get a whole lot friendlier with each other, if you know what I mean. Now get on home."

Smith returned to his squad car and drove on past the Volkswagen, heading towards town. He stuck his hand out the door as he passed, offering a neighborly wave.

Linda was shaking as she got back in her car. And despite the warning, she was going to get right on the phone to Floyd just as soon as she could get home.

Floyd Perkins was aghast. "They did what?" he nearly shouted into the phone. "Those bastards!"

"Floyd, why did you tell them I had told you about that red light? I told you that in confidence."

Floyd was startled. She had, in fact, told him in confidence, in bed. It had been pillow talk, but it had been valuable information since the governor had been obsessed with all things Hyde County of late.

"Linda, I did tell the governor what you told me, but I protected your identity. He, nor anyone one else in the administration, knows your name or anything else about you."

"Well, Floyd, this cop knew everything. I was practically deflowered right beside U.S. 55."

Floyd paused, thinking to himself that the deflowering had happened before today and he personally had participated. But the last thing he needed was to get her even more agitated.

"Linda, don't worry. I will get to the bottom of this. You stay home and stay safe."

####

When Linda and Floyd hung up, a third party stayed on the line a few more seconds, then hung up their receiver as well.

In rural Georgia, almost no one had a private telephone line. The Bishops, like most other folks, shared their telephone line with more than one fellow Astorian.

This loyal Astorian, who had been listening to every incoming and outgoing call made on the Bishop's phone, now had important information to pass on. This wouldn't be carelessly transmitted on an open line. This message would be passed on, face to face, to the people who had asked for it and would pay for it.

####

That night, Linda and her mother were finishing up the dinner dishes. Clon Bishop, weary from a long day of stocking shelves and doing inventory at the Pic and Pay, was in his recliner, feet up, the TV tuned to "The Rifleman," starring Chuck Connors. Mary and Linda were still twittering about Linda's handsome, important, well-placed new beau.

Linda had obeyed Floyd's request not to mention what had happened on the roadside to anyone, not even her parents.

With no warning, a loud blast shook the house. The home's front picture window exploded, glass flying all over the living room. Clon Bishop, miraculously uninjured, jumped from his chair in horror. Mary and Linda screamed.

Through the now wide open window, Bishop saw what appeared to be a black car accelerate up the road. Its lights were off, and by the time he could get to the door, there was no sign of the vehicle. There was a single empty 12-gauge shotgun shell on his driveway, and a streak of rubber on the road. There was no other trace of what had happened other than the shotgun pellets that had done the damage, spread along the wall opposite the window.

Once Linda had calmed down, she knew she had to tell her parents the whole story. So she did.

Clon Bishop was enraged, but as a lifelong resident, he knew the score in Astoria. He knew his daughter had violated the unspoken oath of the town. What happens in Astoria doesn't get passed along to any outsiders, especially those in high places.

"Honey, nothing else can be said to your boyfriend. There will be no talk about home other than what your momma made for supper. We could have been killed tonight. I hope this is the end of it. As far as this family is concerned, it better be. We have gotten the message, loud and clear."

The events of the day were to have quick repercussions in both Atlanta and Astoria.

Ledford, Joey

Chapter Thirteen

The governor was a bit taken back when his chief of staff requested a quick emergency meeting with the topic being Astoria.

Dunlap immediately noticed that Perkins appeared very upset. His suit coat was off, which was unprecedented. His tie was loose around his neck, his face was red, his features agitated and his usually perfect hair was all mussed up.

"Floyd, what is wrong with you, son?" asked the governor. "I have never seen you so afluster."

"Governor, do you recall that I passed on to you information from a confidential informant about the red light in Astoria?" asked the chief of staff.

"Why, yes, I do. That was most valuable information and I appreciate it."

"Governor, did you reveal to Griffin that you knew about the red light?"

Dunlap was surprised at the question. "I felt it necessary to let that arrogant bastard know that we had some goods on him," said Dunlap. "Was that a problem?"

Dunlap laid it all out to his boss, revealing the identity of the informant, how she got the information and how it literally landed in his lap.

"So you was bedding this Astoria girl to get me information?" asked the governor. "Son, I am damned impressed. I done good hiring you, didn't I?"

"Well, that's not all exactly correct, sir. I have a genuine romantic interest in this girl. She just happens to be from Astoria.

"The real problem, and the reason for this meeting, is somehow they found out she was the informant. An Astoria cop pulled her over on some trumped up traffic charge yesterday. He scared her to death. Sir, he actually sexually assaulted her."

"He did what?" Dunlap was incredulous.

"Well, this cop went into some convoluted story about how she was from Atlanta and might be carrying drugs or something. Then he proceeded to feel her up big time and hump her butt."

Dunlap's eyes bugged. "He humped her butt?"

"Yes sir. I mean, he didn't take off his pants and he didn't strip her or rape her or anything, but he humped her butt, scared her some more and then he sent her on to her parents' house."

Dunlap stroked his chin and slowly and thoughtfully relit his cigar. "This sumbitch is better than I thought he was," he mused aloud. "How in the Sam Hell could he have known this girl told you about the red light?"

"I don't know, sir."

"Well, you said she found out from some drunk in a beer joint down there, right?"

"Yes sir. She said he was trying to impress her. All the boys down there do that. He bragged that he actually operated the switch that changes the light."

"Floyd, son, there's your real leak. Griffin got his henchmen to sweat everybody in the whole stinking, vermin-infested operation until they figured out this boy leaked. Then he turned on your girlfriend."

Perkins nodded. "I bet you are right, sir,"

"You are damn right I'm right, son. I'm the governor of Georgia. I'm always fucking right."

But then the governor turned thoughtful and his boastful tone disappeared. His voice softened.

"Son, I suspect your girlfriend, and maybe her whole family, might really be in some honest to God danger. This guy is pure evil and he might hurt these folks. She gave up valuable intelligence to us and that turned these folks into his enemies."

Then, his tone changed again and he slammed his fist on his desk. "Griffin don't scare easily. He has upped the ante in this here poker game!"

"Son," he said, looking back at Perkins. "It is now time for Plan B."

####

Boss summoned two people to his drab little office in the courthouse. This quick summit was the result of some news he had gotten from his unofficial police sources.

Arriving first was Popsi Colanise. Boss gave him the courtesy of a quick pre-brief. The big Greek was not the problem today. Frankly, he had never been the problem. He was a tremendous asset and his value to Griffin seemed to be increasing daily since this latest brushup with Buford Dunlap.

Lagging in ten minutes late was Astoria Police Chief Carl Griffin. He smelled of alcohol and his eyes were bloodshot. He rarely wore a police uniform, and today was no exception. He looked more like a day laborer than the leader of Astoria's finest.

Boss was dead sober, and on those increasingly rare occasions when he had not had a drink, those who had been hitting the bottle really stood out to him.

"Carl, are you drunk?" asked Boss.

"No, sir. I had a couple of beers at lunch, but I am not drunk."

"Lunch? Do you realize it is 10:30 in the morning?"

"I have to check on some collections out at Mel's today, so I ate early."

Griffin rolled his eyes and looked at Popsi, who shrugged his shoulders.

"You have been told you play no role in collections. Do you not remember that?"

"Oh yeah, that's right. OK, I guess I don't have to go after all."

"Carl, your performance has been absolutely atrocious of late," said Boss, his eyes stern, his fingers drumming on his desk, his arms occasionally rising for emphasis. "There are a couple of matters I wish to discuss with you in detail."

"Yes, sir," replied the chief. "Does he need to be here?" He motioned towards Popsi.

"You goddamn right he needs to be here. He follows orders, promptly and correctly. You will understand why he is here in a few minutes."

Properly chastised, Carl Griffin suddenly acquired a forlorn look. He had finally realized this might be something serious.

Earl Griffin introduced the topic of Theo Sullivan. He asked his cousin where he first met Sullivan, and why he trusted him enough to give him an important and confidential job in the Astoria operation.

Carl stammered, hesitated and finally said that Sully was a friend from high school, an old running mate that he felt he could trust.

"Do you realize that this man you hired, some swamp rat you used to shoot pool with, divulged the secret of our red light running campaign to some girl he was trying to impress at a bar?"

Recognition dawned over Carl's face. Now he understood why Popsi had gathered Sully from Mel's and had taken him away. He had not heard from him since.

"No, sir. I am very surprised to hear that."

"I suppose you are, Carl. You seem to be the last one to know a lot of things around here, which is inexcusable considering your position of responsibility.

"Now, I want to know what the hell happened with the Bishop girl."

"Yes, sir. Pop… uh… Mr. Colanise told me you wanted us to keep an eye on her parents. We began … uh, electronic surveillance and determined that she was coming home yesterday. I ordered a unit to stand watch on 55 and stop her."

"Did I say I wanted her pulled over? Didn't I say she was strictly off limits?"

Carl again looked puzzled. He looked at Popsi, whose great stone face did not move. "I do think that was part of the instructions, yes."

"So, she was off limits, yet you had one of your boys pull her over and work her?"

"Yes, sir. That's what I thought we were supposed to do."

Earl Griffin's face got even redder as the rage began to build. "And once she got home, that evening, isn't it true you sent a crew over to her house to scare her family?"

"Yes, sir. I believe the instructions were to ... as I recall ... 'step it up once she comes home.' She came home and we stepped it up."

"You pencil-brained fuckin' idiot!" raged Boss. "You were to step up surveillance, not shoot out her daddy's front window. You were to watch her, listen to her and see who she was talking to. You were not to stop her, harass her, scare her and then terrorize her family."

"How did somebody so God-blessed ignorant get Griffin blood in their body?"

Carl Griffin really, really needed a drink. He had never been so thirsty for alcohol in his life.

"You are suspended, without pay, until further notice," railed Boss. "You are not to carry a badge, wear a uniform -- as if you ever did anyway -- drive a squad car, nor have contact with any employee of the police department. You will hand over all your firearms, uniforms, badge, everything, to Mr. Colanise.

"Now get the hell out of my sight. I will decide your final disposition on another day."

Defrocked of his once proud position, stripped from power and humiliated in front of Popsi Colanise, Carl Griffin stood and stumbled toward the office door. Tears were forming in his eyes. At the door, he turned and spoke once again.

"Boss, I'm sorry. I never meant …"

"Shut up! Get out! Now!"

Once the now sobbing Griffin had ambled down the hall and was safely out of earshot, Griffin motioned to Popsi to close the office door.

"Were my instructions clear to you?" he asked.

"Boss, I passed them to the chief, word for word. I thought he understood, especially when I had earlier told him we were shutting down both the speed operation and the light. Why would we shut down to lay low, but at the same time grab a local girl off the highway, rough her up and then shoot out her family's front window? It doesn't make sense."

Griffin nodded, pursed his lips and continued.

"At least you get it. For now, you are running the police department."

"Boss, I don't have, what do they call it? … police post certification."

"I don't give a fuck," said Earl Griffin. "I hold no elected office myself, but I run this county. Likewise, you will run the police department until I tell you differently.

"I'll call Carole Friedlander and make sure they all understand this change in command. No uniform for you; no badge. You should continue to carry just as you always have. In addition to running the department, you will continue to be at my beck and call for non-police assignments as warranted.

"This is going to be a …. uh, active time around here. I need somebody I can trust and somebody I can count on to follow my orders to the letter."

Griffin instructed that surveillance on the Bishops was to continue unabated, but no further contact was to be made with the family.

"If she talks to her boyfriend again, though, let me know every word that is spoken."

"I understand, sir."

Griffin indicated to Colanise that he was dismissed. The big man moved towards the door, but Boss asked him to stop. Then, a completely different Boss, a softer, friendlier Boss, suddenly emerged.

"Thank you again … Popsi," he said, forcing a half-smile. "Help me get through this."

Popsi could not help from grin from ear to ear as he strode down the hall. This had been a very, very good week!

Chapter Fourteen

The Three Musketeers were riding again. On this muggy July midmorning, Jim Bob, Sassy and Zeke had a plan to make a day of it. Jim Bob's mom had made them a sack of peanut butter and jelly sandwiches, and they each had shiny dimes so they could stop at a store somewhere during their two-wheeled travels to get a cold drink to wash the sandwiches down at midday.

Jim Bob could already taste the ice cold R.C. Cola, his all-time favorite. Most folks always seemed to prefer Georgia-made Co-Colas, but the R.C.s came in twice as big a bottle and tasted so much sweeter and were, in Jim Bob's opinion, just lots better than Co-Colas. Zeke was a traditionalist who always went with Coke, but Sassy loved grape Ne-Hi that always left a purple stripe around her mouth.

Jim Bob really didn't know why, but he loved it when Sassy looked that way. He was just very fond of her, and that seemed so weird because he'd always thought girls were dumb. Sassy was different, though, because she could ride almost as fast as him and definitely faster than Zeke, who always seemed to get a little out of breath on their hard-out peddling sprints.

Jim Bob was experimenting with something he'd just learned from an older boy in the trailer park. If you took baseball cards and borrowed some clothespins from your mom, you could clip the cards onto your wheels. You fixed it so the cards extended into the wheel, just enough that they would scrape on the spokes.

It sounded like a real engine and Jim Bob loved it. And the faster he rode, the better the engine revved!

He was very selective on which cards he would use for his "motor," though. He always picked guys who hit .200 or less or pitchers who lost a lot more games than they won. Jim Bob liked to keep the cards of the best players – guys like Mickey Mantle, Yogi Berra, Willie Mays, Hank Aaron and some others -- in a separate box under his bed. He really didn't know why, but he just felt like those were real keepers and didn't need to get worn out flapping on his bicycle.

Zeke had a new dog, and it was bounding along beside them. His name was Pluto, named after the Disney dog because he was big and brown and had floppy ears kind of like Pluto's. Jim Bob seemed far more worried than Zeke that Pluto would stray into the path of fast-traveling tourists that their dads had been unable to slow down with a ticket. It didn't matter how many tickets they wrote, Sassy often noted, the Yankees always drove too fast.

The three were buzzing today about movies they were hoping to go see at the Bijou Theatre in town. Sassy went on and on about "Sleeping Beauty" because she had seen it advertised on TV. Jim Bob and Zeke kind of looked at each other and shrugged their shoulders. Sassy never even noticed as she continued to describe what she'd seen. The boys were more interested in seeing "The Shaggy Dog," but Sassy wouldn't hear of that.

In the distance as they peddled along the right of way of 55, Bobby saw strange new activity. A crew of men had mounted poles into the soft sandy soil not far from the edge of the pavement. As they got closer, Jim Bob realized the men were about to put up a big sign.

There were some billboards on the roads around Astoria, but not many, and those that were there were touting Stuckey's down south toward Savannah or the Alligator Farm on the edge of the swamp. Jim Bob wondered what was being sold on this sign, so he peddled harder and got ahead of his two friends.

The actual sign was laying off to the right, awaiting the completion of the standards that would hold it up. When Jim Bob read the message, he let go an audible gasp and came close to wrecking his J.C. Higgins.

"Beware!" read the biggest word, painted in big black all capital letters. "You are in Hyde County and approaching Astoria, Georgia. Don't get fleeced in a CLIP JOINT. Don't get caught in a SPEED TRAP!" At the bottom, it was signed by Buford Dunlap, the governor of Georgia.

As Jim Bob was still processing this amazing sight, his two friends rode up beside him. "What's going on, Jim Bob?" asked Zeke, clueless as always.

Sassy had already taken it all in and looked at Jim Bob in disbelief.

"What IS going on?" she said. "Why would the governor of Georgia be against our daddies doing their jobs?"

Zeke finally looked over and processed the billboard's amazingly controversial message. "What's a clip joint?" he asked. "Is that the barber shop?"

"No, Zeke," said Jim Bob. "That's like Mel's. Didn't you know the men sometimes play cards in the back? And I've seen the tourists play that dice game, what is it, Razzle?"

"But Jim Bob, they've always done that. Is something wrong with that?" asked Sassy. "I've heard daddy say that guys like Mel would go under if it wasn't for their dice games."

"One thing's for sure," said Jim Bob. "That Buford Dunlap is a doggone communist. How could he stand up for Yankees over our daddies?"

Jim Bob quickly formulated a plan. "Our daddies got to know about this," he said. "Do y'all know where they are working today?"

Nobody was sure. "Well, let's ride into town and tell Carole. She can dispatch it out to them. They might want to run these guys out of town before they can put this sign up," reasoned Jim Bob.

The two glared at the men as they peddled by. Pluto, apparently understanding their distrust, barked at them as he dashed along right behind Zeke's back fender.

####

Carole Friedlander wasn't surprised to see the Musketeers. They had visited before, but usually it was to see one or more of their fathers. All of them were out doing city business today, however.

"What can I do for you young'uns today?" she said with a big motherly smile, which was somewhat dulled by the ever-present cigarette dangling from her mouth.

"They're putting up a big sign to warn the Yankees that we're here!" shouted Jim Bob.

"They're out to put us out of business!" added Sassy.

"There's three of them! And they have a truck!" Zeke cried.

"OK, kids. Slow down!" said Carole. "Tell me exactly what you saw."

####

The kids were the first to know about Buford Dunlap's Plan B, though they had no idea that was what it was called. Carole told Popsi and he told Boss, and the two of them went out to see the sign in person.

Popsi passed it, did a U-turn and Boss cursed out loud as he saw it. The workmen, apparently state road department employees, initially didn't even notice the two men who were taking in the results of their labor.

"Maybe I should have let you burn down the Governor's Mansion," said Boss. "This man is a lunatic."

Popsi didn't say a word. But his grim visage told the story. He knew this could be big trouble. People had to be speeding before the patrolmen could pull them over. Warned in advance, all the drivers would be on their best behavior and creep through town. The businesses were bound to suffer as well. Nobody thought anything of a little Razzle Dazzle when it came at you all unexpected. But to be warned of a fleecing in advance would definitely throw a monkey wrench into the town's thriving underground economy.

"As the men stood outside Popsi's unmarked car, he heard Carole call for him on the radio.

"Excuse me, Boss," he said. "Sounds like I need to answer."

Popsi climbed back into the big Chevrolet and exchanged a few words with Friedlander. When he got back out of the car, Boss could tell the news wasn't good by the frown on his face.

"Friedlander says there's another one north of town. Two of 'em in all."

Earl Griffin's hand came down hard on the Chevy's hood. The sound was loud enough to make the workmen turn around and look. One looked at the other and they laughed.

Boss was enraged. Not only had Dunlap put signs along his roads, but the governor's men were in his county laughing at him. It was probably a good thing he wasn't carrying because he might have put all three of them down right then and there.

Popsi realized he had better diffuse this situation and quickly.

"Boss, let's go back into town and figure this out," he said. "We can't do anything out here."

Boss pulled his flask from his pocket as soon as his butt hit the passenger seat. He washed down two pills with a big draw of Kentucky bourbon. He had pretty much drained the flask before Popsi pulled into the back alley of the courthouse.

Chapter Fifteen

News didn't break quickly -- it took a while for things to get out in a world with no social media, no Internet and no cable news networks. In fact, even TV network news was glittery and new and had an experimental feel, just 15 minutes during the evening dinner hour. The news business was a bit like being a cop in Astoria; it had a wild, wild west, anything goes kind of vibe to it and it attracted a strange and creative breed of people who might have never found fulfillment otherwise.

The news of the Astoria billboards was officially broken by a young man named Thomas Sentry, though his alias was Cliff Cannon. "Cannon" was the morning jack of all trades for WWGS, the AM radio station in Moxley, serving as much of south Georgia as its "coffee pot" transmitter would cover, and with the flat sandy plains around it, it got out pretty well, as least in daylight.

Cannon saw the billboard on his way into work long before dawn, a few hours before the state troopers would arrive to guard it. It was such an unusual sight in his headlights that he slammed on the brakes to take a closer look. A billboard that shouted,

"Warning?" Wow, you'd expect a road sign saying detour before you'd see such a thing.

But Cannon knew a bit about Astoria, and he knew the local cops were absolute Nazis on traffic enforcement, so he had a bit of the background just by living in the general area. He'd had no idea, though, that the Astoria boys had put a buzzing bee under Gov. Dunlap's bonnet.

Not only was this his lead story on the WWGS morning news, but he talked about it between country songs, farm reports and local obituaries. He loved stuff that would set his show apart from the slick Willie broadcasts streaming across the coastal plain from Savannah.

Once Cannon got to work and let his first report on the billboard fly, however, the sound of the big metalic United Press International teletype clicking nearby reminded him that he could and should do even more with this story.

Cannon was what was known as a "stringer" for larger news organizations. As a news broadcaster, he had a relationship with the Georgia news desk of UPI, a proud international wire service. If he tipped UPI that the governor wanted some Astoria blood, he knew he'd get a stringer check for it. If they liked the story, he might make $5 or even $10. That wasn't bad money for making one phone call, particularly when you considered how little WWGS paid him.

So Cannon picked up the phone and got UPI rookie Lewis Rome on the line. Rome and the other UPI staffers were accustomed to getting calls from radio guys in the hinterlands, but usually the tip was about a single-car fatal accident or sometimes a house fire that had killed someone.

Rome liked what he was hearing from Cannon and took copious notes on his manual typewriter. And when he hung up the phone, he thought he had a pretty good "bright" for the Georgia wire.

He knocked out a quick three paragraphs and filed it to the newspapers in the state. He also did a "takeout" for broadcasters in Georgia to read on the air. He was pretty proud of himself after he filed it.

No sooner had it hit the wire than John Warrington, one of UPI's regional desk men, walked across the room towards Rome. When Rome saw him coming, he was startled, because Warrington, quite frankly, scared him to death. Gruff and imposing, the black-bearded Warrington was known as one of the toughest editors in the company. He was also considered by many to be one of the best writers on the planet.

Warrington had forgotten the rookie's name, so he didn't use it. Instead he launched into the issue at hand.

"I think this is pretty good little story you just filed," he growled, which surprised Rome, who had figured he would cut him to pieces for an error in grammar, spelling, judgment, or all three. "You need to build it up. I want to trunk it."

Rome's heart jumped. The trunk was UPI's A-wire, which meant the story would go all over the nation, maybe all over the world! And as the reporter, it would carry his byline! But the nuts and bolts of "building it up" somewhat stumped the green newsman.

"What do you suggest, Mr. Warrington?"

Warrington could barely restrain his disgust, but somehow he did. The children we're hiring these days, he grumbled to himself.

"This billboard had to have come from the governor's office. Call them and get some background. Why are they doing this? Why don't they just send in the State Patrol or the GBI to clean house? Call the State Patrol and see how many tickets these officers write.

"Do I need to hold your hand, or can you do this for me?"

"Yes sir. I mean, no sir, I'm on it," said Rome.

Rome called the governor's office and explained to the secretary what he was looking for. He didn't even know the governor's press secretary to ask for him by name.

After a brief pause, a familiar voice came on the phone.

"This is Buford Dunlap. How can I do 'ya today?"

Rome was flabbergasted. He had gotten the governor himself! He was smart enough to never doubt the news judgment of John Warrington ever again.

"So governor, we hear you've commissioned a billboard just outside Astoria ... "

"Two billboards. Where you from, son?"

"I'm from Athens."

"You go to the university?"

"Yes sir, I graduated two months ago."

"Well, good for you. What yo daddy do?"

"He's a lineman for the power company."

"Good. He's likely a good Democrat. Son, I'm proud of you. You got through school and you gotcha a pretty good job there with the wire boys. I'm gonna give you a good one today and I want you to give it helluva ride, OK?"

"Uh, yes sir."

"Well, it's like this. There's a bunch of lawless cutthroats down there in Astoria who are riding herd on innocent tourists, unsuspecting folks who are just traveling through our fine state on their way to the beach."

Rome typed like a madman, getting every word down.

"The ring leader of this crooked enterprise is a man named Earl Griffin, but he calls himself Boss. I guess that's fairly accurate because everybody in all of Hyde County appears to do his bidding, including a gang of scoundrels and scallywags who work for him.

"You know to spell scallywags, don't 'ya?"

Rome could barely contain his excitement. He inserted an "uh huh" here and there as the governor proceeded to interview himself.

Dunlap went on for awhile until Rome finally got the courage to interrupt him.

"Governor, why don't you send the state police down to break this up?"

"Well, son, we are looking at all the alternatives at this time. I would note that our resources are somewhat limited and it would take quite a bit of hog rootin' to dig all this manure up."

"So the billboards ..."

"The billboards are designed to dry this festering sore up by word 'a mouth. And if you do your job, people all over the country will know that you need to step lightly when you're passing through Astoria and Hyde County. Keep your foot off the gas. Don't stop and get cornholed in a clip joint. Hey, clean up that cornhole shit, that was off the record."

"Yes sir."

"Governor, I need to call the State Patrol and get some records on these tickets ... "

"Well, you can do that, son, but I got some information for you on that."

Wow, this story was reporting and writing itself, thought Rome.

"Last year, the Astoria Police Department wrote more speeding tickets than the city of Atlanta," said Dunlap, pausing to let that sink in.

"Gee willikers, really?"

"Son, I'm the governor of Georgia. I ain't gonna bullshit ya."

"And also, Lewis," he paused, letting it sink in to the rookie that he was now on a first-name basis with the governor, "They have written more tickets for red light running than the city of Macon!

"And they only have one goddamned red light! Oh hell, that was off the record … clean me up there, Lewis."

"Yes sir."

"I think this'll about do it. If you need any more, call us or the State Patrol back. Remember, do this right, son. You'll be doing your home state and your beloved governor a huge favor if you give this a good write up."

"Thank you, governor!"

"And son, come on out to the mansion some Saturday night. I'll pour 'ya a stiff drink. The good stuff, I promise. And give my regards to yo daddy and yo momma. I'm thinking she's raised a pretty good boy."

Rome began to bang out the story. Warrington, noting from across the room that Rome was off the phone, came over and peered over his shoulder at his typed notes. Rome heard him chortling a time or two as he read Dunlap's quotes.

Within an hour, Warrington had crafted Rome's rough draft into a journalistic masterpiece. In newsrooms around the country, editors were soon giggling about the governor of Georgia waging a verbal and highway billboard war with an old-style county boss and his gaggle of "scoundrels and scallywags" out in the boondocks.

####

Twelve blocks from the grimy UPI office, the city editor of The Atlanta Journal was reading Rome's story on a strip of yellow teletype paper. He walked across the room and plopped it on the desk of Wilmer Montgomery, a young but experienced general assignment reporter at the state's largest afternoon daily.

"Monty, this is a good one. I'd like you to match it."

"Herb, you know I hate rewriting wire copy."

"No, I don't want a rewrite. Drive down to Astoria and get me a reader on this for tomorrow's editions. There's nothing from this Boss Griffin in it, no local reaction, no color other than Buford's gassing on about an apparent criminal enterprise.

"Get me some color!"

"OK, Herb. Let me finish this and I'll get down there."

SPEED TRAP

Chapter Sixteen

Wilmer Montgomery was only three years out of Auburn University, but he was already hard-nosed. Primarily a police reporter, the skinny, dark-haired, goatee wearing man known as Monty was known for getting good quotes from cops. He liked a good whodunit, and even though on this story he had a pretty good idea who had done it, he needed a little more evidence of it before he could write it.

He thought about blaring into town at 80 mph just so he'd get a ticket and meet the key players firsthand, but he knew for a fact his skinflint editors would refuse to pay his fine. And if he got thrown in jail in godforsaken Astoria, Georgia, he might never see his wife again, not to mention taste the Mexican food he loved to eat with his newspaper friends every Friday after the publication of the Journal's final edition.

So he made sure to mind his manners on the road, and went straight into town to the Astoria Courthouse, circa City Hall. He realized quickly it was also the police headquarters when he saw a couple of squad cars parked out front.

He came inside and began to wander around. The first door he saw that was open was that of the city clerk.

"Hello, I'm from the Journal up in Atlanta. I was looking for Mr. Earl Griffin."

The woman gave him a once over. "Sir, Mr. Griffin doesn't see anyone without an appointment."

"Can I make one?"

"Not without seeing Mr. Griffin," she said, apparently failing to see the contradiction of her statement.

"Well, could you get a message to him that the Atlanta Journal would like a comment from him on the governor's billboards, plus some allegations the governor has made against him?"

The woman looked a bit flustered, but she gathered herself quickly. "Why don't you sit out there in the hall and I'll see what I can do for you."

Monty sighed, but since Griffin was his top priority, he complied. Twenty minutes later, the city clerk came out of her office.

"Mr. Griffin said he don't want to talk to the Atlanta Journal and that he had no comment to that fishwrapper," she said.

"That's what he said?" asked Monty.

"It wasn't in Morse Code," she replied.

Montgomery thanked the woman and moved down the hall to what appeared to be the police department. He walked through the glass door and up to a glass window. Carole Friedlander was at her usual post.

"May I help you, sir?"

Montgomery again introduced himself and asked to see the chief of police. Friedlander, knowing the city was without a uniformed chief at the moment, took a slightly different approach. "He ain't around," she said.

"Is there anybody else who could speak for the department, any other officers? Where might I find some?"

Friedlander laughed. "You can find 'em down at the speed trap," she said.

Monty quietly celebrated, because he had his quote. And he could read her nametag, so that was good enough for him. "Thank you, ma'am. Where might this speed trap be?"

To his surprise, Friedlander gave him exacting directions back up U.S. 55, exactly the way he had come. She told him where he could find an officer or two, noting that "they may be parked behind some bushes or underbrush."

Montgomery passed through the town's infamous red light without incident as he turned back north. Being that his Ford had a Georgia license plate and was in no danger of triggering the usual mechanical magic, and he had forgotten Dunlap's quotes in Rome's story about red light running, he didn't think twice about it. But he was a bit surprised to see a Georgia State Patrol squad car parked in front of the now famous Astoria billboard. He pulled over to chat, drawing his notebook and checking to make sure his pen was still working.

Trooper Calvin Bocock had been warned by his dispatchers, via the governor's office, that reporters might come calling. His superiors had made a command decision to let him talk. They knew he was a personable young man, so they briefed him on the message and trusted that he was ready to communicate it.

"Why, hello Mr. Montgomery, I've read your stories. You do a great job covering the police," said Bocock, who'd never had any formal training talking to reporters, nor did he need any. It was all just good common sense. "What can I do for you today?"

Montgomery asked him how it felt to be guarding a billboard.

"We protect the public and public property," said Bocock.

"What are you protecting it from?" asked Monty.

"Let me just say that there are elements in Hyde County that do not like the message this billboard is sending to the traveling public," said Bocock. "Our governor feels this message needs to be sent, and to ensure it is sent, we are stationed here for the time being."

"How long is the time being?"

"As long as we're needed," said Bocock.

"Can you elaborate on these elements who seek to … do this billboard harm?" asked Monty, trying to keep a straight face.

"I'd rather not. I think the governor's office can give you what you need on that," said Bocock with a big smile.

"Would these 'elements' be centered around one Earl Griffin here in Astoria?" probed Monty.

"Mr. Montgomery, I'd rather not name any names. We are here to make sure the traveling public passes through Hyde County without any unnecessary obstacles," said the trooper.

Monty tried his best to get Bocock to go off the record and give him the straight scoop, but he only smiled and continued with the small talk.

"Who would you recommend I talk to?" Monty said.

"The Astoria boys had two units two miles that a way," he said, pointing up the road. "Talk to them. I don't think they are that busy today." That promoted a big smile from the trooper.

"Thank you, Trooper Bocock. Would you like me to bring you a Co-Cola or something?"

"No sir, thank you very much for asking. I'll get away for a bite after a while."

Monty then drove on up the road and found Officer Wesley Crane right where both Friedlander and Bocock said he'd be. His squad car was sitting in the shade of an oak tree amid some underbrush, and was hardly visible from the northbound side of 55, a detail that did not escape Montgomery, who made a note in his pad.

Crane was not happy to see Montgomery stop, but having been warned by Friedlander, he was going to do his best not to make Astoria look even worse in the pages of the state's largest newspaper.

Montgomery launched into full-fledged interview mode, so Crane took a deep breath and tried to carefully choose his words, which had always been hard for him.

"We are here to enforce our laws and protect our town," he said.

"Are you here to generate revenue? That's what the governor says," probed Montgomery.

Crane paused. Then he bristled. "He's such a liar he'd have to get somebody else to call his dog," said Astoria's unofficial police spokesman of the governor of Georgia.

Montgomery cut it short after that. He knew he'd not get a better quote today.

The reporter was soaked in sweat by the time he'd completed his rounds. He'd talked to Luther Bickle, who hadn't said squat, some ladies in the stores downtown, and even ran into a looker named Flo Riley in the grocery store. She had seemed very friendly until she heard what he did for a living, and then she quickly clammed up. Having a highly developed skill of knowing what makes sense and what doesn't, something he called "his bullshit meter," Monty had come to the conclusion that the people in this town were scared of Griffin. They might not be crazy about what the police did on the roads in and around town, but he'd found nobody who lived here who was going to publicly criticize it.

He called the city desk to dictate his story, a laborious process that involved writing on the fly while Herb typed it all out on the other end. He'd started with a stack of dimes to feed into the pay phone, and he only had two left when he was finished.

"Well, Bud, this is a pretty good story," said Herb, who was an expert at editing on the fly. "I wish we had more from Griffin, but what you got was good. The police dispatcher's quote was really good, and nothing beats what that cop said about the guv'na. Any chance you could find somebody who just got pulled over and put them into the story?"

"Herb, I saw nobody pulled over," said Montgomery. "I think Buford's billboards must be working."

Earl Griffin was motionless in his bed, nearly despondent. CeCe, weary of Earl's restlessness, had decided to sleep in another bedroom, which only added to Earl's depression and despair.

He'd had no idea the governor's billboards would create such a media storm. The UPI story had swept the nation, and Wilmer Montgomery was not the only reporter who had reported and written their own Astoria billboard story. The phones in city hall had rung all day with reporters seeking his comments. The Mutual Radio Network, CBS, NBC, The Associated Press, The Boston

Globe, The New York Times and even the BBC had called. No one got as colorful a no comment from Boss as Montgomery, but all of them wrote stories, each of them small daggers striking at Astoria's secret economic empire. Boss was terrified that these developments signaled the passing of an era that went back to his father, a gut-wrenching fear that Astoria was no longer his quiet little fiefdom. That lit a fire that raged within him. He had never felt so besieged.

And suddenly, he realized he had never been so determined to fight back. This war has only begun, Boss vowed.

Chapter Seventeen

It was clear to just about everyone that the governor's billboards, along with all the negative publicity, had created a significant economic downturn in and around Astoria. Those who read about Astoria before starting their trip north or south had highlighted Hyde County on their gas station maps and made sure to do nothing wrong on the roadways anywhere close to the area. Obviously, the trick red light was impossible to ignore, but word had come down from on high that since the state trooper billboard guards and reporters were roaming around town that there would be no red light enforcement activities until further notice.

Wes Crane and his fellow officers were of the opinion that even overall road traffic was down. The tourists were avoiding even passing through, meaning they were taking the north-south routes that tracked west of U.S. 55. That meant longer trips for many of them, but apparently they considered that a small price to pay for bypassing what Crane and his colleagues considered legitimate traffic law enforcement and what Gov. Dunlap was calling "ill-advised, over-zealous, locally condoned police misconduct."

As a result of the downturn, Crane, Tony Wiggins and Colin Smith had significant downtime. Crane was worried one or more of the cops might even be laid off, which wasn't out of the question considering that revenues were down to nearly nothing.

So partly to take their minds off their idleness, and partly because the three were party animals at heart, they were spending more and more time at Bart Taggart's bar. Bart was getting a little tired of having them around, since their presence unnerved many of his regulars who were wary of a drunken driving or public drunkenness charge. But his biggest concern was the fact that the officers always expected to get lots of free drinks.

Bart poured them their first beer of this day, but decided the time had come for a little meeting before the alcohol could take effect and make his message harder to absorb.

"Boys, you know I like you guys, I like you a lot," he said to the three uniformed officers, who were belly up at his well-worn bar. "When you're here I don't have to worry about brawls and all the usual shit that happens. But I do have to give y'all some bad news."

"What's that, Bart?" said Colin Smith.

"Business is down, guys. It's down for me just like it is for you. And I can't afford to give you guys free drinks every day –

even one or two. You have to admit, y'all was never here this much when you was out enforcing and shit."

"So Bart, you are cutting us off?" asked Tony, a look of amazement on his face. "You know we give you a lot of extra benefits."

"I know, Tony, I mentioned that. But times is hard. Beer and whiskey ain't free. I gotta pay my bills, you know."

Tony and Colin were clearly agitated, but Wes Crane quickly diffused the situation. "Bart's right, boys. Before, he was giving us some free drinks a coupla nights a week. Hell, we been here every day since them fricking signs went up. We have to be reasonable."

Tony sighed, then pushed his bar stool back.

"You're right, Wes," he said, pausing only for a second and then standing up. "Let's go to Flo's!"

Since that first visit to Astoria's best-known cathouse, the trio of burly cops had quickly become regulars there. Each of them had become incredibly enamored with Fancy Fontaine, Flo's hottest property. Just the thought of Fancy in her red negligee was incredibly arousing. And not only was Fancy a stunning looker, but she was extremely talented in her profession, in more ways than one.

The boys piled into Colin's cruiser and set off for Flo's. This was only the second time all three men had decided to go for afternoon delight at the same time, and also the first time they'd had a minute to share some thoughts on Fancy.

"You know, boys, that Fancy is really something," said Wes. "She's purty as a speckled pup."

"Yes sir, you got that right," echoed Tony. "I'd lick her down like a newborn calf."

Colin Smith burst into laughter. "You sumbitches shickle the tit out of me," he said.

They pulled up to Flo's and drove around to the back of the former restaurant so the squad car could not be seen from the road. As was the practice, they had to check in with Flo before knocking on any doors.

Flo Riley saw them pull in and rolled her eyes. It was nice to run a house where you didn't have to worry about getting busted by the cops every two weeks. But just like Bart Taggart, Flo was worried about offering too much of a good thing to Astoria's finest.

"Are you boys here again?" she said, opening up with her usual friendliness.

"Yes ma'am," said Colin. "I can't speak for these boys, but I'm hornier than a billy goat."

"Don't you boys have wives?" Flo probed.

"We got wives," said Tony.

"But Flo, have you ever lived in a trailer park," asked Wes.

"A few years ago. You know a couple of my girls live there. What's the big deal?"

"It's high summer," said Wes. "It's hot and the winders are open. Sounds get around and trailers are close together. Bed springs are screaky. We all got kids."

"Besides," laughed Tony. "It's two in the afternoon. We can't show up at home and demand our mommas give it up."

Colin jumped into the debate. "And that noise thing. These women tend to cry out loudly when they's, you know, getting pleasured."

Flo shook her head and laughed out loud. "I've heard about all three of you boys. You ain't exactly administering a lot of pleasure around here, especially to Fancy."

"What 'ya mean?" asked Colin.

"Colin Smith, you know good and well all of us are here doing what we do to make money. You boys always expect fringe benefits. I can't let my girls go on giving y'all freebies. You got to pay up like all my other customers."

"We aren't here to provide y'all with your own personal concubine," Flo concluded.

"Cock what?" said Tony.

Flo laughed. I guess I shouldn't expect johns to be literate, should I?"

"My name ain't John," said Tony, clearly a bit flustered.

"OK, here's what I'm going to do, boys. I'm going to give y'all one more on the house. This is it. Next time you come, full price only. And even this time, Fancy's off limits.

All three looked downcast.

"I'll do one of you," said Flo. "Delores and Desiree will handle the other two."

"I was kinda worried about sloppy seconds behind these clowns," said Tony, who earned a disapproving look from Flo.

"But Flo," said Colin, figuring he was third man out. "Delores is so homely she needs paintin.'"

"Colin Smith, you better just watch it!" Flo raged. "I do not appreciate any crap like that about my girls, especially when we're doin' y'all one hell of a favor, for free to boot!"

"OK, OK, sorry Flo," said Colin as the boys dispursed to the respective cabins.

In the adjacent room, out of sight but within earshot, Fancy Fontaine breathed a huge sigh of relief. She was sick and tired of the freeloading cops. To be perfectly honest, she was pretty tired of this whole wham, bam, thank you ma'am business. It was just a matter of time, she kept telling herself, until she had saved enough money to get the hell out of Astoria. She had her sights on a beautician school down in Savannah.

####

A similar scene was about to play out a few miles away at Melvin Guthrie's place. Mel was not happy with recent events in town. He hadn't even pulled his Razzle board out from under the counter in a week and that just would not do. The very few tourists who were stopping at his ramshackle business wanted no part of any dice game, having been warned by media accounts and the devil governor's stinking road signs.

Mel could not make a go of it just selling soft drinks and Moon Pies and a few odd pieces of souvenir junk. Business depended on the big money that was generated by Razzle Dazzle, and every pitch he gave was being received by the wary. Most would politely refuse and walk out. Others got a bit angry and would say things like, "So this is what the billboard was about, huh?"

Mel was getting hesitant to even make a pitch. His mark would be just as likely to run back to the billboard and get one of the troopers to come back and hassle him, arrest him, or worse. He knew they could bust him for illegal gambling with a witness and he couldn't take a chance on providing any.

He was in a particularly dark mood when Carl Griffin once again walked through his front door. Guthrie had endured Griffin out of necessity when he was chief of police, but it was pretty clear to Mel that Griffin had been permanently terminated. He didn't know that for sure, but Popsi Colanise's comments the last time the big Greek had stopped by pretty much sealed the deal for Griffin as far as he was concerned.

"Carl, what you doin' here?" Guthrie asked, not too politely.

"Hi, Mel. I figured we could have a coupla drinks and maybe play a hand or two of poker."

"You got any booze? You got any money?"

"I got a few dollars," said Griffin. "But Mel, you know times is a bit tough for me right now until I get reinstated. I expect that'll happen pretty quick and I can pay you back what I owe you."

"Carl, you are one stupid son of a bitch. You know that?" Melvin raged.

"What you mean, Mel. C'mon, I can buy at least one beer from you."

"You ain't gonna get reinstated. I don't have any idea what you done, but you done something and Boss ain't hiring you back. In case you never noticed, your cousin ain't exactly the forgiving type."

Griffin paused and pursed his lips. He was clearly hurt by Guthrie's outburst. He was still used to getting the respect he thought his title brought him and this fall from grace was becoming increasingly painful.

"You tellin' me we're not friends anymore?"

"Carl, right now, right here, you're as popular as an albino wino at a family reunion," said Guthrie. "You're a fuckin' freeloader. You drink my whiskey. You lose at poker and don't have no money to pay. Hell, I had already decided to rearrange your skull just like a New York Yankee who can't pay at Dazzle. But why should I even work up the sweat?

"You get a job and you get some money, you can come back here. Until then, you need to get your ass a fer piece down the road."

Melvin's son Kelley appeared out of nowhere and took extreme pleasure out of grabbing Astoria's suspended chief of police by the collar and pushing him to the door. He opened it and shoved, and Carl went sprawling into the gravel in front of the store.

Tears were forming in Griffin's eyes and his knees and elbows were bloodied by the impact. He got into his car and started to drive away. But first he looked back at Mel's in all its glory.

"Fuck you, Melvin Guthrie," he said to no one but a crow perched on a nearby branch. "You are an asshole. I never liked you anyway."

His tires squealed and gravel went flying as Griffin drove away.

Chapter Eighteen

Georgia State Trooper Oscar Sloan, who'd been the very first officer to report for billboard duty more than two weeks ago, was doing his best to stay awake on a sultry south Georgia Saturday night. It was 2 a.m. or thereabouts, and there was very little traffic on U.S. 55. He had his cruiser's AM radio on a country music station he liked out of Atlanta that carried well in the nighttime, so well he could pick it up way down here in Astoria. Even with the music turned up high, it wasn't easy to keep from drifting off when there was nothing to do but guard a godforsaken road sign.

Oscar had found that when sleep was hitting him hard, it helped to sing along, so he was accompanying Johnny Cash. Quite loudly, in fact.

His truly bad imitation of the Man in Black came to an abrupt end as his police radio came to life.

"APD 1 to GSP, over."

This was truly strange, Sloan thought. Why would the Astoria PD be calling us? One, they don't do much at all after dark, and two, they're kind of hating us right now.

"GSP to APD, go ahead," he replied.

"Requesting assistance on a 10-26. Have 10-32 and … uh, 10-35, over."

This made no sense whatsoever. Astoria was telling him they had detained a subject and needed backup, the subject was armed and the subject was transporting liquor? So maybe they had an illegal rum runner?

"APD 1, what's your 20?"

"North city limit line on 55, over."

"Standby, APD."

Sloan's instructions had been to not leave the billboard unless instructed by State Patrol dispatchers that he was needed elsewhere. It was standard policy for a local jurisdiction to ask for help when something was too big for them, but it sounded like they had things under control. He decided to ask GSP Dispatch for help, so he radioed them and they decided after a quick consult with the shift supervisor that he should go take a look.

It didn't feel right to Sloan, but as far as he was concerned, he'd covered his ass by asking dispatch, so he cranked his engine, put on his blue light and roared exactly 2.8 miles up the road to where he found APD 1, which had pulled over a 1952 Buick Roadmaster titled to one Lester M. Carlyle of Philadelphia, Pennsylvania.

Officers Wesley Crane and Colin Smith were stomping around the Roadmaster, acting important and official and waiting for Sloan to get out of his cruiser and come up to them.

Sloan had never known Astoria PD to be this active on the roadways before dawn, nor had he ever seen two city officers riding together.

"What are you guys up to?" asked Sloan.

Crane proceeded to explain that they had pulled over Mr. Carlyle on a routine traffic stop. He had acted extremely suspicious, so they had asked him to let them search the car. In the trunk, he said, they had found this package containing suspected narcotics and a .38 Special revolver.

Sloan rolled his eyes. "You found a handgun, just sitting in the trunk beside the drugs? Let me see."

He was shown a bag that contained what might have been a quarter-pound or so of marijuana and, sure enough, a .38 Special snub-nosed revolver.

"Does it make any sense to you that the gun would be with the drugs and not on the suspect?" asked Sloan.

"Well," said Crane. "I thought about that. But I'm just reporting what we found and when we find narcotics and firearms, we call for assistance."

Sloan smelled a rat, a skunk and a pole cat, all at once, but he had to do his job. "Let me speak to the suspect," he said. Smith went to get him out of the back of the Astoria patrol car.

"He's cuffed, right?" asked Sloan.

"Yeah, he's cuffed."

"I'd like to talk to him in private, if you don't mind," said the trooper with a glare.

"That's kind of ... irregular, ain't it?" asked Crane. "I thought this was a teamwork kind of thang."

"Officer, produce your suspect and back down!" Sloan said with authority.

"Whatever," said Crane. "Colin, bring the perp over here."

Caryle, a black 38-year-old encyclopedia salesman, was clearly terrified. Once the trooper had managed to calm him down, he told Sloan he'd been assigned to try to sell the reference books in black middle-class neighborhoods in Florida and was planning to drive all night to get there. But then he'd been pulled over. He said he knew he shouldn't be driving this late at night and had no idea he'd been speeding.

"Speeding?" asked Sloan. "That's it?"

"Yes sir," said Carlyle, clearly confused.

"Do you realize these officers say they have found narcotics and a firearm in your trunk?"

"WHAT??" cried Carlyle, his eyes bugging almost beyond belief.

"Had they not reported this discovery to you, Mr. Carlyle?" asked Sloan.

"No sir, not a word. I could not understand why they had cuffed me and put me in their car.

"Officer," he continued, his voice breaking, "I swear on a stack of Bibles I don't have any drugs and I don't even own a gun."

"You wait right here."

Sloan was fuming as he approached Crane and Smith.

"You assholes planted this contraband on this man, didn't you?" asked the angry trooper. "It is because he's black?"

The two Astoria officers looked at each other and almost laughed out loud.

"Oh shit!" exclaimed Sloan as it dawned on him that he'd been duped. He dashed for his cruiser. "Let this man go! Right now!"

He floored it, and sure enough, a half-mile from the billboard, he saw a plume of black smoke rising through the moonlit sky. "Jesus, Jesus," he exclaimed. "The governor's gonna kill me!"

The smell of gasoline was strong and the wooden billboard structure was still ablaze. There was not a soul there other than the red-faced trooper. He watched in stunned silence while what remained of the governor's billboard continued to burn, lighting the night sky.

####

On the other side of town, at about the same time Oscar Sloan was pretending he was a country music superstar, Cal Bocock, who had also drawn night shift billboard duty, was also passing time. Cal liked country music as much as his State Patrol colleague, but he found it easier to stay awake if he was engrossed in a good book. By the light of a flashlight strategically placed between his legs, Bocock was getting close to the climax of a bestselling horror thriller, "The Haunting of Hill House" by Shirley Jackson.

Approaching headlights, as always, prompted him to stop his reading and look up. A car he quickly identified as a 1948 Packard pulled off the highway and stopped on the other side of the billboard.

Bocock took no chances at any time, especially in the wee hours, even more so when he was on edge because of being pulled from deep within a haunted house, so he pulled his service revolver and got out of the car. An obviously distraught young man met him halfway between the two cars.

"Officer, you gotta come help me. They've shot him!"

"Calm down, son," said Bocock. "They've shot who?"

"My friend! My lifelong friend!" The man burst into tears, and when his hands went to his face, Bocock, still wielding his flashlight, immediately noticed bandages over one of the man's hands.

"Put your hands in the air," he said.

"Hey, hey, don't be afraid of me. I didn't do it," said the man, who obediently raised both his hands.

Bocock approached him and did a quick search. He found no weapon and observed that the bandage was covering what had once been the man's right index finger.

"You gotta come with me," he said, tears streaming from his bloodshot eyes. "He's been shot."

"Who has been shot?" asked Bocock.

"His name is Carl Griffin. He's the police chief here in Astoria."

Bocock could not have been more surprised. He recognized the name, and realized the man's probable relationship to Earl "Boss" Griffin. But he was puzzled as to why this young man would not report this alleged crime to Griffin's department, so he asked him why he'd come to the billboard instead.

"I don't trust any of those damn bastards," said the young man, who refused to identify himself to the young trooper. "They done it. I know they did. So why would I get them to come check on him?

"Those bastards'll kill me too if they get a chance," he said. "Look what they done to me already?" He held up his bandaged hand.

"The Astoria Police cut off your finger?" asked Bocock.

"I already talked too much," said Theo "Sully" Sullivan. "I ain't sayin' no more. But you gotta come."

Bocock was in a quandary. Should he leave the billboard?

His gut told him to go. Not only was there a suggestion of a shooting or possibly a murder committed by Boss' gang, but there was also an apparent witness, albeit a reluctant one, who had come to him for help.

He returned to his cruiser and picked up the police radio.

"GSP Unit 64, 10-7. 10-75 with subject reporting a shooting."

"10-4," said dispatch.

The dispatcher, a bit sleepy herself, had failed to realize that both Astoria billboard guards had been called away from their posts within minutes of each other.

"Follow me, officer," Sully said, so Bocock did as he was asked, leaving the second billboard unguarded. The two cars drove a mile or so up 55, then turned off on a local road.

Fifteen minutes later, a dark panel truck was flying up 55, only to slam on its brakes and come to a dead stop just on the other side of the billboard.

"Where's the other trooper?" Luther Bickle asked his son, Slim.

"He ain't here, is he?"

Bickle could not believe their luck. "How much gas you got left?" he asked.

"Enough," said Slim, who was giggling like a school girl.

"Boss gonna love this," said Luther. "Let's do it!"

Slim flew out of the truck, opened the side door and pulled out a 10-gallon gas can connected to a spraying pump. He proceeded to aim the spray at the governor's billboard, soaking the canvas message board.

Bickle got out of the truck himself, and pulled out a different apparatus. It was a World War II vintage flamethrower. The weapon was very heavy, so he labored with its weight. The gasoline Slim had applied would help ensure it did its job since the weapon's burn time was pretty limited.

He aimed it at the billboard and fired. It ignited with a small explosion as the gasoline caught fire.

"Burn, baby burn!" said Bickle. "Slim, did I tell you this reminds me a lot of our Klan cross burnins?"

"No daddy. You need to take me on one of those," said Slim. "I bet they's lots of fun."

"Let's get out of here before somebody rolls up," said Bickle.

He cut loose with an evil cackle when the two were safely down the road, the flaming billboard lighting up his rearview mirror. "Who woulda ever guessed the other trooper would be fucking off somewhere?" he asked his son.

"Maybe he went to Flo's to get a piece of tail," said Slim.

The two exploded in riotous laughter.

####

Bocock followed the Packard to a farmhouse at least a half mile from any other residence. It was a white, wood frame house and it was probably 50 years old. He got his evidence bag from his trunk, and taking no chances, drew his service revolver as he approached the house. This could be a trap, he realized.

The front door was open a couple of inches and lights were on inside. He motioned to the man to lead the way, and he followed him into the house. It was not what he expected at all – it appeared to be a family homestead.

In the living room, he saw what his witness had reported. A 30-something white male was laying prone on the living room floor in a puddle of blood. A Colt Python revolver was in the man's right hand. Much of his jaw had been blown away. At first glance, it appeared to be a classic suicide, with the Colt having been put in Griffin's mouth and fired. But who knew for sure?

Bocock was not a detective, but he'd been raised by one and had been trained to think like one. His dad had been a detective for years and was a retired chief of police. So the young trooper knew he was in a potential crime scene and proceeded to treat it as one.

"Is there a phone here, son?" asked Bocock. Sully, tears flowing again as he gazed upon his fallen friend, nodded and pointed. Bocock proceeded to make a series of phone calls, first calling his night commander and then the Georgia Bureau of Investigation. The Astoria Police Department would be bypassed on this one and he wasn't worried about being second guessed. He figured the governor of Georgia would have his back on this call.

Cal then proceeded to carefully search the house and the area around it. Meanwhile, he continued to question the young man, working hard to try and win his trust and hopefully learn his identity and any other information he could contribute to this budding investigation.

There were things that didn't make sense in Griffin's house. Many things, in fact. It was long after dawn before Bocock learned the billboard he had been guarding, as well as the second one guarded by his colleague, had been charred beyond recognition.

Chapter Nineteen

Calvin Bocock was the kind of officer who took his job seriously. So seriously that he had taken it on himself to continue to investigate the death of Carl Griffin, even though he'd officially turned the case over to the Georgia Bureau of Investigation. Despite the governor's intense interest in Astoria, Bocock had a feeling the GBI would not get as personally invested in the apparent suicide as he already was.

Monday was Cal's day off, but it also happened to be the day of Carl Griffin's funeral. So Cal got into his only Sunday suit and drove his personal car to Astoria and pulled into the parking lot of the Astoria Baptist Church.

He had figured that since the late chief was a Griffin that there would be a house full that rainy August afternoon. So he was surprised to find that only a few cars were in the church parking lot when he pulled in 15 minutes before the service was to begin.

Bocock figured he would not likely know a soul in attendance, and he liked it that way. The shoe was also on the other foot, so to speak, since no one would know a Georgia State

Trooper, the very one who answered the call of Griffin's death, was there in his Sunday best to pay his respects.

There were only 15 people in the pews, Cal quickly noted as he entered the sanctuary. And he was surprised that he recognized one of them right off the bat. An elderly bald man in a crumpled black suit turned and looked his way as he made his way to his seat. It was Earl "Boss" Griffin! Cal had done his homework and he'd seen pictures of the town's top man and the governor's arch enemy.

There was a woman beside Griffin that Bocock figured was Boss' wife – Cecelia – if memory served. She seemed the only distraught person in attendance, sniffling and wiping her nose on occasion with a white handkerchief.

There were four men sitting together only a couple of rows in front of Bocock and the trooper surmised they were Astoria cops. Three of them looked enough alike to be brothers, and Bocock couldn't help but wonder if they were Griffins too.

And one row in front of the trooper on the aisle was a woman so beautiful she took his breath away.

She had long black hair and wore a simple black funeral dress. She turned and smiled at the newcomer and flashed the most stunning set of eyes he'd ever seen. Bocock took a deep breath. He was going to have a hard time keeping his mind on his business with this gorgeous lady sitting so near him in the church.

The funeral began as most do, with music. A somber-faced elderly lady walked to the piano and began to play a series of hymns. The tiny congregation dutifully sang along, often struggling to stay in key, especially on "Amazing Grace."

Finally, the minister came to the pulpit. Cal was not surprised when he introduced himself as the Rev. Thomas Griffin and said he was a cousin of the dearly departed. Cal quickly surmised that three other members of the congregation, in the front on the opposite side of Boss, must be the preacher's clan.

"Friends and neighbors, we are here to pay our final respects to Carl Eugene Griffin, who was taken from us far too early on Saturday," began the Rev. Griffin. "Carl was a fine man, a true law enforcement professional. I see his colleagues from the Astoria Police Department are here, as they should be, to say goodbye to their beloved colleague."

Boss Griffin turned and glared at the four cops, wiping a sarcastic grin off the face of one who had clearly been amused by the preacher's description of their former supervisor.

"As you know, Carl's parents are no longer with us, and I'm certain that played a role in his recent …. troubles," continued the minister. Cal made a mental note. The young man – who ominously, was not present -- had made no mention of Griffin having been troubled in any way, other than being dead on the floor, of course.

"I will always remember Carl as the happy and somewhat mischievous boy who loved to play baseball and basketball," the minister continued. "As an adult, he worked hard and got his police certification, and served our fine police department with distinction."

Again, Bocock noticed a rustling among the officers, and some whispering in the ranks. They obviously had a different opinion, and found entertainment in the minister's message. The striking young woman, however, remained stoic. Bocock wondered if she was a significant other, or perhaps an ex. That might explain "the troubles." Losing a catch like the dark-haired lady would not have been easy for any man.

Bocock observed no other movement or reaction from Boss Griffin. And he saw no one else in the congregation who would be likely to be a bodyguard or a key aide, which Bocock thought a bit strange. But then, where would Griffin feel the safest if not in his own church, with one of his relatives presiding over the funeral of a third?

But then the trooper noticed another couple, near the front and behind the Griffins. The woman was also quite lovely – though far from the caliber of the lady in black. Bocock wondered if that could be Boss' daughter, Patsy. Who was her husband? Oh yes, Marvin Justus, the lawyer, said to be a player in Boss' organization. He was rail thin, dark-haired, and Bocock noted he wore a much nicer suit than his apparent father-in-law's.

The Rev. Griffin was wrapping up what had obviously been a difficult chore for him. Bocock had quickly concluded that Carl Griffin had always been a ne'er-do-well. He had risen far above his deserved station due to family ties. Bocock was still confused, however. He had not found one police uniform – nor a badge or even a service revolver – in Griffin's home the night of his death. The death weapon was not a typical police issue. There were no awards, no trophies, nor plaques that commemorated his exalted status. How could this man have been the chief of police? That was one of two truly baffling discoveries in the house.

The other was the result of information he had gained from the young man, who had grown up with Griffin. When Bocock learned the two had played baseball together in school, he knew he could trust his answer.

He still remembered what the friend had said: "He always played first or the outfield because that was all he could play. He was a lefty."

And Bocock had found the gun in Griffin's right hand.

The four police officers, Marvin Justus, and a sixth man Bocock had not figured out rose to perform their duties as pall bearers. They began the processional to the church cemetery behind the red brick, white spired structure. As the congregation filed out, Bocock got himself in position to speak to the mysterious lady in black.

Bocock introduced himself, describing himself only as an acquaintance of the deceased.

"I'm Fancy Fontaine," she said, melting his heart with a big smile and a blink of those incredibly enchanting green eyes.

"What was your relationship to Carl?" probed Bocock.

"We haven't known each other too long," said Fancy. "I guess you could say we did business together."

"What kind of business are you in?" asked Cal.

Fancy blushed. "I'm in personal services," she said. "We'd better get to the gravesite, don't you think?"

The graveside service was thankfully short and sweet, and the plain brown casket was lowered into the ground. Bocock again maneuvered himself into position, this time to chat with Boss Griffin himself.

"I don't think we've met. I am Trooper First Class Calvin Bocock of the Georgia State Patrol."

Griffin looked a bit startled, but quickly regained his composure.

"What are you doing here?" he asked, his eyes flashing an angry glare. His tone had been soft, however, and sounded no alert with the cops or the lawyer or anyone else who might have rushed to Griffin's side.

"Mr. Griffin, I worked the crime scene the night the chief died," he said.

"I wondered why that happened," said Griffin. "How did you get there and why wasn't our department called?"

"I'm not at liberty to say," Bocock said slyly. "As you know, crime scenes anywhere in Georgia are within our jurisdiction."

"Why do you keep calling this a crime scene?" asked Boss. "The stupid sumbitch offed himself. Surely you saw that if you was over there Saturday night."

"Mr. Griffin, the chief's death remains under investigation," said the trooper.

Griffin looked concerned, but again, only for a moment. "If you folks want to waste taxpayers' money, that's your prerogative," he said. "We move on here in Astoria."

"You don't seem too concerned about the death of your, what was he, a cousin?" probed Bocock.

"Listen, asshole. I ain't answering any of your questions. You just told me his death is, what did you say, 'under investigation?' You work for that asshole Buford Dunlap, so for all I know, you probably think I killed my own cousin, poor stupid bastard."

"Did you, Mr. Griffin? Or did you have it done?"

"Fuck you. Get off my church property. You aren't welcome here."

"Mr. Griffin, do you know anything about the arson of the governor's billboards?"

Griffin's snarl turned into a narrow, toothless smile.

"I think the people of Astoria, whoever it was, just sent a strong message to your ass-wiping boss in a most unique and creative fashion."

"Which people of Astoria?" asked Bocock. By this time, one of the Astoria officers was moving closer to the pair, obviously concerned about Griffin's reddening face and rising voice.

"All of them, motherfucker," said Boss. "All of them."

Bocock chuckled. "I seriously doubt that," he said. "Well sir, it was …. interesting to make your acquaintance."

"You ain't got nothing left to guard," Griffin said. "So you and your state trooper brethren need to get the hell out of my county. For good. None of you are welcome here anymore for any reason."

"Sir, I don't think you can overrule the state constitution."

"Screw the state constitution. Screw the whole communistic state of Georgia," raged the Boss as Wesley Crane, who'd only heard a little bit of the conversation, looked on with concern. "This is now an independent state, the State of Hyde.

"Officer, show this man to his car," said Griffin. "It is time for him to go."

Griffin turned and joined his family, which by now had gathered in a tight knot nearby and looked on with concern. Nobody argued with Boss, much less at church. Who was this young handsome stranger?

"You heard the man," said Crane, who started to put his hands on Bocock's shoulders.

"You'd better not touch me, Astoria, unless you want assault charges," said Bocock. "I'm with the Georgia State Patrol."

"Hot shit! Boys, he's with the State Patrol," Crane said to his colleagues.

"Yeah," laughed Colin Smith. "They's the ones that can't even guard a coupla billboards!" The city cops erupted in laughter.

"Laugh all you want, boys," said Bocock with a confident smile. "It is pretty funny, isn't it?"

Bocock got into his car, cranked it and headed towards home. Within a mile, however, he noticed he was being followed by a dark Plymouth sedan. He could not see the driver well enough to draw any conclusions, even his or her sex. When he slowed, his pursuer did the same, keeping the distance between the two vehicles constant. Bocock thought about a lightning quick turnaround and pursuit of his own, but decided against it since he was not in uniform, on duty, or even armed. And besides, he thought with a chuckle, he was alone in enemy territory, the Independent State of Hyde.

As soon as Bocock crossed the Hyde County line, though, he saw his tail pull off the road and do a hasty U-turn.

Bocock chuckled again. I love this place, he thought. It's really too bad I'll be going back to regular patrol.

Inevitably, his thoughts turned to Miss Green Eyes. Wow, what a marvelous specimen of womanhood. Personal services, huh? That doesn't sound good at all.

Chapter Twenty

Bocock was quite surprised when he was advised by radio two days later that he was to come to Atlanta for a meeting. For a state trooper, having to report to headquarters on Confederate Avenue was not usually welcome news. He wondered if he and his colleagues would be called to task for deserting the billboards and allowing them to be torched by "the citizens of Astoria," as Boss had so aptly put it. So he got up well before dawn that Thursday and headed to Atlanta, getting to GSP headquarters about the same time that most of the top brass were arriving for work.

However, instead of being asked to report to the office of the top man – known as the colonel – Bocock was ushered into the smaller office of Maj. Samuel Westbrook, a career trooper who was often his shift supervisor.

"Bocock, they don't tell me much, you know," said Westbrook. "All they told me to tell you was to report to the governor's office at 10 a.m."

Bocock was again surprised. "You or the colonel are going with me, aren't you? And how about Sloan and Pickens?"

"They're not up here," said Westbrook. "And my instructions are to tell you to report up there alone."

This was a bit disconcerting, but Bocock's face didn't give any clues to his boss. "Yes sir," he said. "I'd better get over there."

It was a few minutes after 10 when the young trooper arrived at the Capitol. This was a first for him, a native Georgia boy being asked to visit with the governor in his office under the Gold Dome. He'd never met Buford Dunlap, so all he was aware of was the governor's folksy persona on radio interviews and in the newspapers. He'd never even seen him on television. So Bocock literally had no idea what was going to happen.

I'm in high cotton, he thought as he passed through the stately glass office doors from the Capitol's main corridor. Unless, of course, I'm about to be drawn and quartered, or demoted, or fired, or something worse.

Secretary Bonnie Triplett greeted Bocock by name and quickly ushered him into the governor's inner sanctum. Sitting at his mahogany desk was the governor and in the seats facing the desk were the governor's fresh-faced chief of staff, Floyd Perkins, and a tall, thin, distinguished-looking silver-haired gentleman that

Bocock soon realized was Herman Sneed, the director of the Georgia Bureau of Investigation.

Bocock, hat in hand, greeted the three men and sat in the only vacant seat in the half-circle in front of the governor's chair, which was the seat in the very middle.

"Governor, I apologize that I'm late," Bocock said with a smile.

"Not a problem, son," said Dunlap. "I realize you've driven in from the coast this morning. Long morning for you already."

"We're used to it, sir," said Bocock. "We work some crazy shifts."

"That brings me to our agenda," said Dunlap. "I understand you were working the night we lost the billboards."

"Sir, you don't know how much I regret what happened," said Bocock.

"Son, son, son!" said Dunlap. "You misunderstand. I am not upset that the bastard torched my billboards. I have looked at all the reports and have talked to several folks about all this, including Mr. Sneed here. I ain't mad at you boys at all.

"You … we… was tricked by a devious, conniving psychopath," said Dunlap. "His plan was actually pretty damn smart.

"We got what we wanted out of them," he said of the billboards. "We warned a lot of drivers first-hand, and we got newspaper stories all over the place alerting people to what goes on down there. I don't have the discretionary money to put 'em back up. But screw that, we don't need to. What's done is done!"

"Sir, I'm still not 100 percent sure that Carl Griffin's death was a murder," said Bocock. "I have my suspicions. But I can't say for sure he was killed, nor can I say that I was intentionally diverted to Griffin's home."

Dunlap nodded and noted he was aware of the "confidential informant" who had lured Bocock away from the billboard. He then looked at Sneed, and asked the GBI Director to talk briefly about Griffin's death.

"Trooper Bocock, our investigators have come to the same conclusion as you – we don't know for sure what transpired that night. Our best evidence that it might not have been a suicide, to be honest, came from your preliminary investigation.

"No police uniforms and such in the residence, considering he was the chief, is most curious," Hickman continued. "And with no close relatives available to interview, we would not have learned that the victim was left-handed, as you did, which creates questions considering where you found the death weapon."

The governor leaned back in his chair. "And son, the report you sent up on Griffin's funeral was also quite revealing. You might not know that Earl Griffin has flatly refused to talk to the GBI about his cousin's death, so your talk with him is all we have to work with for now. I guess we could subpoena him, but I figure that's probably a waste of time."

"That's the way I feel as well, governor," said Sneed. "We can't place him at the house. The only man we can place there is the trooper's CI."

Sneed went on to reveal that the only fresh fingerprints found at the house were Carl Griffin's and those of one Theo Sullivan, whose prints were on file due to brief service in the military. "Could this be your CI?" asked Sneed, who showed Bocock a picture of a young man in a military uniform.

"That's him, sir," said Bocock. "I'd hoped to have him identified by now myself. In fact, I thought he would come to the funeral. The fact that he didn't leads me to believe he is not part of the inner workings in Astoria."

"Which supports the conclusion that Griffin's death, and your diversion, was a complete coincidence," said Sneed.

"That is the way I'm leaning," said Bocock.

"I just don't see that it makes any sense to send us to a murder scene and a drug plant during a traffic stop at the same time," said Bocock. "Both of which then cleared the way for two counts of arson."

"That's probably too much criminal activity, even for Boss," interjected the governor.

"I think they were willing to take out one billboard, to send us a message, while the second one was just dumb luck," said Sneed.

"But isn't that a bit of a leap?" Bocock interjected, until Sneed interrupted.

"Well, there's one piece of evidence that I haven't mentioned – at the billboard you were watching," said the GBI chief.

"Oh, do you mean the rubber tire marks on the road just beyond the billboard's location?" asked Bocock.

"Exactly!" said Hickman with a smile. "Excellent observation, Bocock."

"I didn't study the marks, as I'm not yet qualified in that area, but I did notice them, sir. I regret I cannot say if they were there during my watch."

Sneed leaned forward. "We studied them in detail, Bocock. And it is our belief that they were left the night the billboards burned."

Dunlap got up and began to pace around his office.

"So you think the arsonists were making tracks, so to speak, from the billboard vacated by the traffic stop when they noticed while passing the second one that Bocock was gone?"

"Yes sir, governor," said Sneed.

"That's pretty good, boys," said Dunlap. "So this idiot cousin of Griffin may or may not have killed himself just in time to do his cousin a big favor, a favor that allowed his henchmen to complete a billboard-burning double play, so to speak?"

"That's certainly our best theory at this time," said Hickman.

"Well, I don't want to give up on this murder investigation," said Dunlap, and Sneed nodded his head in agreement. "Bocock's observation on where the gun was found certainly suggests somebody made it look like a suicide when it really wasn't."

"But there were no signs of a struggle," said Bocock.

"That's true. Even if Carl Griffin was drunk as a polecat, which he likely was, I can't see him just sitting there and letting one of Boss' thugs open his mouth and insert a .38," the governor said. "But I guess they could have cleaned things up before this Sullivan character found the body.

"We're sure he didn't do it, right?" asked the governor.

Bocock shook his head. I got honest grief and disbelief from him," he said. "If he did it, he's a regular Jimmy Cagney."

The other men laughed.

"OK, enough is enough," said the governor. "Bocock, let's get to why I called you up here in the first place.

"I have suggested to Mr. Sneed, and he has agreed, that you be promoted to special agent of the Georgia Bureau of Investigation."

Bocock's eyes bulged. He was speechless, which did not happen often.

"This is a new position, son. I want you to move to Hyde County and become a permanent fixture in that hellhole of a community. I want you to find out how that place runs. I want you to get enough evidence to put Earl Griffin in the state prison. Or better yet, Old Sparky, providing you can tie him to his cousin's murder or anybody else he might have killed, raped, robbed, torched or goat-fucked."

Old Sparky was the nickname for Georgia's electric chair.

The governor was rolling now. "Floyd, go get that box."

The chief of staff got up and went to a corner of Dunlap's office and returned with a suitcase-sized cardboard box.

"Son, these are all the letters I and other state agencies have received from travelers regarding their misadventures in Hyde County. Track these people down by phone, talk to them, and determine whether criminal activity occurred. Hell, they was mad enough to write us, so they may still be mad enough to come down there and testify against those peckerwoods if we can get enough evidence to charge anybody."

Dunlap suddenly realized he was overstepping, which he certainly did on occasion. "I apologize, Mr. Sneed. Agent Bocock now works for you. I don't have the authority to be giving instructions to this fine young public servant."

Sneed laughed. "Why sure you do, Governor! I work for you and Bocock works for both of us now."

Dunlap snorted. "I've always liked you, Herman, going all the way back to my days in the Legislature. You have always served our fine state with distinction."

"Governor, you already got my vote. Flattery won't get you anywhere," chuckled the veteran investigator. "However, anything you can do for my budget in the next cycle would be appreciated."

"Sneed, you're killing me, man," said Dunlap. "I just gave you a free body here, and he's a good one. Second generation law enforcement. Daddy's a police chief, right, Bocock?"

Cal nodded.

"Korean War veteran. Wounded in action. Excellent trooper. Self starter. Born to be an investigator. Hell, he went to a fucking funeral on his day off and nobody even asked him to. Good thing he did, by the way, since you boys didn't."

Sneed looked uncomfortable. "You're right, governor. We should have," he said.

"Let's nail that sumbitch," said Dunlap, switching gears again.

Dunlap paused and looked over at Perkins, who had done nothing at this meeting other than fetch the box of letters. "Floyd, can you put Bocock in touch with your lady friend?"

"Well, sir, she told me her parents don't want her talking about Astoria," said Perkins.

"Floyd, do I have to answer to her damn daddy? I'm the governor of Georgia. Give Bocock her address and let him go talk to her. She might be more willing to talk about Astoria when she's here in school in Atlanta and she knows nobody from down there is watching. And I don't want you there while he's talking to her. There will be no interference in a criminal investigation from this office.

"And besides, Floyd, Bocock might be able to loosen up some information from her that she won't share with you."

The chief of staff squirmed in his seat. At least Dunlap had not revealed his relationship with Linda Bishop to the young agent.

As if it was going to remain a secret.

"So I guess we're done here, right? Floyd, I gotta go give a speech and knaw on some rubber chicken today, don't I?"

"Yes sir, governor. The Georgia League of Insurors."

"Lord God," said Dunlap. "The bullshit I go through for the good people of Georgia.

"Good luck, Bocock. Let us know anything we can do to get this done. I want to nail this fucker."

He rose and shook Bocock's hand. The new agent looked the governor in the eye, smiled, and the governor noted with satisfaction he had a man's firm grip.

Dunlap smiled. "We done good here today, boys," he said, looking at Sneed. "We put a good fox hunter into the field. He's going to bring that weasel back to me on a stick!"

Chapter Twenty-One

Cal Bocock completed a dizzying pile of paperwork that officially transferred him from the State Patrol to the GBI – which also brought a decent pay increase. He was very proud of his new position and couldn't wait to call and tell his dad. But he also realized he would miss being a uniformed trooper and patrolling the open roads of Georgia. He knew he didn't want to be a trooper forever, but he never dreamed that chapter of his career would end so soon.

Being an efficient public servant who wanted to save the state as much money as possible, Bocock had decided that while he was in Atlanta, it made sense to go interview this Linda Bishop, friend or acquaintance of the governor's chief of staff. He sensed that Perkins wasn't too happy about giving up Bishop's address and telephone number and wondered why that would be the case. He was probably a friend of the girl's family, he reasoned, remembering Perkins' comments about Bishop's reluctance to talk. It had not been a willing exchange of information, especially the details Bishop had originally shared about the alleged workings of Astoria's revenue-generating traffic signal.

That information excited Bocock. He knew from experience it was not easy to churn up criminal offenses based on the nuts and bolts of speed enforcement. There were too many moving parts, so to speak, to try and prove that a law officer had an inaccurate radar gun, or regularly lied about its readings, or wrote illicit tickets with trumped up charges. That was a sticky wicket at best and even though he would investigate with gusto, in his heart he felt his chances of success were rather small.

But a red light that was doctored to skip yellow? That could be the Holy Grail that could end this investigation to the state's satisfaction pretty quickly. He was grateful to Dunlap for remembering the girl's role in all this.

He arrived on the Georgia Tech campus about 3:30 in the afternoon. Students were lounging in the campus' common areas when Bocock rolled through. The girl lived in an apartment only a few blocks from Grant Field where Coach Bobby Dodd and his Ramblin' Wreck played football on autumn Saturdays.

When he knocked on her door, there was no answer, so Bocock decided to wait. There was a convenient park bench only about 50 yards from Bishop's door.

At around 4, he saw a girl that fit the description Perkins had provided heading for the apartment, school books in hand. Bishop was a real beauty, with curly blonde hair and long, well-tanned legs. Bocock smiled as he quickly realized why Perkins knew this girl and why he hadn't wanted to throw her into the middle of his investigation.

He came up behind Bishop while she was fumbling for her apartment key in her purse.

"Miss Bishop, may I talk to you for a minute?"

Bishop turned and smiled at Cal. Girls tended to do that a lot because Calvin Bocock was just as attractive to them as girls like Linda Bishop were to the average Georgia boy.

"Who might you be, sir?"

"My name is Calvin Bocock and I'm with the Georgia … Bureau of Investigation," said Cal, happy he was able to catch himself before he mindlessly recited his old job title.

Bishop's smile evaporated and her features became stern. "I know why you are here, and I'm not interested in talking to you."

"Miss Bishop, do you fear for your family's safety down home in Astoria?"

Bocock could see that the words he had spoken literally had hit close to home.

"I'd rather not say."

"Miss Bishop, anything you tell me will remain confidential. Your identity is safe with me and will not be disclosed at any time unless you agree it be disclosed."

"I thought that before I told all this stuff to Floy... somebody else," said Linda. "This other individual did not protect me from ... those people down home."

Bocock was not going to take no for an answer now. So he laid it on thick, just like his dad had taught him.

"Miss Bishop, it could well be you disclosed information to someone who is not a trained law enforcement investigator. You can trust me. I swear to protect your identity on a stack of Bibles, King James version."

Linda laughed. That's a good sign, he thought, as her blue eyes twinkled.

"I guess you can come inside," said Bishop, and Cal could not resist giving the rest of her the once over as she turned her back to him and stepped through the door. "But I'm not promising I will tell you anything. I am thinking about it, though."

With an opening like that, Bocock felt like a Tech fullback taking a handoff with only a few yards to gain for the winning touchdown.

Bocock continued to try and make the attractive coed feel comfortable in his presence. "I bet you're extremely popular on this campus," he said.

"I've had my moments," she said. "But a lot of the boys on campus are pretty shy."

Bocock laughed. "They are intimidated by your looks," he said. "They figure, probably correctly, that you are out of their reach."

"You think so, huh?" said Bishop, who was still angry enough at Floyd Perkins that she saw nothing wrong with flirting a bit with this very handsome, well put together GBI agent.

Within 10 minutes, Linda had told Cal about how she had been abused on the side of U.S. 55 by an Astoria police officer. "I want you to know I'm telling you about this because you need to understand what kind of people you are dealing with," she said. "That officer was … pure evil. I could tell that by the way he looked at me and how he ... touched me, all over."

"Was this officer wearing a name badge?" asked Bocock.

"No, I looked because I thought I remembered them always wearing one. But he didn't have one on. I even asked him his name."

"What did he say?"

"He said his name was Officer Friendly and he'd be even more friendly with me the next time we met. God, more friendly than feeling me up?"

She offered a good description of the officer, and Bocock quickly realized he'd seen at least three men at Carl Griffin's funeral who would fit it. "Could you identify him if you saw him again?"

"Yes, but Agent Bocock…

"Call me Cal, Linda."

"OK, Cal it is. I won't press charges. I can't. My momma and daddy live down there and you don't know what already has happened." As soon as she'd uttered the words, she knew she'd made a big mistake and was about to break her promise to her father.

"Linda, what else happened, other than the traffic stop and the sexual assault?"

"I promised my daddy I wouldn't tell anyone," she said. "I can't. They'd be in more danger than ever."

"Linda, you have forgotten what I promised you," Cal said sincerely. "I will take no actions that would jeopardize you or your family. Remember, a stack of Bibles is in play here."

"King James version," added Linda with a smile. "Cal Bocock, if you ever, ever break that promise, I will personally kill you."

Great, thought Bocock. Less than one day on the job and my life has already been threatened. But gee, what a way to go, at the hands of this exceptionally attractive young lady!

"Don't worry. Your secret, and for that matter, any and all secrets you share with me today and forever, will remain confidential."

Linda liked the sound of that and felt she could trust this Cal Bocock. There was a sincerity to him that impressed her. That and his piercing blue eyes. Wow, what a dreamboat!

So Linda proceeded to tell the story of her arrival home after she was pulled over and what had happened. "My daddy was in the same room when they shot out the picture window," she said, tears coming to her face. "He was lucky he wasn't killed."

Bocock frowned. These people are hard core, he thought. There may be more unreported crimes down there than in most northern ghettos.

The student told Bocock that her father had run outside, but he had been too late to see who had fired the shotgun. And she repeated that if Cal went to Astoria and began asking questions, her parents would deny that anything had happened and would also know she had betrayed their trust.

"Linda, this is helpful to me because I needed more insight into what these people are capable of," said Bocock. "I have no intentions of asking the first question about your traffic stop, this sexual assault and the attack on your home. That is, unless any of you change your minds and decide you want to prosecute. That changes the game."

"I don't think we'll ever change our minds," said Linda. "You've never lived down there. I never should have told what I heard in Bart Taggart's that night."

That gave Bocock the segue he needed to go where he really wanted Linda to take him. Tell me exactly what you were told that night, he asked her.

"He was bragging that he pushed the buttons. He's the guy who made the light change to red so the cops could pull them over."

"And he did this from where?"

"He said it was a hotel room. It has to be the Astoria, it's the only hotel in town and it's right there by the light."

"Did he say how often they do this with that light?"

"He said it was hundreds of times. I really couldn't believe he was telling me all this, but I think he thought I'd be impressed and go parking with him or something. He did buy me a beer, and I shouldn't have taken it, but I did."

"Don't apologize, Linda. You didn't do anything wrong. This guy telling you all this, he's the bad guy. And he's working for even worse guys."

Bocock asked his informant to describe the man in the bar. That was a little tougher, she said, because of the time that had passed and the fact she'd been drinking, but she was able to offer a few pertinent details.

"Did he ever introduce himself?"

"I think he did, but I honestly can't remember what he said his name was."

Bocock thought for a minute about the description Linda had offered. There's no way, he thought. Or is there?

"Linda, I'm going to show you a picture of a man who lives in Astoria. It's an old picture, so the guy will be a little older now, but maybe you will recognize him, or at least know who he is from seeing him around town."

Linda laughed again. "Everybody knows everybody in Astoria," she said.

Cal reached into his briefcase and pulled out the military picture he'd been given just hours earlier at the Governor's office.

"Do you recognize this man?"

Linda gasped. "How in God's name did you know? It's him! It's the very guy."

Bocock could not help himself and burst into a most unprofessional fit of laughter. "I've met him myself," he said.

"I know I shouldn't do this," said Cal, "but just to confirm, did he possibly tell you that his name is Theo Sullivan?"

Realization dawned over Linda's lovely face. She pulled the blonde curls back from over her eyes and looked the agent directly in the eye.

"He told me to call him Sully," she said. "I would not have remembered, but that is what he said. I am sure of it!"

Bocock was exhilarated. What a first day on the job and what a great lead. Not only was his confidential informant a possible source of additional information on the death of Carl Griffin, he was also a tongue-wagging blowhard who had given a total stranger unprecedented insight into a lucrative piece of Boss Griffin's criminal empire.

"Linda, I want to thank you for talking to me today," he said. "You have helped me in more ways than you can imagine. Please remember what I told you. Your secrets are safe and will continue to be."

"Can I call you if I need more information?" he said.

Linda smiled her best beauty pageant smile. "Cal, you can call me anytime, for any reason."

Bocock noticed that Linda's farewell handshake seemed unusually affectionate. She used two hands and she held on a bit too long, like maybe she was expecting more.

God, I think I'm going to love this job, Bocock thought to himself as he literally bounded to his car. Now I have to find a place to live and move to Astoria!

Chapter Twenty-Two

Once you have decided that it is important enough for you to actually risk your life to accomplish something that seems to be an important rite of passage, there are few forces on earth that can stop you. It had come slowly but inexorably that summer, the decision to fly over The Pit on the tire swing and jump into the impossibly deep waters of the Altamaha River.

Over many lazy summer days, the Three Musketeers had discussed the plunge, and the long swim back to the safety of shore. They had done this in leisure, from underneath the mighty bridge over U.S. 55, their secret sanctuary that gave them a magnificent view of the river, The Pit, and the tire swing that would allow them to accomplish this once impossible quest.

They had sat in silence and watched as the older kids of Astoria had enjoyed the secret pleasures of The Pit. Most made it look effortless as they had let go of the tire and dropped the long distance into the deep waters. Most had postponed the long swim back to shore, choosing to tread water and watch as their companions made the long fall and splash into the cooling green waters. It was more than envy at this point in early September. It was do or die and the Musketeers had made up their minds that it was something that they must do.

Or at least two out of three had so decided. Jim Bob was the driving force in this crusade. It was important to him that he not turn 13 without having taken the tire swing plunge into The Pit. Slowly and patiently, he had persuaded Sassy that it was also incredibly important for her to accomplish this monumental task.

Meanwhile, Zeke had listened with interest, but with no real desire to participate. Zeke, being a lot smarter than most believed, understood his limitations. He knew that his lungs were not as strong as his two friends (asthma they called it, though he spelled it "as-mah"). It didn't really bother Zeke that he had no plans to jump. He knew he could at least swim a little bit, but he had no dreams or aspirations of that marathon swim from the depths of The Pit to the shallows of the Altamaha.

The three had come prepared this hot, steamy day (how many weren't hot and impossibly humid along the Georgia coast this time of year?). Their original plan had been to ask for official parental permission, but that had somehow never happened. Instead, Jim Bob and Sassy had put on swim suits underneath their usual summertime riding outfits of tee-shirts and shorts. Zeke had done the same, planning privately to paddle around in the shallows near the shore while his friends did the courageous deed.

Pluto had been their constant companion most of the summer. Zeke, after lots of nagging from Jim Bob, had become much more concerned about Pluto's safety. So much so that he had worried that the dog would attempt to jump into the river himself, where he would likely drown since dogs weren't very smart, right? Zeke had brought in his bicycle basket a very long run of rope, the plan being to tie it to Pluto's collar and stake it on the soft sandy shore where the dog could run freely and watch the kids' antics but not venture too deeply into the water.

Jim Bob had been adamant about how important it was to swim The Pit.

"If we don't do it this summer, we are the weenies of all time," he had told his friends. "Nobody waits until they are 13 to do The Pit. You will never be smart enough, or brave enough, to live a real life without doing The Pit, and if you wait too long, you might as well go up to Atlanta and dedicate your life to a church choir school or some other weenie-like ending. I'm being dead serious."

Sassy had heard this lecture repeatedly and, slowly it had weighed upon her. There were no public swimming pools in small south Georgia towns and no officially sanctioned swimming lessons. To be honest, nobody really knew if they could swim until they had to. Most never ventured into deep waters until fate finally forced it upon them. It seemed that today was that day, like it or not. Sassy was pretty sure she didn't like it, but Jim Bob had finally convinced her it was so important that today was the day to find out. Sink or swim. Live or die. She honestly believed she was ready.

As always, they had ridden their bikes from the trailer park to the bridge and then down the steep path to the concrete pillars where they usually sat vigil, plotting their future and discussing the deep dark secrets of 12 year old life. But today was different. They left their bikes and walked the steep path to where the older kids had propped the tire swing near the launch point.

It was here that Zeke made his public loss of face announcement. "It's my as-mah. I can't do this," he said. "I'm going to go down to the bank with Pluto. I'll tie him up and watch you guys."

Neither Jim Bob nor Sassy were truly surprised, and because all three were such close friends, there was no derision directed at Zeke. It was as if they had known that Zeke would not be making the leap. They were at peace with that – he just wasn't up to it.

"Bobby, are you really sure this is the day?" Sassy asked with much apprehension.

"It's now or never, Sassy," said Jim Bob. "Don't worry. We can do this. We will be doing this the rest of our lives."

Zeke staked Pluto on the water's edge, and Pluto endlessly ran the length of the shore as his master sat up shop nearby to watch the show overhead.

Jim Bob and Sassy, stripped to their swim suits, climbed the rocky path to the tire swing. Bobby pulled the big truck tire free, and while holding it both hands, looked with much trepidation to the long swing and the deep waters far below.

"Sassy, promise me you will follow," he said.

"I will, you lug," she replied. "Just make sure the tire gets back up here."

That was something they hadn't even considered. "The big kids have to grab it as it swings back," said Bobby. "Can you do that?"

"If you go first, I guess I'll have to," she said, somewhat timidly.

Jim Bob steadied himself and looked out over his task. He was scared as hell, but he sure as heck didn't want Sassy to know that. And he knew the longer he thought about it, the harder it would be, so after only a few seconds, he launched himself into the void overhanging the mighty river.

Once Jim Bob realized he was at the apex of the swing, he let go. The drop seemed endless. He hit the water off center, his backside taking much of the blow. The impact hurt, but the amazing thing was that he went so deep underwater. Deeper than he had ever been in his life!

Jim Bob worried for a second or two that he would never come to the top. But he did, and he emerged, with a sputter, and then a cough. There was no thought of ever touching the bottom. It had to be down there …. somewhere. But where?

He looked back at Sassy, who seemed so tiny on the ledge so far away. Amazingly, the big tire had come right back to her, and she had grabbed it at some point while Jim Bob was coming back to the surface.

"That was great, Sassy!" he yelled lustily. "C'mon, girl!"

Zeke was in water up to his waist near the shore, watching nervously. Pluto was barking like crazy, running up and down the shore on his stake line, watching the unexpected action.

Sassy, to put it mildly, was terrified. She suddenly had no idea if she could do this. But she was not willing to let Jim Bob do something she couldn't.

The height was dizzying. The old tire seemed so slippery. What if she couldn't hold on and fell too quickly? What if she lost her nerve and couldn't let go? What if she died in the fall to the water?

Most urgently, what if a big alligator was in the water and decided to eat her?

These are urgent questions for a 12 year old girl about to risk her life for the first time, and Sassy wasn't ready to go deep on any of them. So against her better judgment, with the knowledge that Bobby was waiting below, she launched herself into the void.

God, it was so high! It was so scary! But she had committed, and the last thing she wanted to do now was test the rocky ledge on the return trip. So she closed her eyes. And she fell. And she fell. And finally, she hit the water with an explosion of sound and a violence of sensations throughout her body.

Sassy forgot to hold her breath, and that was probably what caused all the trouble. She found herself deep in the waters of the Altahama, and not only was she struggling to find the surface, she was already in trouble with her breathing.

She surfaced gasping for breath and slapping the surface. Bobby, luckily not far away, moved in her direction immediately. But even though he was a far better swimmer, he was not equipped to deal with his friend's increasingly violent panic.

"Sassy, calm down! I got you!" he said.

But Sassy was feeling her life slip away. And lifesavers know that even the most experienced are in big trouble in such situations. Sassy latched on to Bobby and her death grip around his neck made it that much more difficult for him to tread water.

Zeke was watching this closely. And he grasped the danger of the situation immediately.

"Bobby, you OK?" he called.

There was no answer. Sassy's panic was clearly pulling Jim Bob under. He was having trouble holding both of them afloat even though he was kicking harder than he had ever kicked in his life.

Zeke's 12-year-old mind went into overdrive. Within seconds, he had an idea. He dashed to Pluto and took off the dog's collar, which was still attached to the rope staked to the shore. Pluto was a bit shocked to be free, but stood his ground, watching his busy master.

Zeke climbed the slope to where the tire had returned after Sassy's plunge. He grabbed it and climbed higher to the launching point. He looked out over the now roiling waters of The Pit and saw his two best friends, clearly engaged in a struggle for their lives.

"Bobby! I'm going to drop you this rope! Catch it!" he screamed.

Zeke had no idea if Jim Bob had heard. And he knew he had only one shot at dropping the collar and the rope near his friends.

With no thought about his life or safety, Zeke swung out over the void. When he saw he was directly over Bobby and Sassy, he dropped the collar.

It hit Jim Bob right on top of his head!

Somehow, Bobby grabbed the rope. Zeke held on to the slippery tire and rode back towards shore. He let himself go dangerously late and hit hard in the soft, sandy bottom about 10 feet off shore. He hit the bottom hard, went underwater, and saw stars. Later, he realized he had never "seen stars" before.

Despite a sprained ankle, and a woozy head, Zeke sprinted to where he had staked Pluto. And he was most pleased to find that Bobby had not lost purchase on the rope. With all his might, he began towing his two friends to shore. Bobby had regained hope and strength with the arrival of the unexpected lifeline, so he had managed to keep Sassy's head out of the water. Within a minute, the two choking swimmers arrived in the shallows where they were greeted by the excited Pluto, who had no interest in going deep.

Jim Bob pulled Sassy onto the shore, and there, the three friends collapsed in a pile of collective exhaustion.

No one could speak for what seemed like forever. Sassy coughed and coughed, expelling what seemed to her to be about half of the waters of the murky river.

Finally, she rolled over and looked at her two male friends.

"You guys – both of you – you saved my life," she said, bursting into tears of joy. "There was no way I was going to get out of there alive."

"Honest to God, me neither," said Jim Bob, looking at Zeke with admiration.

Zeke couldn't even think about his bad ankle. He was proud of himself, but he quickly decided that modesty was more important today than being a braggart.

"You guys would have done the same for me," he said. "We's the Three Musketeers. One for all and all for one."

All three fell into a collective hug that lasted several minutes. Tears were shed and lifetime memories were made.

Across the Altamaha, there had been a silent spectator. A young black boy, 13 years of age, had watched this entire drama with intense interest. His family's river bottom cabin wasn't far away, and it wasn't unusual for him to watch the white kids swimming in the river. He had never seen any of them almost drown before, which almost certainly would have been his fate in the same situation, as he wanted nothing to do with the deep waters of The Pit. He was awed by the bravery he had witnessed. And he was determined that he was going to meet these three kids. He made this vow even though such meetings between black kids and white kids were strictly forbidden.

Chapter Twenty-Three

Cal Bocock would have preferred to jump headlong into his fledgling investigation of criminal corruption in Astoria and Hyde County, but it was deemed more immediately important for him to be settled into a proper local "office." But rather than brick and mortar downtown, Herman Sneed, director of the Georgia Bureau of Investigation, had decided Bocock would have a home office among the natives.

So a state truck with a trailer hitch was bringing in what Bocock would learn was called a Palace Ranchhome. This two-toned, 50-foot-long mobile home would, upon arrival, be one of the nicest residences in the Astoria Trailer Court. Bocock had already secured a rental spot nestled in the third row of the bustling community.

Bocock arrived on the site about 30 minutes before the trailer, and used the time to sit with the manager of the trailer court and pay him three month's rent in advance. The skinny, plain-talking property manager wasn't the least bit nosy about Bocock's business, and Cal didn't offer any details about why he was moving to Astoria.

He had preferred to blend into the woodwork, but when the trailer pulled in, he realized that was not going to happen. It was like he was immediately spotlighted as one of the wealthiest of the Astoria mobile elite. The Palace's upper and lower sections were dark green with an oscillating white stripe circling the dwelling's midsection from stem to stern. The trailer had five rooms in all, a large sitting area or living room adjacent to the front door with big picture windows on either side. That adjoined the kitchen, which featured a washer and drier, freeing Bocock from having to access the community laundry.

Furthest from either door was a bedroom, where a full-sized double bed was poured into a space that left little room for walking, though there were barely accessible closets and built-in drawers. Further back was the bath, close quarters but functional. Bocock had directed that the bed be removed from the back bedroom, which had its own door to the outside, so he could convert it into a working office. The bed had been replaced by an old wooden desk. He had not even started sifting through the big box of letters and notes of complaints from mistreated out-of-state motorists.

A telephone was to be installed within days, and Sneed had specifically ordered that it be a private line. The GBI director was well aware of the party lines universally used by Ma Bell and it would not do to have an agent who was talking with confidential sources being overheard by Aunt Clara listening in from down the road.

Just as Bocock was gazing wide-eyed at his future home being pulled into his new space, he was greeted by a slender little slip of a blonde-haired girl riding a Schwinn bicycle with tassels trailing from the handle bars.

"Hi mister, moving in?" Sassy Smith said, coming to a stop beside the handsome, sandy-haired man, who was dressed in casual clothing.

"How'd you guess?" Cal quipped. "My name's Cal. And you are?"

Sassy blushed. "My name's Sarah. But they call me Sassy."

"Because you are, right?"

"Huh?"

"I meant Sassy. No offense intended."

"None taken. Me and my friends live here so you'll probably see us riding our bikes through here a lot," she said.

"I wouldn't want it any other way, Sassy. When does school start?"

"Why do grownups always have to bring up the worst things?" Sassy exclaimed, pulling back her curls and frowning at her new friend.

Cal laughed. He liked this neighbor girl, and couldn't help but hope the people here would be this friendly. His greatest hope was that within time, the locals would help him to ferret out the undesirable elements in this otherwise happy little community.

"What does your daddy do, Sassy?" Cal offered.

"My daddy's a patrol officer for the Astoria Police," she said, which Cal accepted without a change in expression. "My two friends are cop kids, too."

"That's interesting," said Cal. "I guess that means I'll be living in a very safe place here."

"Oh, yeah. Daddy and the others keep everybody from getting too crazy on the weekends and all," said Sassy. "But we all manage to have a pretty good time."

Right on cue, Colin Smith, uniformed and driving a squad car, pulled down the driveway toward the conversing pair. As Bocock turned to look at the new arrival, he saw a look of recognition flash across the elder Smith's face.

So much for arriving incognito, Bocock thought.

Without any kind of greeting, Smith pulled up alongside his daughter's bicycle.

"Sassy, what have I told you about talking to strangers?" Smith asked sternly.

"Cal ain't so stranger," Sassy said confidently. "He's my friend."

"Sassy, this man is no friend of ours. In fact, he is our enemy. He works for the Governor of Georgia."

Sassy's smile evaporated and she looked nervously at her new acquaintance. "You don't like speed traps?" she said to Cal.

Before Cal could respond, Smith's rising voice interjected. "Get on home or go play with your friends. I don't want you talking to this man ever again."

Sassy nodded and rode off without another word to Bocock. The agent took a long pause to carefully choose his words.

"Smith, I'm no threat to you whatsoever if you are on the up and up," he said. "However, if you and your friends are crooked and corrupt, I will ride your ass all the way to the Reidsville State Prison."

Smith's face was quickly reddening and veins were standing out on his neck. "I ain't got nothing to say to you. I think Boss told you none of y'all are welcome here. I can't believe you have the unmitigated gall to move into our community amongst us and right away start flirting with my 12-year-old daughter."

"You paranoid punk," said Bocock, putting his chest near the open car window. "Your daughter rode up and introduced herself. She seems to be a friendly, confident and intelligent young woman. From what I have seen thus far of her father, I'm surprised she's turned out this well."

Smith came close to getting out of the car and physically confronting Bocock, but good judgment somehow prevailed. He realized he needed to seek instructions before going off half-cocked, which was always his tendency.

"You are an asshole. This ain't going to be a pleasant experience for you if you really are planning on living here."

"Do you see this magnificent residence?" Bocock replied with a magnanimous smile. "This is home. You are stuck with me."

"We'll sure as hell stick you. Hell, I don't even know your name."

Bocock quickly decided to play a trump card. "My name's Agent Friendly," he said. "The longer you know me, the friendlier I get."

Smith did not provide any body language for Bocock to decipher. Instead, he put the car into gear and proceeded to pull out. "Nothing and nobody in this town is going to be friendly to you. Count on it, motherfucker."

Smith hit the gas, his wheels throwing gravel and a cloud of dust at Bocock. The young agent smiled.

Home, sweet home, he thought.

####

Smith quickly got on the radio and asked Carole Friedlander if the chief was in. When he got an affirmative, he made a beeline for the courthouse to advise Popsi Colanise of this newly-discovered intelligence.

Fully briefed by Smith, Popsi made his way to Boss Griffin's office. He found Boss sipping coffee likely laced with bourbon, pouring over a ledger sheet.

"Colanise, I thought I told you we shouldn't see much of each other. Routine matters need to be discussed with Marvin Justus, my attorney."

"Boss, this isn't really routine. The state moved a man into the trailer park today."

Griffin pursed his lips. He leaned back in his chair and looked up at the Greek. "Did we get a name? Do we know for sure he's a state plant?"

"Colin Smith saw him face-to-face. Said he was the same trooper who went to Carl's funeral."

"Oh yes. He was … Calvin Bitemycock or something like that."

Popsi smiled. Boss didn't make many jokes and he wanted to let him know he'd liked it.

"Colin says he's got a big, nice trailer there. No signs he was going to be uniformed or anything like that."

"I don't think Dunlap would bother just to put a uniformed state trooper among us," Boss mused. "What the hell good would what do? Look over our shoulder on traffic stops?"

"Maybe he's here to guard the Alligator Farm billboard," offered Colanise.

That earned a snicker from Boss. He rolled his chair around and looked toward the blank wall to his right.

"I'd say he's now a GBI agent and he's here to dig dirt on us," Boss said. "So there will be no dirt. We're going to keep it clean."

In the days following the burning of the billboards, the town's operations had pretty much returned to normal. The uniforms were out writing speeding tickets as before, and Slim Bickle had moved into Room 16 at the Astoria Hotel to push the button on the magic traffic light. Even the clip joints had reported a slight uptick in business as the public's collective consciousness had moved on from billboards and news alerts about Astoria.

"Boss, spell it out to me what clean means," said Popsi. "I want to be very clear in what I tell the men."

"Turn off the light," Griffin said. "Bocock could spend 20 minutes watching it and know we were doing exactly what Dunlap said we were doing. Keep the room, though. I don't want to rile up Biff Carlyle about losing revenue at his sleazy little hotel. I could see him mouthing off to Bocock.

"On the roads, play it strictly by the book," said Boss. "Legitimate speeders still get a ticket. Cash bond. No treatments at the jail for those who can't pay. No trumped up charges. No smashed tail lights, no punctured tires."

Popsi nodded. He then asked Boss for directions regarding the town's other illicit commercial establishments.

"Go talk to Guthrie, Flo and the others and advise them there is an investigator among us. These are their businesses and it ought to be their decision how they should proceed. Make sure they know what this snake looks like, what he drives, and that we can't protect them from him and charges the state might bring.

"We'll tell them that," Griffin said, thinking out loud. "I can think of some ways we can protect them, if it comes to that. But it hasn't come to that yet."

Popsi nodded. This was the clear direction he needed to do his job, the kind of information he had never gotten from Carl Griffin.

Boss looked thoughtfully at his muscular aide, and after a long pause, he continued.

"We don't know how good this guy is at his job, but we have to proceed on the assumption that Dunlap has sent the best man he has. Hell, there may even be others we don't know about yet who'll work with him.

"We need good, timely information. Tail him, but do it carefully so he never knows for sure. Get people in the trailer park to keep an eye on him and keep you advised of his comings and goings.

"Does he have a phone in his trailer?" Boss asked.

"They just parked it today, so I doubt it," replied Popsi.

"If and when he gets a phone, you know what to do," said Boss.

"Yes sir," said Colanise.

"That's all. Let's get all this done and let things just run exactly this way for awhile. We'll reassess early next week."

The big acting chief nodded and walked out of the room, closing the door behind him.

Boss took a big draw of coffee, and pulled a couple of pills from his pocket and tossed them into his mouth. He looked at his pocket watch, which told him it was 3:30 p.m.

It's a little early, but I'm cutting out, he decided. I am still the Boss of this place and I ain't going to get all rolled up just because Dunlap has tossed a new snake into my hole.

I have bigger and meaner snakes than he does, Boss thought with a smile. And mine are poisonous.

#####

Chapter Twenty-Four

The trailer had been blocked, which means concrete blocks had been placed in the proper areas to make sure the living quarters were level and as stable as a house on wheels could be. Electric service had been established, and incredibly, Ma Bell's men had arrived in a timely fashion and had installed a private line, black rotary telephone. The trailer had come with twin propane tanks, which allowed cooking on the unit's gas stove. Cal had moved his few personal belongings inside.

In short, he had set up housekeeping. And for the first time, he sat down at his desk in the back bedroom. He started scanning some of the governor's letters.

The third one he read made him laugh out loud. A woman named Shawn Summers of King of Prussia, Pennsylvania, had written a colorful narrative of her trip through Astoria.

"North of town, I get pulled over and the cop says I owe $35 for speeding," she wrote. "I paid him, in cash, though I had never heard of such a thing, and I moved on, passing through town without incident.

"South of town, I am pulled over yet again. It almost seemed like the same cop was coming back for more! And sure enough, he wanted $35 again!

"Is this the way of life in Georgia? Do you guys have to have tourist dollars to survive? I'd suggest you open more swamp zoos and other places to come see armadillos, snakes and crocodiles, since, other than cops, that was about all I saw down there."

The woman included her telephone number, so, on a whim, Bocock dialed it. A woman answered on the second ring, and sure enough, it was this same Shawn Summers.

It took awhile for Mrs. Summers to figure out what the call was about since the letter was six months old. But once she understood Bocock's purpose, she basically repeated the story she'd written to Dunlap.

"So Miz Summers, I guess the key question I have for you is, was there anything inappropriate about these traffic stops?" asked Bocock.

"You want to know if I was speeding?" she asked.

"Well, yes ma'am."

"Damn right I was speeding. Both times. It is a long way from Pennsylvania to Palm Beach and I wanted to get there in as little time as possible."

She admitted that she'd written the letter in the passion of the moment upon arriving at her family's beachside second home in south Florida. "It just seemed queer to me that the only times I got pulled over in 1,200 miles of driving were in clodhopper city, what is it? Astoria, Georgia."

Cal laughed. "Did it disturb you that you were not allowed to post a cash bond, that you had to pay the entire $35, in cash, on the spot?"

"Agent Bocock, I did think that was a little bizarre. The thought crossed my mind that if I had not chosen to carry a big chunk of cash, what would have happened to me? Do you know?"

"Let me say we have heard a few things," Cal replied. "I'm not at liberty to discuss them, but some of the allegations involve, let's say, unpleasant experiences."

"I had no desire to get anywhere close to those twin cops," said Summers. "The only other thing I'd tell you is, it seemed kind of like an assembly line, like they were used to drivers just stopping by and coughing up the cash."

Summers said she'd cooled off a lot and had no desire to return to Astoria for any reason. "My husband and I decided we'd either be flying or taking the train from now on," she said. "The main reason I drove that week was to get one of our cars to Palm Beach."

Bocock briefly considered such a lifestyle – two homes, one at an exclusive beach, cars at the ready at each, and no worries about dropping $70 – a lot of money -- to greedy country cops.

"OK, Miz Summers," he closed. "I greatly appreciate your time today."

"Thank you, agent. I'm happy to hear somebody down there has some morals. Yes, I was speeding, but I didn't endanger anybody and I wouldn't have. It was totally unnecessary."

Bocock hung up the phone. He'd written a lot of tickets during his years as a trooper, and he knew well nobody was happy about getting one. But if you didn't keep speed in check, the roads would become lawless and extremely dangerous. As if they aren't already, he laughed.

Two tickets to one driver in less than an hour, he said. I'll have to share that with my trooper friends.

He thought again about the blind efficiency of the Astoria Police Department. Then he considered the town's only traffic signal, and its alleged triggerman, Theo Sullivan.

Enough of this office time today, he thought. It's time for sightseeing.

Bocock locked his trailer door and strolled to his 1957 Chevy BelAir, his personal wheels, a two-toned turquoise and white classic that he truly loved. As he got behind the wheel and started the engine, he couldn't help but feel he was being watched. He had felt that way ever since he had moved in. Part of that, he knew, was just the nature of the job. GBI agents always got a wary eye from the general public, providing the general public knew they were GBI agents. And thanks to Sassy and Colin Smith, everyone had learned really quickly that he was a GBI agent.

The other part of it was Astoria itself. The place seemed confined, on alert, guarded, even hazardous. He dismissed the thought as paranoia as he drove into town and parked at a meter not 100 yards from the famous traffic light. He quickly got out and put a dime in the meter. Hell, he thought, you might get 30 days down here for a parking ticket!

He sat in the stuffy Chevy, windows down, for more than an hour, watching traffic move through the intersection. He timed the red, yellow and green phases of the light with the stopwatch his father had given him when he graduated from the police academy. Not once did he see anything out of the ordinary. Nor did he witness a traffic stop, or for that matter, did anyone run the light.

And frankly, he wasn't surprised. Boss Griffin had run this place for more than 30 years. Nobody did that unless they were sly, crafty and cunning. Cal knew he wasn't messing with dummies. But he hoped there might be one or two that might help him solve this mess.

That brought him to his next target today, Theo Sullivan. It hadn't been too hard to determine where Sullivan lived – he had been listed in the Astoria telephone directory. He drove to his small, wood frame home, which was not more than a half-mile from the house where Sullivan had brought him the night Carl Griffin died.

Bocock parked his Chevy in the driveway and just before he knocked on the door, he noticed a dark Plymouth sedan drive towards him on the lazy country road. He suddenly remembered the car that had followed him after Griffin's funeral – same make, similar if not the same color.

He turned and stared at the car. The male driver turned his head so Bocock didn't get a good look at his face as he passed. But Bocock got the license plate number from the back bumper as it moved away.

"I have you now, secret shadow," Bocock said aloud.

Bocock knocked on the door, repeatedly. No one answered. He knew Sullivan was home, however. The same car that had parked near the billboard the night they met was in front of the BelAir in the driveway.

Bocock walked around the house and peered into the windows. In one room, apparently the bedroom, shades were drawn. But behind the house, in what appeared to be the kitchen, the window over the sink was open and Sullivan was sitting with his back turned, facing the front door where Bocock had knocked.

"Hello, Theo," said Cal. Sullivan, obviously startled, fell out of his chair into the floor. He got quickly to his feet, unleashing a stream of profanity.

"I don't want to talk to you, trooper! Our business ended the night we met."

"Let me in, Theo. We have to talk."

"No. Get the hell out of here. Get off my property."

"Well Theo, if you won't let me in, we'll talk like this, with me sticking my head though your kitchen window and you dog-ass drunk at your dining room table at one in the afternoon."

"I ain't drunk! I'm just ... having a cocktail."

"Vodka right out of the bottle. Real social, Theo. All by yourself on a weekday. Don't you have a job?"

Theo's guard dropped for a second. "I had one. But those bastards took it away."

"It was at the red light, wasn't it, Theo? In a nice room at the Astoria Hotel?"

Sullivan got to his feet, clearly a bit unsteadily, but deliberately none the less. He walked toward Bocock, who was leaning through the window. The two got close enough for Bocock to sniff the liquor on Sullivan's breath.

"I don't know what in the Sam Hell you are talking about," said Sullivan. "Who would work at a red light?"

"You would, Theo. You made them lots of money, pulling that switch at exactly the right time to get those silly tourists in trouble."

"You're full of shit, man. I told you to get out."

"Think of all the money they made, Theo. How much did you get? Minimum wage? A dollar an hour? Five dollars a day?"

Theo Sullivan was drunk. He was drunk most days and was almost out of money. And he was mad as hell at his current state of life, with his best friend dead and his status in the town being persona non grata.

"No, I didn't get shit for shinola," he said, ironically mangling the old expression for possessing poor judgment. "You obviously don't give a shit about me, man. You just talking to me can get me killed. Don't you know that? Don't you care?"

"Sure I care, Theo. Help me take them down, Theo. I'll protect you. You won't do any time. Help me convict the people who keep all the money."

"What you gonna do, trooper? Put a guard on me? Like you did that billboard? I see how you state guys guard. That billboard is still smoking. Just like I'd be in no time if they knew we was talking."

Bocock frowned. They already know we are talking, he thought. Secret shadow had likely already informed Boss Griffin. This investigation is not going to be easy, he thought for at least the one-hundredth time.

"Trust me, Theo. We'll put you up someplace safe. Atlanta maybe. And when we're ready to go to trial, you can tell it all."

"Yeah, tell it all. You see what happened to my friend Carl."

"Tell me about Carl. What had he done to them?"

"He hadn't done shit! He was just doing his job and they got mad at him and they took his badge, they took his uniforms, they took his guns. Hell, they took his goddamned dignity."

"So he'd been fired?"

"They called it suspended. Man, I can't tell you all this. I'm gonna be dead. Deader'n a squashed skunk on the road."

"Theo…"

But Cal couldn't get another word in. Theo Sullivan closed the window, and even though it was more than 90 degrees outside, he'd decided he'd rather go without a hint of a breeze than continue the conversation with Calvin Bocock.

Bocock watched as Sullivan turned his back on the window, righted the chair out of which he'd fallen and picked up the vodka bottle. He took a long swig, and turned to see Bocock still looking at him.

Theo Sullivan lifted his middle finger in the universal gesture, took the bottle and walked out of the room.

Cal returned to his BelAir and took his time departing. He looked long and hard for the dark Plymouth sedan, even doubling up and driving by the house again, but he never saw it. He'd have the patrol run that license plate number before this day was done.

He couldn't help but be disturbed by what he'd heard from Theo Sullivan. It looked like the most promising lead he had wouldn't lead to anything after all.

Chapter Twenty-Five

Boss Griffin was drunk and bordering on disorderly. It was the dinner hour and he was sitting at the head of the dinner table in his very ordinary Astoria home. Across from him sat his wife, Cecilia, who was not in a good mood herself. She was pissed off about Earl's constantly dark moods, and she was also dreading the impending start of school and her daily battles with the riff raff that populated her institutions of alleged learning.

Also at dinner this evening was their daughter and son-in-law. Patsy was 30 and had managed thusfar to preserve her beauty queen figure. Even though she was a married lady, she was still a Southern debutante at heart.

Marvin Justus, the dark-haired lawyer, was so thin it sometimes seemed he didn't take up much space. But he was a substantial mass and force in Hyde County, doing much of the daily work that kept the place running. And, most importantly, he kept the dollars flowing in.

Boss was fuming about the state of the dinner. Their maid and cook, Carla Weaver, had cooked her usual Sunday feast of fried chicken and gravy, green beans, fried okra and biscuits, but the man of the house was not satisfied.

"Carla, this chicken is dry as the fuckin' Sahara!" he raged after Carla, wide-eyed with fear, had emerged from the kitchen. "And the biscuits taste like they came from the same sand pit. Damnit woman, is this why I goddamn pay you?"

"I'm sorry, Mr. Griffin. Do you want me to fry up another chicken?"

"No. But I want this done right next time! Especially when we have the kids over. Now get the hell out of here before I take a whip to you!"

"Earl, there's no need for such an attitude," said CeCe. "And just in case you forgot, we don't whip the niggra hired help anymore. Can you not evolve with the times?"

"My house, my fucking attitude!" replied Boss, his bald head practically glowing red with fury. His hand shaking, he picked up his water glass, stood and threw it against the wall, where it shattered.

His family was speechless. They had never seen such a tantrum from Boss.

"I'll clean this up in a jiffy," said Carla, obviously happy the heavy tumbler had not hit her en route.

The breaking of the glass pretty much broke up the dinner. Patsy looked at her snarling father with disgust.

"Daddy, what has gotten into you? Troubles in town?"

"Honey, I think your daddy is nervous," said CeCe. "Do you remember that young state trooper who confronted him over at the church?"

"Good looking man," Patsy replied, which earned a truly dismissive smirk from her father.

"We think he has moved into town and is conducting some kind of witchhunt," said CeCe.

"What in the world?" asked Patsy, who honestly had no clue why her father was wealthy and she was heir to a wide swath of the lands of south Georgia.

"It's no concern of yours, Patty," said Boss. He was the only person on earth who called her that, and even though she hated her lifelong nickname, she tolerated it because even though her dad was taciturn and could be nasty, she loved him.

"Patsy, come on in to the living room. There's new doings over at the country club," said CeCe. She'd learned many years ago that when Earl got this way, the best thing to do was leave him alone and let him stew in his own juices. Besides, Marvin was there and they could do what they do in the study, which was mainly smoke cigars and conspire to fuck up all the people who fucked with them.

Earl and Marvin adjourned to the mahogany-paneled study, which like all the other rooms Griffin frequented, was windowless. Griffin poured himself a big glass of bourbon and a second, smaller one for Justus, which he gratefully accepted. He also handed the younger man a Cuban cigar.

Both made use of Griffin's engraved, double-edged cutter and then lit the expensive cigars, the finest in the world. Within minutes, the small study was cloudy with pungent smoke.

"Are you really worried about this agent? He's not going to find anything on us," Justus said reassuringly.

"Things just seem to be slipping out of control and spinning around a little bit," said Boss. "Ever since I had that tussle up in Atlanta with Dunlap, I've just been a little bit out of sorts.

"I want to change the subject. Tell me about our projects."

Justus smiled, because that was his specialty. He proceeded to tell Boss about a big shipment of cocaine that the boys had picked up from what had otherwise appeared to be a fishing boat over in Darien.

"You would not believe how much these Negros love this white powder," he laughed. "They will take every dollar they make and buy cocaine and I suspect they then laugh and fuck, and laugh and fuck until they finally pass out."

Griffin laughed. "Are they really open with it? I mean over there at Dolly's?"

Dolly's was the black version of Flo's. Astoria's secret underground economy had two sides – black and white. Dolly's actually generated more money for the cause than Flo's, mainly because the saucy redhead refused to let her girls or her customers indulge in illegal drugs. Sometimes, Earl thought the white cathouse was being run by a Sunday school teacher!

"There's also, on occasion, some heroin coming in," said Justus. "We're reselling most of it down in Savannah, but Dolly moves some of it here at her house."

"Those boys start much shit when they get high on all this dope?" asked Griffin.

"Most of the time, they just fuck their brains out with Dolly's girls and then pass out," he said. "Then they wake up and do it all again. But don't worry, she polices her house. She knows when they're out of money and she runs them off. Most of them get right back out on the shrimp boats or the turpentine farm and get enough money to get back there and start it all up again."

"What about the nigger women and their kids? Their men are spending all their money on booze and dope and whores."

"Boss, it's always been the same. Before drugs came in, it was shine. Male niggers are a sorry sort; they have kids but they don't provide for them. But the woman are hard workers. They make their own money and they take care of the kids. Like I said, it's always been the same."

"I know that," said Boss. "I guess I just wanted to hear that this new element we are introducing ain't really changing nothing."

"The only thing that's changing is our bottom line," said Justus with a toothy grin. "We are doing so much better with drugs and these guns that we sell up in Atlanta that you'd almost never know we shut down for a spell because of those ridiculous billboards."

"This Bocock, he'll figure some of this out," said Griffin. "Dolly lets things run so wide open that he'll get some ideas, somebody will squeal, and he'll probably make some busts."

"Boss, we're extremely well insulated. None of our primary people have any dealings with the drugs. Hell, Popsi and the cops don't even know a lot of this. I have guys that know guys that nobody else knows. And almost nobody knows me. Absolutely nobody knows you."

"Good, son. You are making me feel a lot better."

Justus smiled. "Let me make you feel completely better."

He stepped over to the older man and passionately kissed him on the lips. His right hand roamed down to Boss' crotch. The old man groaned with pleasure.

Cal Bocock had awakened in a good mood despite the obstacles that faced him. He was frying himself some eggs and bacon for breakfast before another day of sorting through letters for good leads and wandering around town hoping to make some friends for his cause.

He had his transistor radio on WWGS listening to some kick ass country music. He was singing along with this new one from Marty Robbins that he absolutely loved, "El Paso."

Cal sang along, imagining that he sounded good enough to be on stage with Marty himself. He continued to sing until the cowboy, sadly, dies in his lover's arms. At that point, he was through flipping the eggs and preparing to eat them.

"This is Cliff Cannon, and this news bulletin is just in from Astoria ..."

That got Bocock's attention. Cannon was the young radio newsman who had broken the story of Gov. Dunlap's billboards hitting the roadways of Hyde County.

"There was a house fire overnight in the Hyde County seat. Authorities say one man, apparently the only resident of the house, is dead.

"The victim was identified as 28-year-old Theodore Sullivan. Authorities say he apparently died of smoke inhalation. The cause of the fire remains under investigation. Officials say the house was beyond saving by the time the local fire department arrived about 2:30 this morning."

Cal threw his fork against the wall and cursed. Waves of guilt destroyed his good mood along with his appetite. He spooned the eggs into the garbage and wrapped the bacon in a napkin.

He got on the phone to headquarters and arranged for the state's best arson investigator to get to Astoria as quickly as possible. That task completed, he jumped into his BelAir and drove to the burned house of Theo Sullivan just as quickly as he could.

Fire trucks and police cars packed the road around the house where he had confronted Sullivan just two days before. He showed his state ID to Officer Wesley Crane, who huffed a bit, but waved him inside the roped off fire area. Inside, he noticed Officer Tony Wiggins talking to a firefighter. He didn't see anyone else he knew, but concluded that a grey-haired man still poking around inside the still smoldering house must be Dr. Grady Bennett, the town's physician and the Hyde County coroner. Sullivan's body was covered by a sheet on a metal gurney, apparently near where it had been found.

Bocock introduced himself to Bennett and showed him his credentials. Bennett quickly told him he had no doubt Sullivan had died from the smoke.

"My only expertise here is the body itself," said the doctor. "His lungs were filled with smoke. He was laying prone on what remains of that couch there. There was an ashtray of cigarettes and two empty vodka bottles. I can only assume he passed out drinking and his cigarette caught the house on fire."

"Any signs of an accelerant?" asked Bocock.

"As I said, I have no experience in arson investigation," said Bennett. "I'm primarily here just to examine the body. I'd ask one of the officers about any evidence like that."

But Bocock knew better, knowing what kind of answer he would get from either Smith or Wiggins. He returned to Smith and informed him the state would assume control of the scene and GBI arson investigators would be in place within hours.

"You are in charge, right?" he asked Smith.

"I guess I am. But it ain't no business of yours what I decide to charge." Smith thought that was hilarious and laughed in Bocock's face.

The young GBI agent was not entertained. He had no reason to doubt that his dealings with Sullivan had resulted in the young man's death, just as the victim had predicted. And with Sullivan's demise, Bobock had also lost his best witness in the similarly questionable death of Carl Griffin.

From down the street, safely shielded behind a police van, Popsi Colanise was hearing via radio about everything Bocock said or did. He had been careless the other day when Bocock had spotted him in his county-owned car. He would make no further mistakes. Too much depended on his performance being flawless from here on out.

Bocock stayed at the burned out house the rest of the day and deep into the evening, literally guarding the crime scene until his colleagues could arrive. The crime scene technicians did their work with great care, but arson investigations had not yet become well developed science. It was pretty clear by the time Bocock returned to his trailer for the evening that there was no evidence at the scene that Theo Sullivan's death had not been accidental.

Bocock's heart was heavy. He knew almost certainly that Sullivan would still be alive had he not been seen visiting his house. He made mental notes to have several heart to hearts with his father and with Director Sneed on how to conduct an investigation that could consistently escape the prying eyes of those looking to protect Boss and his evildoers.

Chapter Twenty-Six

The Musketeers were together again and all three were feeling the heat of the dreaded school year looming in the near distance. There were only a couple of blessed summertime days remaining and they were making the most of them, lounging under the bridge that spanned U.S. 55.

Naturally, the conversation focused on their near-death experience of just the day before, the fateful event that had occurred right beneath them in The Pit. Jim Bob maintained at length that he could have made it back to shore safely. After all, he dawdled in the water waiting for Sassy to jump in and then kept her afloat when she began to struggle.

As for Sassy, she made it clear she'd had enough of the Altamaha once and for all. "I don't like that river, and that river don't like me," she said.

Zeke didn't have much to say. His ankle was a bit swollen from his drop off the tire swing near the shore. He confessed he'd told his mom he'd hurt it in a bike wreck.

Across the river, the same little black boy saw them, and occasionally heard their voices rising over the green waters of The Pit. He decided to do something he'd never done before.

He climbed up to the roadway on his side of the river and crossed the bridge on foot. He saw the worn path down to the kids' secret sanctuary. He was going to meet these kids, face to face. He'd seen white kids before, in town, and on the roadsides, but he'd never actually met and talked to any. Now seemed like a good time, he decided.

He didn't want to scare them, so he called out right before he climbed up to the overhang where the three were sitting and chatting.

"Hello!"

"Hello yourself," said Jim Bob. "Who is it?"

The newcomer showed his face. There was no noticeable reaction from the two boys or the girl. "My name is Kimmie."

"Nice to meet you, Kimmie. I'm Bobby, but these rascals here call me Jim Bob. This is Sassy, and that ugly freckle face there is Zeke."

Kimmie was usually very shy around strangers, but these kids made him feel very comfortable. So he told them why he had crossed the bridge to visit today.

"I saw you guys in the river," he said. "And I thought both you boys were very brave, the way you saved her ... I mean, Sassy."

"You was over there whole time? Like that's crazy!" said Sassy. "Why didn't you jump in and drown along with us?"

All four shared their first laugh together. Kimmie immediately felt like he'd known these kids for years.

"I don't swim at all," he said. "I guess I knew better."

"I wish I had," said Sassy. "I sure know now. I guess I don't learn real easy."

Talking about learning prompted Zeke to ask Kimmie about school. He told his new friends that the black school had two rooms and two teachers. One classroom held the older kids, and other the younger kids. "There's never as many older kids because they end up quitting," he said.

"Quitting? They quit school?" Jim Bob had never heard of such a thing.

"Yeah, a lot of Negro folks don't think school's worthwhile. They think it's a waste of time. I like school myself. At least most days."

"Well, maybe it is a bit of a waste if you only have two classrooms," said Sassy. "That don't sound right to me at all. We have one for each grade."

Kimmie was amazed. "You have 12 classrooms?"

"At least 12," said Zeke. "Some classes are bigger and are split into two classes."

Kids being kids, the four climbed down off the bridge and walked down to the river bank. Kimmie picked up a flat rock and, throwing it sidearm, skipped it off the water. Sassy counted six skips.

"Wow, that was amazing!" said Jim Bob. "Show me how you did that."

"It comes natural to me," smiled Kimmie. "I've always thrown this way."

After some practice, all four kids were skipping rocks. In fact, after several minutes of marathon skipping they were having trouble finding flat stones because they'd gouged most of them off the bank.

"I bet you're a great baseball player," said Jim Bob. "I really like Willie Mays and Hank Aaron. They're black, you know."

"I've heard of them, but I've never seen them," said Kimmie.

"Don't you have TV?" asked Zeke.

"No, my folks can't afford TV. We have a radio, though! Sometimes late at night on stations a long ways away with lots of … my mom calls it static … I hear the St. Louis Cardinals. But you know, when you can't see them, it isn't that great."

Jim Bob said he'd seen both Mays and Aaron play on the Saturday game of the week. "Those guys can hit the ball a mile!" he exclaimed. "And both of them are great outfielders, though I think Mays is probably the best 'cause he plays center and covers more ground than Aaron."

Sassy was bored with all the baseball talk and proposed an idea.

"Kimmie, we have swings and a slide at our trailer park," she said. "Why don't you ride up there with us and let's play on them?"

Kimmie admitted he didn't have a bicycle. "But I run all the time," he said. "I can run alongside you'uns."

"And we can go slow," said Zeke, who preferred that anyway.

So the four proceeded to climb back up to the roadway and journeyed along the right of way back to the Astoria Trailer Court. The makeshift playground was located in a field adjacent to the trailers, an area occasionally used for pickup baseball games.

Kimmie had never been on a real swing before and loved it. He was swinging so high Sassy was afraid he'd loop over the iron bar on top of the swingset.

"You guys have a lot of neat stuff to do," said their new friend. "At home, I pretty much just have to help my mom do chores. I can play a little bit, but there's lots of work, too."

The kids didn't notice it, but they had gotten a lot of strange looks from the other trailer park residents who had seen them ride in and saw them in the playground. No one had said anything to the kids, but there were some adults who were not happy about the visitor.

Then, as the day was turning to dusk, an Astoria squad car pulled up the driveway closest to the playground. Wesley Crane was at the wheel, and when he saw the four kids, he came to a sudden stop.

He was out the driver's side door in a flash.

"Bobby, what in the blue blazes are you kids doing?"

"We's playing, daddy. Like we always do."

"Who is this?"

"This is our new friend Kimmie. He lives across the river."

"I know where he lives. What's he doing over here?"

"We asked him to come play with us," said Zeke, bravely offering support to his friends.

Crane was seething with anger. He walked closer to his son and towered over him. "We don't associate with niggers. And you don't either!"

Jim Bob was shocked. And he was getting angry himself. "Daddy, kids are kids. Kimmie is a kid just like we are. Just like Sassy and Zeke."

"He's a nigger! Niggers belong on their side of the river!"

"That's just not right!" said Jim Bob.

Crane backhanded his boy in the face, the blow making an audible sound. Jim Bob went sprawling into the dirt and his nose began to bleed. The other kids backed up and their faces showed how shocked they were.

"You are wrong, wrong, wrong!" said Jim Bob through clinched teeth and red, tear-stained eyes.

"You get your ass home, right now. And you go straight to bed without any supper," fumed Crane. "Sarah, you and Zeke go home, too. Your folks are going to hear about this."

"And boy, you get on across the river, right this second. You ain't welcome around here and you ought to know that. Maybe I need to ride up there and tell your momma that you're over here sucking up to the white kids."

Kimmie's lip trembled, but he didn't say a word. He looked at his new friends as tears mounted in his eyes. Without a word, Kimmie simply bolted off -- he ran away. He galloped right out of the trailer park. He would not see the area again for many years.

####

Late that night, in his trailer only about 100 yards from where Wesley Crane had slapped his son and run off his visitor, Cal Bocock awoke with a start. Sometimes, your subconscious mind thinks of things you never considered while you were awake. And Bocock could not believe he had overlooked such a potentially significant detail.

He had had two encounters with Theo Sullivan in life. During both of those encounters, the young man was stressed out and emotional. During neither of those meetings, though, had he ever seen Theo Sullivan smoke a cigarette. He knew well people who smoke light up much more frequently when they are stressed out and emotional. His own mother was a prime example of that. He'd seen her go into a chain smoking fit when he had gotten in trouble or had gotten hurt.

During their last meeting, Theo had been drunk. Drunks who smoke tend to smoke constantly. He had seen no evidence of smoking on Theo's kitchen table. He had seen no packs of cigarettes, nor an ashtray.

Yet Doc Bennett had said there was an ashtray full of smoked cigarettes by the couch and Sullivan had likely caught the house on fire when he passed out smoking and drinking.

All of which is physically impossible to do when you don't smoke.

All of this had popped into Cal's head when he had finally fallen asleep. He began to wonder who he could contact to confirm his suspicion that Theo was a non-smoker. The obvious choice was Linda Bishop. Though she had only met Sullivan once, it had been in a bar. If Theo was puffing away that night in Bart Taggart's bar, perhaps Linda would remember and shoot his theory down. He decided he'd call her the first thing in the morning.

So now I have two deaths with little things that don't add up, he thought. Carl Griffin, a lefty, supposedly shot himself with his right hand. And Theo Sullivan, who had not smoked in Cal's presence the night Griffin had died, nor later when Cal popped in through his kitchen window, was supposedly chain smoking the night he died in a house fire.

How can I prove either death was a murder? That was the million dollar question with no apparent answer. He could not remember if the GBI crime scene techs had examined, nor even saved, the cigarette butts. Had they burned in the fire? Cal honestly could not recall seeing them.

Were there even cigarette butts there in the first place? Or had Bennett simply parroted a theory he had heard from one of the cops, or somebody else?

This somebody else, if there was such a person, knew a lot more about the death of Theo Sullivan than he did.

Chapter Twenty-Seven

The door flew open at Bart Taggart's bar shortly before 6 p.m. and in walked Patsy Griffin Justus. Bart immediately greeted her with a big smile. Patsy was as close to a regular as Bart had, as long as you eliminated the extremely regular members of the Astoria Police Department from the list of usual suspects.

Patsy tended to show up just about now, before dark but after what, for most folks, would have been a long work day. Patsy didn't work, though, unless you counted her extracurricular activities at the country club or at the Hyde County Junior League or the Daughters of the American Revolution as work.

"Hi Bart," she said, batting her heavily mascaraed eyelashes at her favorite bartender. "Get me the usual, and if you don't mind, sweetheart, bring it back to my usual table."

Patsy looked especially comely tonight. She was dressed in a tight red skirt, and her white, lacey blouse was unbuttoned to the point where there was a pretty decent view of what most men would think was spectacular cleavage, at least during a time when visible cleavage was relatively uncommon.

As Bart poured her double scotch, on the rocks, Patsy ambled over to the jukebox. With a ready handful of dimes and quarters, she proceeded to select a heavy menu of Hank Williams, her namesake, Patsy Cline, Johnny Cash, Skeeter Davis, and, just to show she was current, a few by the red hot Johnny Horton, who'd had four big hits within a year, including two number ones.

Bart took the drink to a little table Patsy preferred in the back corner, which was near a mirror where she could keep an eye on her appearance and whether it remained suitable as the night wore on. It hadn't gotten busy yet, so Bart sat down to shoot the breeze with his wealthiest regular.

"How's it shaking, Patsy?" he asked with a friendly smile.

"Bart, life is extremely unfair and unkind," she said without elaboration. "Your little honkytonk, and its great jukebox, helps me ... let me say, moderate my mood swings."

"Is this going to be one of those nights?" he asked.

No elaboration was needed. Ever since Patsy returned to Astoria from college, there had been an understanding that Bart would make sure Patsy got home safely if she had imbibed too much. The message had originally come directly from Boss himself, and had later been reinforced by Marvin Justus, who Bart had secretly begun calling "Mr. Patsy."

"Perhaps," she said. "I'll let you know."

"You know I'll make sure you and your car get home safely," said Bart.

"Good, love," she said, flashing that beauty queen smile. "Keep 'em coming."

About an hour later, Cal Bocock came in. He too was becoming a regular. He liked Bart because, unlike most Astorians, Taggart would talk to him. And his gut had been that Bart was a straight shooter about most things, although Cal had not been so bold to ask him about Astoria's underground economy. Cal assumed the bar was legal, but frankly he hadn't taken the time to explore whether it had the proper licenses. He had larger targets, and he was happy there was a place close to home where he could come for a cold one after a long day pursuing his multi-faceted case.

It had been a particularly frustrating day for the GBI agent. Linda Bishop, though extremely happy to get a phone call from Bocock, had not been able to recall whether Theo Sullivan was smoking the night she met him. Cal's other encounters with townspeople had been similar. Those who knew who he was and what he did shied away from his advances. Those who didn't know who he was saved the shying away part for after they learned who he was.

Cal noticed most people seemed extremely nervous around him – like they were criminal suspects themselves, not just residents in a town run by criminal suspects. Some seemed overly paranoid, sometimes even clearly looking around to see if anyone was watching them as they talked to the agent. He understood that concept all too well, still believing that it was his interactions with Theo Sullivan that resulted in the young man's death.

He knew that his chance encounter with Sassy Smith and her police officer father had sped up the identification process for the Astoria Powers That Be, but only by a short time. This town clearly had a lot of eyes and ears that focused their input toward Boss Griffin and the tight little group that ran not only the town, but the entire county.

So it was a frustrated and even exasperated Cal Bocock who walked into Bart's and ordered a Blue Ribbon draft. But his mood quickly brightened when he looked into the corner and recognized Patsy Justus. Patsy caught the gaze head on and appeared to recognize Cal as well.

Cal realized he needed a moment to prepare, so he kept his seat at the bar and began to sip the refreshingly cold beer. And with Bart nearby, he decided to be as bold as he had been to date with the bartender.

"Bart, is that who I think it is at that corner table?"

"Yes sir, Cal. That is Mrs. Patsy Justus her own self," said Bart. "Have you ever met?"

"Not officially," he said. "I have seen her from a distance."

"She looks even better up close," said Bart with a laugh. "Patsy's one of the best looking women in this whole damn county."

"She's here alone? Isn't that ... unusual for a married woman?"

"Cal, Patsy is one of a kind. She is independent, headstrong and strong willed. Let me put it this way, Cal. What Patsy wants, Patsy gets."

It wasn't 30 seconds later that Cal felt a soft tap on his shoulder. He turned around to see Patsy in his face, her big smile framed by luscious ruby-red lips.

"Hello, cowboy," she said. "I haven't seen you in here before."

"I can say the same thing about you, Mrs. Justus."

"Screw that Missus shit," said Patsy. "Call me Patsy."

"Why don't you let me buy you another beer and you come sit with me? We ought to get to know each other."

"Let's reverse that a bit. Let me buy you, what is that?"

"Double scotch on the rocks."

"Strong drink."

"For a strong woman."

With a fresh beer and Patsy's third double scotch of the night in hand, the two moved into the back corner. Cal looked around to see who might be watching, but at this point, Bart was the only apparent witness to this meeting. He busied himself by pretending to clean the bar and wash up some beer mugs as the two had chatted. Cal noticed what his daddy would have called a "shit-eating grin" on the barkeep's face.

Back at the table, Cal pulled a chair to directly face Patsy, who had resumed her back to the wall position. He wasn't crazy about not being able to see the entire bar, but he noticed there was a mirror that would give him some heads up if somebody was watching or approaching. He felt he couldn't sit too close to the long-legged lady without appearing to be too forward.

"Tell me about yourself, cowboy," Patsy began, batting long eyelashes over piercing brown eyes. There was no doubt in Bocock's mind that he had this woman's undivided attention.

Cal told it straight up, that he was a career law enforcement officer recently assigned to the GBI. He neglected to note that his primary assignment was to nail Patsy's father to a wall.

"You married?" asked Patsy. Cal shook his head.

"Never had time. At least not yet," he said with a suggestive smile. Better lay on the honey, he thought. At least up to a point.

"But I know you are. I've seen your husband ..."

"That son of a bitch don't count as a husband," said Patsy. "Do you see a ring on this finger?" She displayed a well-manicured left hand with long red fingernails.

"I think you could best describe me as a bored housewife," she said. "And I'm describing you as one damn fine-looking man."

Cal blushed. "Why Patsy, that's mighty sweet of you."

"Honey, I can be unbelievably sweet."

Patsy slipped off her high-heeled shoe under the table. Before Cal could notice, her foot was in his chair, slowly massaging his crotch.

"Patsy, you're getting a little ahead of yourself, aren't you," Cal laughed, keeping his composure.

"I could go for a little head," she laughed. "Let's cut out of here."

Both laughed aloud. "Maybe we should just have another drink instead," Cal suggested.

"OK," she said, motioning for Bart to come over. "Another round! On me, Bart." This time, Bocock did not resist the offered drink.

Inevitably, the conversation turned to Patsy's father.

"So Cal, I understand you are investigating my daddy," she said, her expression unchanged from its consistent interested woman on the make mode. "What are you contending he did?"

"Patsy, I can't tell you things like that," said Bocock. "It has been reported in the press that the state is investigating the activities of the police department, as well as allegations of ongoing criminal activity down here. I'm not confirming or denying anything. I'm just telling you what people think they know."

"Cal, let me tell you what I know. My daddy has worked hard all his life. He has earned every dollar that he has. He has turned this shithole of a town into a pretty decent place. My momma is principal of a pretty good school, a school that's much better than those in nearby counties. Most people here have honest jobs and a safe place to live and raise their families.

"What could possibly be criminal about that?"

Bocock smiled. "I've said all I'm going to say on that subject."

"I'm not under investigation, am I?" Patsy laughed.

Cal shook his head. "No ma'am. Not to my knowledge."

"Good. Then let's go sightseeing. I want to show you some things you haven't seen yet in my little hometown."

Against his better judgment, Cal agreed. The bar tab had already been settled, Patsy apparently having an account that required no cash. So they walked out of the bar, Bart giving them a friendly wave. Cal's trained eyes roamed the clientele and saw no immediate threats -- other than Taggart, of course -- and there was nothing he could do about the bartender's steady gaze.

Cal opened the passenger door of his BelAir, and Patsy quickly moved all the way into the middle of the couch seat, straddling the car's big transmission hump. And as soon as he had gotten in and closed the door, she grabbed him and kissed him, deeply and passionately. Cal kissed back.

"Nice to meet you, Patsy."

"Same here, cowboy. Now take a right out of here, and then the second left.

That route led directly to the local version of Inspiration Point, the closest thing the flat coastal area had to high ground. It was on the river, about two miles downstream from The Pit where the Three Musketeers liked to hang out.

Once parked, Patsy began to work Cal with enthusiasm. She forced his hand into her blouse. He initially withdrew, but she persisted. She began to massage his crotch, and Cal realized this was going to get out of hand unless he took command.

"You know, Patsy, I'm a bit of an old fashioned guy," he said.

"What does that mean?"

"You are drop dead gorgeous and I like you. But we don't know each other well enough yet to be going where you are taking us."

"Shut up and let's go anyway, sweetie. You'll like where I'll take you."

"I know I will, Patsy. But not tonight, sweetie. Let's slow this down. Can I take you home?"

"To your place? Sure!"

Bocock laughed. "No, yours!"

Patsy sighed. "You know, cowboy, this may well have been your only chance to ride this cowgirl. I'm used to getting what I want."

"That's what I've heard," Cal replied with a knowing smile.

Patsy pulled him close and once again kissed him passionately. "I want you to think long and hard about what you are missing. And I want you to tell me one more time what you are thinking."

"I'm thinking about you, no lie," laughed Bocock. "But I'm sticking to my guns."

"You could be shooting that gun, you know," Patsy continued to flirt. "Or I could give you that head we were talking about. Sweetheart, I can take the chrome right off your trailer hitch."

Cal laughed, even though he had heard that one before.

"Can I drive you home – your home?"

"Take me back to Bart's, cowboy. Take your blue balls and go on home."

"This has been an unforgettable evening that I have truly enjoyed," he said.

"Well, it's a first for me," she said.

"What do you mean?"

"It's the first time in my life that I have failed to get the britches off a hot cowboy I wanted," she said. "And I am not happy about that at all."

"I am flattered to be one of your first at anything," Cal said.

"Remember what I told you," Patsy said as she got out of her car at Bart's. "What I want, I get."

"I'll remember that, Patsy. Good night."

Cal did as he was told and took his blue balls on home.

This time, however, he completely missed that he was being watched from Bart's parking lot. And the tail that followed him home did a most professional job of not being spotted.

Chapter Twenty-Eight

The last time Cal Bocock had gone to church, it got him this job. And he had developed some interesting leads and insights during that early afternoon at Astoria Baptist Church. So on the Saturday afternoon that Theotis "Sully" Sullivan was to be laid to rest, Bocock once again brightened the insides of the town's newest and nicest church, allegedly rebuilt through the generosity of Boss Griffin himself after an untimely fire destroyed the original sanctuary.

Bocock was 15 minutes early for Carl Griffin's funeral. Today, he arrived within seconds of the scheduled 2 p.m. service. He found the parking lot nearly empty, which was not a surprise. He knew from asking around town that Sullivan had very few friends. His best, Carl Griffin himself, beat him into a wooden box by weeks.

Again, the Rev. Thomas Griffin was presiding. Only a scant handful of people dotted the sanctuary, nearly all finding an aisle seat on the hard wooden pews. Bocock's eyes were immediately drawn to the very same woman who had attended Griffin's funeral, the magnificent dark lady with the green eyes, who was wearing the very same black funeral dress. She was seated in the same pew.

He never forgot a name, and he would never forget hers – Fancy Fontaine. Was it real, or an alias? She looked his way when he padded in and found a nearby pew. She flashed a brief but friendly smile.

This was very interesting and unexpected. Had the three of them – Carl Griffin, Sully and the woman – run in the same circles? She had described herself as working in "personal services." That covered a wide range of possibilities. Bocock welcomed another opportunity to talk with this woman, who suddenly loomed in his mind as the biggest mystery in town other than the inner secrets of Boss Griffin himself.

There was one other person in the sanctuary that Bocock recognized. It was Colin Smith, the Astoria cop and father of Sassy Smith, the trailer park girl. Smith was certainly the surliest of the surly at APD, and had never had a kind word for Cal. He was obviously one of Boss Griffin's most loyal pawns.

But he appeared to be the only cop present. Had he worked with Sullivan on the red light detail? It had been frustrating to Bocock that he had never once seen it skip yellow, though he had managed to sneak up on it at all hours of day and night from all four directions. Was this fraudulent light a big myth? Or had

Griffin shut it down because he knew Bocock was in town and watching for unscrupulous traffic stops?

There were two other men that Bocock did not recognize. One was nearly Boss Griffin's age, dressed in a cheap suit. The other was middle-aged, dressed in what was probably his work clothes. Bocock surmised that one or both of these men were Sullivan's relatives, possibly a father or uncle.

But that was it. What a life for Theo Sullivan. Unlucky in life, nearly friendless – what a tragically sad way to meet your maker. Five people at his funeral, one of them a former state trooper whose untimely intervention probably caused his death. It was a sobering thought for Cal.

No Griffins, other than the minister, came to the funeral. Sullivan was at best a bit player in the inner workings of Astoria, obviously ostracized at the end.

The Rev. Thomas Griffin walked to the pulpit after the same elderly piano player completed an uninspired version of "He Walks With Me." What would he say about Theo Sullivan? What was the official Griffin version of Sullivan's life?

Not much, it turned out. Griffin gave the typical, "I didn't know this man, but today he walks with God" eulogy.

"Theotis wasn't a member of our church, and I did not have the pleasure of knowing him," he said at one point. "Sadly, he has only one relative present, Mr. Clon Sullivan, his uncle who lives in Slaton County."

Bocock shook his head. That explained the plain-dressed man, who acknowledged the introduction from Griffin with a nod of his head. Only two mysteries were in church today. The other elderly man, and the enigma in black, that beautiful green-eyed woman.

Griffin didn't say what Theo did for a living, and that was probably because he was unemployed. And obviously, since Theo's only known previous job had been to perform an illegal function for a criminal enterprise, it wasn't the kind of thing a minister would mention, even if he knew. The handful of facts Griffin threw out probably came from his uncle – he played baseball as a youth, he had recently lost his best friend – ironically not identified as a relative of the minister -- and he had died in a tragic house fire.

A fire that Bocock believed was arson, set to commit murder. How he'd ever prove it was yet another mystery.

The uncomfortable eulogy finally ended, and the pianist plunked her way through "What A Friend We Have in Jesus." Griffin invited the five to the graveside, and apparently only then realized there were no official pallbearers.

"Gentlemen, we have a problem today. This is a pauper's funeral, and I'm happy to perform it as God's servant and the pastor here in God's House. But can I ask you men here in the sanctuary to be honorary pallbearers?"

Bocock realized he had no choice. There are usually six pallbearers; today there would be only four. Obviously, the good reverend felt he was doing his part by working for free.

So, a bit uncomfortably, Cal realized he was going to be up close and personal with Sully Sullivan one more time. He and the uncle assumed one side of the casket, Officer Smith and the unknown elderly man on the other. And the latter was the most unhappy draftee at all. "I don't want to do this," he said.

"Melvin, you gotta," said Smith. "Three of us can't get him out to the hole."

How classy, thought Bocock. What would Jesus think of this?

It was probably lucky that Sullivan was a thin man. The casket and the corpse amounted to a pretty good weight for each to bear, but the four did just fine until they got into the grassy cemetery.

The man Bocock later learned was Melvin Guthrie, the owner of a decrepit little country store called Mel's, slipped in the grass. The casket teetered in the balance, the top opening and poor Theo appearing to decide he wanted none of this casket thing.

Somehow, Smith, who was strong and fairly agile, managed to slide down and assume much of the weight Guthrie had lost purchase of. Bocock grabbed the top of the casket and managed to close it, somehow keeping Sully from taking his premature leave.

Guthrie cursed, wiped some mud from his knee and reassumed his position. He moaned about his aching back and then further defamed the funeral.

"I fuckin' wish I had stayed home," he griped. "I didn't like the sumbitch anyway."

The four finally got to the graveside and laid the coffin on the device that would lower it into the ground. Bocock managed to escape and slide alongside the Lady in Black.

"Quite an adventure, huh?" she said with a smile.

"I think Theo wanted out," said Cal, prompting Fancy to muffle a laugh.

"I really want to talk to you," Bocock said quickly. "Can I buy you dinner?"

"Why Mr. Bocock," smiled Fancy. "I don't think I've ever been invited out at a funeral before."

Then her mood turned serious. "You know I shouldn't be seen talking to you," she said.

"It has proven to be a problem for some, that's for sure," Bocock glumly admitted.

"Let me think about it during the service," she said. "If I decide I will, it has to be under my circumstances, in a way I arrange. If the answer is yes, I will slip you a note as we shake hands after the service. It will detail how we must meet."

Cal, dumbstruck, nodded. He purposely moved away from Fancy, sitting a few seats away in one of the precarious folding chairs set up at the graveside.

At one point during Griffin's graveside prayer, he snuck a look at Fancy. He was pleased to see her laboring away with a pencil.

Bocock smiled. Funerals seem to serve me well, he thought. But then for some reason, he thought of his mother up in the north Georgia mountains.

If she only knew I had been to church just twice since I've been here, and both of them were funerals for people connected to my case, she would kill me, he thought.

And that would mean yet another funeral.

After the service as the tiny gathering mingled just enough to be polite, Cal offered his hand to Fancy Fontaine. As expected, in her gloved hand was a tightly folded piece of paper. Cal nodded and smiled, and clandestinely slipped it into his trouser pocket so no prying eyes would see.

He turned and saw Guthrie moving toward the parking lot. He hurried to catch up with the breathless, gap-toothed storekeeper.

"Sir ... Melvin ... are you all right? I wanted to check on you after that nasty spill."

Guthrie turned and growled back at Bocock. "I'm OK, I guess. Damn grass is slippery."

"I don't think we've formally met," said the young agent.

"I don't think we need to," said Guthrie. "I got no business with you."

"I just wanted to talk about Theo. You must have known him. I just thought you might share a thought or two."

"Sully didn't have many thoughts," said Guthrie, showing his gapped teeth. "He was so dumb he couldn't pour piss out of a boot with the instructions written on the heel."

Bocock chuckled to be polite. "You must have liked him though, taking time on a Saturday to attend his funeral."

"He was OK in the good times," he said. "We, uh, played cards on occasion. You know, he was good friends with Carl Griffin and he and Griffin used to hang out at my store sometimes."

"Interesting," said Bocock, surprised that after such a surly opening that the old man had opened up a bit. "Can I ask you one more thing?"

"Oh I guess, but I do gotta go," said Guthrie.

"Did Sullivan smoke?"

Guthrie surprised Bocock by laughing out loud. "You're a GBI agent, so I guess you're interested in the illegal things he did. He did smoke."

"Smoking is illegal?"

"You know smoking ain't illegal," Guthrie said sharply, looking at Bocock like he was a 12-year-old. "He liked to smoke the wacky weed. I had to toss him out of my place a couple of times when he'd light up a marijuana cigarette. I don't want to get in trouble with Colin here or the other APD boys."

"I didn't know that," said Bocock. "Did he smoke cigarettes?"

"God you ask stupid questions," said Guthrie. "I don't rightly know, but I don't think I ever saw him smoke a cigarette, other than the Mary Jane he carried back when he had some money."

"Any idea where he got it?"

"Jesus Fracking Christmas," said Guthrie, now becoming peeved. "Do you think I'd tell you if I knew where he got it? Hell, for all I know, he probably grew a patch in his front yard. Or maybe in his bathtub."

"Thank you, Mr. Guthrie. May I come to your store sometime?"

"Only if you're going to buy something," said the county's foremost Razzle Dazzle dealer. "I'm in business to make money."

"Of course, sir," said Bocock. "Have a good day."

The uncle had disappeared. There just had not been enough time to talk to him. Cal made a mental note to track him down by telephone up in Slaton County.

Bocock turned only to almost run into Colin Smith. Smith snarled and sidestepped out of Cal's path.

"Hey trooper, don't you have a billboard that needs guarding? I think the Alligator Farm put up a new one." Smith, as always, laughed at his own bad jokes.

"I'm out of the billboard guarding business," said Bocock. "Haven't you heard?"

"Yeah, that was a definite loss of inventory, huh? That job was eliminated, wasn't it?"

"Watch your top knot, officer," said Bocock, repeating a phrase that police officers often shared. It means, "Be careful out there."

"You're the one that needs to keep eying that top knot," said Smith. "I ain't in no danger."

Bocock dismissed Smith's latest insult. He couldn't wait to read Fancy Fontaine's note. But he was going to be very careful and not even look at it until he was in the privacy of his own trailer. There are too many unfriendly eyes and ears in Astoria.

And sure enough, during the short drive from the church to the Astoria Trailer Court, Smith watched him warily, trailing at a distance in his squad car.

He did this up to a point. Cal watched in his rearview mirror as Smith pulled off into Bart Taggart's parking lot, obviously seeking some post-funeral adult lubrication.

Chapter Twenty-Nine

Fancy Fontaine's note was brief to be so detailed. She wrote that she would meet Bocock at 7 p.m. sharp the following Tuesday in the alleyway behind Grizzle's Country Store.

"I reserve the right to refuse to answer any question," she wrote. "Let's have dinner out of county. Private!"

Bocock was elated about what he had read in school-teacher perfect small cursive style. For a reason he could not quite understand, this felt far more important than just a lead in his investigation.

As the days passed, life seemed to be returning to what had long been normal in Astoria. Gov. Dunlap's billboards were a distant memory for travelers, as were the media accounts about the speed traps. With only the United States Automobile Association's published warning to protect the traveling tourists,

Astoria's patrolmen were again pulling numerous people over and writing speeding tickets.

Cal borrowed a radar gun from his former colleagues at the State Patrol and on several days, spied on Wesley Crane, Tony Wiggins and Colin Smith at different times as they worked speed. He didn't witness a single stop that was out of line. He knew it annoyed the local cops like crazy, but he stayed close enough to watch what happened on the traffic stops he witnessed, and he often followed the motorists after they pulled away. Once, when a motorist who had been pulled over stopped for gas down the road, he stopped to chat with him. Cal never saw or heard anything out of the ordinary.

It seemed more and more like Astoria's magic traffic light was an optical illusion. He checked on it at least twice a day and never saw any light cycles not within the norms. As best as he could tell, Astoria was still in the traffic enforcement business, but it appeared they were following the rules. That was frustrating to Cal, but also strangely satisfying. It had to be his presence that had prompted the city cops to toe the line.

As it appeared less and less likely he would catch any of Astoria's finest red-handed, he began to delve more into the box of letters, as well as continue to work the streets of Astoria, hoping to find someone, anyone, willing to talk about the heavy-handed rule of Earl "Boss" Griffin.

####

After two very routine days, it was finally Tuesday night, and Bocock picked what he considered his best-looking casual clothes for his dinner date with Fancy Fontaine. He had scouted out Grizzle's store in advance. It was a typical south Georgia country store, stocked with groceries and dry goods. It sold bait for fishermen and even had some farm supplies. What Bocock didn't know was that Slim and Lettie Grizzle were on the up and up. There was no Razzle Dazzle at Grizzle's, no gambling of any kind, no alcohol nor any drugs or guns. The Grizzles were God-fearing, honest, hardscrabble south Georgia business people. And frankly, that was why Fancy Fontaine liked and trusted them and had selected their store as her rendezvous point with the GBI agent.

Bocock was extremely careful as he drove the BelAir from the trailer park to Grizzle's, making certain he wasn't being tailed. At one point, he thought he might have spotted a suspicious tail, so he promptly pulled off on a residential street and made a brief tour of a blue-collar neighborhood before pulling back onto U.S. 55. He had lost whoever it had been. He passed Grizzle's, did a U-turn, again watching for tails, and, as Fancy had requested, made a beeline for the alley behind the store. It was a narrow, gravel affair that fronted a dense pine forest.

Almost as soon as he pulled behind the store, Fancy emerged from Grizzle's back door. She was dressed in a simple blue dress, her long black hair pulled into a bun. She clutched a small white handbag.

She started to come to the passenger door, but Cal was out his door before she could get there. He greeted her with a warm smile and opened her door.

"You are such a gentleman!" she said, her green eyes twinkling in the dusk of the late summer night.

"I don't have many opportunities to dine with beautiful women," said Bocock. "I'm going to be on my best behavior."

His date smiled, and climbed into the seat last used by Patsy Griffin. Cal considered the contrast, and decided Fancy Fontaine was quite an improvement in class, attitude and behavior. But then, to be perfectly fair, he knew nothing about her.

"OK, as we pull out, I'll have to ask you to lower your head onto the seat," he advised his passenger.

"Why Mr. Bocock, we don't really know each other that well now, do we?" she said.

Cal laughed. "In case we are being followed, I don't want them to know I have a passenger," he explained. "Remember your concerns about privacy?"

"Of course," she laughed. "How silly of me!"

Bocock wasted no time getting back onto 55, and the county line was behind them in only seconds. He studied his rear view mirror as well as the vista ahead and declared the coast clear. Fancy had rolled onto her side in the BelAir's big front seat, and even though she could have easily touched the driver, she made no contact whatsoever. Again, Bocock thought about how different his drive with the ravenous, sex-crazed Patsy Griffin had been.

"So where is dinner?" asked Fancy.

"There's a place in Moxley called Cleo's. They have probably the best menu in Moxley, as if that's saying much," said Cal. "Have you been there before?"

"I don't get out much," she said. "It sounds wonderful."

Tuesday nights being sleepy and slow in Moxley, a slightly bigger town 26 miles from Astoria, the young couple had plenty of privacy. They were seated at a booth and there were only two other couples in the restaurant, both well out of earshot.

Cal had thought long and hard about how he was going to begin this interview. He had numerous opening lines, but at the end, he kept going back to the tried and true of just being a mildly curious interested listener.

"Fancy, tell me about yourself," he said.

Rarely had he been so surprised at a subject's response.

"Cal Bocock, I want you to promise me you won't put me in jail for anything I am about to tell you," she said.

"Jail? What have you done, Fancy?"

"I haven't killed or robbed anybody, but I do commit what you would consider criminal acts," she said.

Cal rubbed his chin. Luckily, the waiter came to take their order, which gave him time to think. He changed the subject to the menu. "You know, they have what they call pizzas here," he said. "Cleo's has a cook who was a U.S. Marine and he served in Italy during the war. He learned while he was over there how to make pizzas."

"I've heard of them, but I've never had one," said Fancy, who seemed honestly excited. "Let's do it!"

So Cal ordered a cheese, pepperoni and mushroom pizza. He asked for a Coke, Fancy picked iced tea. The waiter advised them they'd made a great decision, and left them alone again.

"Now back to these criminal acts, Fancy. You have to help me a little bit here. Are there victims involved?"

"I think you would consider them victimless crimes," she said. "My victims, umm, clients, almost always leave satisfied."

Cal had his suspicions from the beginning, but now he knew what Fancy was signaling.

"Fancy, I am not in Astoria to bring morals charges against anyone," he said. "Now if you are running a huge criminal enterprise, you could be a target. Am I offbase here?"

"Cal," she started slowly, "I run nothing but me. But I am a part of an illegal business."

Then, like a Catholic girl sitting in confession for the first time in many years, she broke into tears. "Cal, I'm a two-bit whore. I'm a call girl -- a prostitute.

"If my confession gets me the jail, so be it," she continued, those enchanting green eyes becoming red with tears. "I've thought about this a long time. I'm ashamed of myself and decided I've done this long enough."

Cal had been a law enforcement officer for a long time, and he could almost always tell when someone was telling the truth, and when someone was being sincere. He also realized he was touched by Fancy's unexpected breakdown.

"Fancy, it's OK," he said. "As I said, I'm not going to get you on some morals charge. Yes, prostitution is illegal, but what's going on in Astoria is bigger than that."

"Yeah, but it's part of it," she said. "I love the lady that took me in, and I don't want her going to jail either. She's what I guess you would call a madam and there are now four other girls at her place, but she's honest and there's no drugs or real terrible kinky stuff.

"Can I be frank?" she asked.

"Your secrets are all safe with me," said Cal.

"We pull tricks, we do blowjobs," Fancy said. "But Flo draws the line there. She won't let us do butt sex or handcuffs or any of that hard core stuff."

Cal blushed. He'd never heard of such a thing. OK, maybe he had, in a deeply recessed part of his north Georgia mountain upbringing.

"I've embarrassed you," said Fancy. "And you don't think much of me. Let me tell you my story."

Fancy took him back to her poverty-stricken childhood, and her mother's sad, but well-reasoned plan to provide Fancy with a pathway to a better future. Fancy would never talk ill about her sainted mother, so it was clear to Cal that Fancy believed she had merely done what she had to do to survive.

Even though it was not exactly the way most men might think, all this made sense to Cal Bocock, who had been raised to be open-minded and objective about viewpoints he had never before considered, as well as lifestyles he might have originally considered wrong. Organized prostitution was against the law for a reason and would always be wrong, Cal believed, but why should society have a say about what a man and a woman chose to do behind closed doors?

In short, Cal Bocock was impressed with Fancy Fontaine. And despite what she had said, he now thought more of her than he had before her tearful confession. Any person who started with nothing, someone alone in the world who had to fight just to survive, especially a woman with no man to provide for her, had Cal's respect.

Then the pizza arrived, giving another perfectly timed break to a very serious conversation. Once again, Cal and Fancy were just a man and a woman eating dinner together.

Fancy had come so very close to not meeting Cal at Grizzle's. And even after she had decided to meet Bocock, she had come even closer to merely continuing her mysterious ways. But now that she had confessed her terrible sin to the man who had been brought to Astoria to clean things up, she felt like a new woman.

She looked across the table at this man who was not even close to what she had imagined. He was completely different than any man she had ever met. Cal Bocock had just been told she was a worthless prostitute. But nothing had changed about his attitude, his manner of speaking or the way he looked at her with those twinkling blue eyes. There was no difference in his casual wisecracking and his obvious, but not offensive flattery.

Most men she'd met thought of nothing but sex, especially when they knew how she made her living. And she had always been happy to oblige, for a price. But this man seemed immune to her dangerous profession. He kept asking questions about Fancy herself, what she read, what she liked on TV, what happy memories she'd had from childhood. He wasn't just focused on the job he was sent to do. He was focusing on her.

Fancy was impressed. And deep in her heart, she felt she had done the right thing, no matter how risky it had been, and would continue to be. She had no way of knowing what was going to happen next in this crazy life she lived. It had clearly gotten a lot more complicated in the last couple of hours.

Fancy Fontaine didn't know everything about Astoria and its inner workings, nor would she ever. But she knew a lot, and she had decided she was going to help Cal Bocock as best she could. She could never hurt Flo, but maybe she could protect her. He was obviously so hungry for information. And information, like sex, always has a price.

Her price would be immunity for not only her, but for Flo, who was like a mother to her.

Chapter Thirty

Cal repeatedly offered to discreetly drop Fancy at Flo's, but she insisted he take her right back to Grizzle's. Storekeeper and friend Slim Grizzle was ready and waiting to take Fancy the rest of the way back to her cabin behind Flo's. She reminded Cal that they should take no chances that would put either of them in danger.

Back in the alleyway behind the faded white clapboard store, Cal scrambled around the BelAir and opened the door for Fancy. She climbed out of the big car, and Cal, holding her hand, raised it to his lips for a gallant kiss.

A tear formed in Fancy's eye, and for a brief second, she pulled him close. She kissed him on the cheek, and quickly disappeared inside the unlocked back door of the old store. They had planned to repeat this meeting in eight days, not seven so they would avoid slipping into an observable routine.

Cal's heart was beating hard in his chest, a fairly amazing response from just a simple peck on his cheek. He took the same careful approach in his departure from Grizzle's, and then began to think about all the things Fancy had told him during and after dinner. He decided he needed some time to wind down and consider all this new information, so he pulled into Bart Taggart's for an ice cold nightcap.

He quickly panned the bar, which was fairly busy for a weeknight. Happily, there was no sign of Patsy Griffin, but he did notice two of Astoria's finest at the bar. Wesley Crane and Tony Wiggins noted Cal's entrance with icy glares. Cal decided he'd get his beer from Bart and sit at a table instead of his usual bar stool. He wanted no trouble from the disagreeable cops tonight.

Bart was his usual self, friendly and chatty, and Cal was pleased there was no joking reference from the barkeep to his recent departure with the woozy Patsy. He took his Pabst to a table on an opposite wall beneath a glowing neon Falstaff beer sign and sat down so he could keep Crane and Wiggins in view.

The cops apparently were interested in détente as well, making no move toward the GBI agent. However, within a minute or two, Crane got up and Bocock steeled himself for a confrontation. Instead, the big crew-cut patrolman passed him by without even a glance and moved to the pay phone near the door. Out of the corner of his eye, Cal watched Crane deposit his nickel into the coin slot and proceed to have a brief conversation. Then he returned to his stool beside Wiggins and loudly ordered up another round from Bart.

Bocock thought briefly about a second beer, but realized after a time that he had nursed the first for more than 20 minutes. So he took a look at the two cops, who appeared to be drinking scotch, nodded at Bart, stood up and hit the door. His BelAir was parked near 55 in the gravel parking lot and Cal pulled to the edge of the highway to make sure the way was clear to pull out.

Without warning, his windshield exploded in a shower of glass. Cal immediately knew he was being fired upon with a rifle, and his training instinctively took over. He threw his car into park, grabbed his sidearm from where he had stashed it under his seat and rolled out of the car, protecting himself behind the driver's door.

He looked at the direction from which the shot had been fired and saw nothing. But through the moonlight and his still-burning headlights, he did see what appeared to be a perfect ambush point, a flat collection of concrete blocks, almost like an old wall from a demolished building, right across the road.

Bocock boldly came around the door and raced toward the wall, holding his sidearm in the classic two-handed defensive position. He saw and heard nothing, but once he got to the wall, he detected what could have been someone racing into the woods immediately behind the wall.

Cal realized that a sidearm was no match for what was probably a hunting rifle, but he instantly decided to pursue the running gunman anyway.

About a quarter-mile into the woods, there was a country road leading to the river and endless points beyond. Just before

Bocock reached the road, he heard the screeching sound of wheels being engaged. When he emerged from the woods onto the road, there was no sign of the escaping vehicle, though there was still dust in the air from the spinning tires.

Whoever had ambushed him had made a clean getaway.

Typical for this case, Cal thought. But he realized that for once, there had been some evidence left behind. He would call the GBI crime technicians once again.

Upon returning to his still running Chevy, Cal quickly determined that a single shot from the rifle had entered on the passenger side and had penetrated both the front and back seat and was probably embedded in the trunk. That would provide some ballistic evidence – at least he would know what kind of weapon had been used.

Retracing his path, he also found three spent cigarettes that seemed freshly smoked in the area where the gunman had likely crouched behind the wall. The sniper had waited for him long enough to chain smoke three butts. The cigarette butts were stamped -- Lucky Strikes. More evidence, and some irony. It had been lucky he was not hit, but he knew that from that range, with a hunting rifle, he would have been dead had that been the shooter's intent. This was nothing but an attempt to scare.

Cal Bocock didn't scare easily. This was nothing to him except more motivation to nail these cowards.

He decided to confront the two cops who had been sitting idly in the bar. After all, there had been a crime committed in their jurisdiction just yards from where their worthless asses had been planted, getting plastered.

Even though the shot had drawn some attention and several people were watching Cal move about making crime scene observations, he didn't see the two cops.

He went inside, and both were gone.

Bart Taggart, honestly looking concerned, asked Cal what had happened.

"Somebody took a pot shot at me while I was pulling out of your parking lot," Cal replied. "I thought about reporting it to the Astoria Police Department, but I notice they turned tail and ran away."

Bart snickered. "They downed their drinks and walked out the back door almost as soon as you left," he said. "They usually park in the back lot because, as you might understand, a squad car in my parking lot isn't great for business."

Cal went to the back door and looked around and saw no signs of the squad car. The cops obviously wanted no part of the scene in the aftermath of the shooting.

Cal went to the pay phone and called GBI headquarters. They told him the obvious, to leave everything in place, that they would dispatch a team within hours. It was going to be a long night, not unlike the evening Theo Sullivan died in the fire.

Bocock thought again about Wesley Crane's phone call. There had been plenty of time for the sniper to get in place after Crane's tip of his arrival at Bart's. Enough time, apparently, for him to take his position and smoke three cigarettes before Cal came out of the bar.

But still, it had only been a matter of minutes. This had to have been planned well in advance, and the sniper must have either been on call or close by. He could see no physical way it had been either of the two cops, but it might have been the third patrolman, Colin Smith.

Or it could have been some of the frightful riffraff that Fancy had described to him. The guys behind the scenes, she had said, do most of Boss Griffin's dirtiest work. They were most certainly the guys who had torched the billboards. They had most likely offed Carl Griffin. And he felt they had almost certainly killed Theo Sullivan.

Now they had tried to kill a GBI agent. Again, Cal's professional opinion was that it had been only a scare tactic. But scare or not, in the eyes of the law, it had been assault with a deadly weapon at best and attempted murder at worst.

Now that the adrenaline rush had passed, Cal was more angry than anything. They had shattered the windshield of his beloved BelAir and a rifle bullet had pierced the seat where Fancy had been sitting only hours before. These people were incredibly reckless and dangerous, and there was no question in Cal's mind that he could be killed at any time. As guarded as he had been since Theo's death, he resolved to double that caution.

For the first time in days, Cal thought about the governor. He knew that Herman Sneed would personally be advising him of this attack, probably the first thing in the morning. This would rile him up one more time, and Cal had already learned that when Dunlap was riled up about something, he tended to get aggressive and sometimes creative.

Finally, after what seemed like eternity, two crime scene techs arrived from the GBI's Savannah office. Cal began the painstaking task of showing them all he had observed while hoping they would find other clues. He sat to write his longhand report, spelling out in detail the events of the evening.

The motive for the attack was incredibly obvious, and Cal was a little surprised he had not thought about it until now, but that tended to be the case when an investigator was putting pen to paper. It was not the kind of detail that *could* be put in a report, because even though it was obvious, there was no proof, nor was there a politically acceptable way to report it.

Sure, Cal was investigating an increasingly dangerous crime boss. He poked around and irritated his lieutenants almost daily. His presence had curtailed the use of the traffic light, one of Astoria's most tried and true revenue sources.

But that wasn't the real reason Cal had been attacked this evening.

Cal had messed around with Boss' daughter. And even though he had not been the instigator, it was clear to the agent that his one-nighter with Patsy, as innocent as it had been, had been reported to the highest source – her old man.

And he was clearly pissed off. This was a warning shot across Bocock's bow from Boss to stay away from his daughter. She was an adult and perfectly capable of making her own decisions, but it was more evidence that Boss controlled everything.

Or at least he tried to.

Chapter Thirty-One

Fancy had dreaded this day since the night of her first date with Cal – and there had been two since. But she decided she couldn't put it off any more. The worst part was the work itself. She couldn't escape into fantasy land and be a sex servant like she could before she met Cal Bocock. Every trick felt like a betrayal to Cal; not only the promise she made, but also what she was coming to feel in her heart.

So on the Thursday after the couple had again visited Moxley for dinner – and this time a movie as well – Fancy walked from cabin No. 1 to the front office where she knew Flo would be because she had just seen Popsi Colanise come for yet another collection. She made sure the leering Greek was gone before she let herself in the back door.

Flo was counting what Popsi had not taken, and she obviously wasn't too happy about the remaining sum. Fancy realized this probably wasn't the best time to knock another big chunk off Flo's bottom line, but she had decided to do it and putting it off again would mean nothing but continued misery.

Flo glanced up and was surprised to see her best girl come into her office, if one could call it that. "What's up, hon?" she asked, managing a smile as she pulled back her long red curls.

"Flo, I know this is a terrible time, but I need a new start," Fancy said.

"What do you mean, sweetie?" Flo asked, concern obvious in her face.

"When I came here, I told you it wouldn't be forever. You have been great to me, and I consider you the mom I lost when mine died. But I'm going back to Savannah."

The affection melted from Flo's face. A bitter frown took its place. "You are cutting out on me? Now? When business is already in the toilet because of all this bad publicity and this state investigation and all this bullshit?"

Fancy gulped, took a half step back from the suddenly confrontational Flo, and continued with her planned speech. "I've made some calls and I can start at the beauty school in Savannah. Flo, I told you whoring was not going to be a permanent thing with me. I can't do it anymore."

Flo was fuming. "I take you in off the street. I give you a home – my best cabin – and I don't charge you one red cent for it. And just" – she counted in her head – "seven months later you're leaving me high and dry? How much money did you save? Were you skimming more than you were supposed to?"

"I don't have enough money," Fancy said. "I'll probably have to get a job waiting tables or something to get by. But I will."

"Bullshit!" cried Flo. "You're going to go down there and become a high-priced call girl, aren't you? You figure you can do better than being a sweet little black haired whore at Flo's."

Fancy paused. She had not planned to go where she was now headed, but Flo had forced her hand.

"My whoring days are over," she said. "I've met someone."

"You meet someone every day!" said Flo. "Is one of those lawyers from downtown going to set you up to be his getaway girlfriend? The least you can do is tell me the truth."

"I have met someone that hasn't come here, not once," she said. "And he promised me he would never come here."

"So he knows what you are, what you do, and he's sweeping you away?"

"No, not at all. I'm going. He's staying."

"Here? Who the hell is it?"

Fancy decided to lay it all on the table, just as she had with Cal on their first trip to Moxley. "It's Cal Bocock, the GBI agent."

Flo stopped dead for an instant. Her face soon matched her hair. She was almost apoplectic in her rage. She picked up a coffee mug that had been sitting on her desk and flung it in Fancy's direction. Some of the lukewarm coffee hit her, but she dodged the mug, which shattered on the wall behind her.

"You gave me up to the GBI? How could you? You little ungrateful bitch!"

Fancy came forward and grabbed Flo in a bear hug, corralling the older woman's arms before she could do some real damage. "Hear me out, Flo, just for a minute. Hear me out before you do anything else."

Somewhat against her better judgment, Flo went limp and backed away from Fancy's hold. She turned her back and walked back to the little antique table she used as a desk and a makeup table. "Talk to me, girl. But make it quick because I don't know what I might do to you."

"Cal has said more than once that he isn't interested in making any morals charges against anybody, including you or any of the girls. He considers this small potatoes compared to the traffic stuff and the Razzle Dazzle. He really wants Boss, not you or anybody else."

"And you believe this bullshit? You think you walk out of here and then he gives me and my business a complete pass?"

"Yes, I believe him. He's given me his word and he's honest. He's … like nobody I ever met."

"Honey, you're in love with this man and you're going to believe anything he tells you. And I suppose you've told him everything you know about this town and what goes on here?"

She nodded. Flo fumed again, turning and pulling her hands through her hair. "Well get the fuck out of here," she said. "Moe still lives in Savannah, you know, and he's going to be watching for you on the streets down by the riverfront. If I hear you are down there turning tricks, I don't know what might happen."

Fancy shook her head. "Flo, I told you the truth. I have turned my last trick. I'm done."

"Yes you are, sweet ass," Flo said. "Go!"

Fancy was crying now. She had hoped it wouldn't end this way, but it had. Luckily, she had suspected that it might, so Slim Grizzle was waiting for her at her cabin. Her few possessions were already in the trunk of his box-like Ford sedan.

"Flo, I love you," she said tearfully. "Thank you so much for what you have done for me."

"Thank you for what you have done for me," Flo replied angrily. "I don't know what you think is going to happen to me when the GBI padlocks this place. And they will.

"I can't go to beauty school. I'm a madam and that's what I'll be until the day I die."

Fancy wiped away the tears and backed out the way she had come. She ran back to her cabin, climbed into the waiting storekeeper's car, and told him she was ready. She was Savannah bound, this very day, her life savings in her purse.

Not many miles down the road, all the tears and heartache was gone. She was ready for her new life.

Chapter Thirty-Two

Meeting Melvin Guthrie at Theo Sullivan's funeral had been a lucky break for Cal Bocock. He'd actually been on the lookout for Guthrie – he was developing a good criminal case against him for illegal gambling.

Working the pile of complaint letters supplied by the governor's office, Bocock had seen a consistent story develop. Tourists who happened to stop at Guthrie's store – which he now knew was Hyde County's most notorious "clip joint" – would consistently leave with empty wallets. Or worse. He'd read numerous accounts of Dazzle losers being beaten by a younger man in or near the store.

Over time, Bocock had developed a rapport in repeated night time telephone calls with three different losing gamblers, and all three had agreed to come to Astoria to testify against Guthrie on gambling charges. All three understood they had broken state law just playing the illegal game, but the GBI had agreed to waive any charges in exchange for their testimony against Guthrie. Besides, all three had been told by Guthrie – or at least by an elderly man described as being a dead ringer for Guthrie – that Astoria had a special "local ordinance" that made Razzle Dazzle legal.

A prosecutor for the state attorney general's office had managed to get an indictment against Guthrie on three counts of illegal gambling. Bocock had expressed his doubts that the local grand jury would indict, but they had. It had not been easy, but finally he had a case to prosecute, and his hopes were high it could be the beginning of the end of Boss Griffin's notorious rule.

Criminal cases moved a lot quicker in Georgia and the rest of the country in those days, and soon it was time for the trial to begin. Bocock had more friends in town than he had ever had before – the state prosecutor, a young lawyer who was assisting him and two of his former state trooper friends who had been assigned to stay with the three star witnesses at a motel in Moxley and get them to the courthouse in time.

Bocock had been told about the attorney defending Guthrie, so it was not a surprise when Marvin Justus strode into the courtroom carrying an expensive briefcase. The well-dressed attorney dismissed Bocock and the two state prosecutors with a cursory glare.

Jury selection had been fairly brief and painless. To no one's surprise, not one potential juror admitted to knowing about any widespread gambling taking place in Astoria. All professed to be stout opponents of gambling, with several noting that they considered gambling a sin against God and man. All denied knowing anything about alleged police corruption in Astoria and Hyde County and none professed any allegiance or connection to an individual discussed in questioning during the voir dire process, one Earl "Boss" Griffin.

Bocock knew just one seated juror, and in a bit of an ethical breach, he had to pretend he didn't know him. It was Clon Bishop, the manager of the Pic & Pay Grocery Store who was also the father of Linda Bishop, who had helped Cal identify Theo Sullivan. The GBI agent rationalized his failure to report his knowledge of Bishop by telling himself he didn't actually know the man. He knew of him because of Linda, a confidential informant.

Richard Kilgallon, the portly state's attorney, got up to begin his opening statement. Bocock observed that the jury was alert and showing no expression as Kilgallon began his argument.

"Ladies and gentlemen of the jury, this illegal game, this Razzle Dazzle, has been practiced in your community for years," he said. "We will prove that this man," he said, pointing to Guthrie, who grimaced and turned to whisper something in Justus' ear, "cheated each and every one of our witnesses out of sums of money ranging from $382 to $2,146 by persuading them to play this game that they had no chance on earth to win."

In Justus' opening, he surprised the prosecution by not denying that games of chance had been played in Mel's store. The local attorney noted that it was a free country, nobody had been forced to play, and nobody, he said, had been forced to pay. "People do what people have to do to make a living," said Justus. "Times are hard and sometimes consenting adults will engage in business practices that might be interpreted by some as illegal when in fact they are not."

Guthrie, maintained Justus, was providing legal entertainment and no one had been forced to participate. Bocock, well versed in the state code's definition of gambling, found himself wondering what kind of legal argument Justus was trying to present.

Kilgallon's first witness was none other than ironworker Vernon Crabtree of York, Pennsylvania, who testified that his unfortunate stop at Mel's had not only cost him $968 in cash and his Bulova watch, but also his long-planned summer vacation in Miami and, for a lengthy period, the affections of his wife.

Crabtree was a good witness, Bocock thought, providing convincing details and taking no time whatsoever in identifying Guthrie as the man who had conned him. He also identified Guthrie's son Kelley, sitting with his father, and told Kilgallon he had no doubt about what would have happened to him had he refused to pay and give up his watch.

"He had a baseball bat, and he was a swinging it back and forth," Crabtree said of Kelley. "He would'a beat the hell out of me with it if I had not paid his daddy."

On cross examination, Justus asked Crabtree if he had been coerced to play the game. "Well, he told me one roll was free," he said. "I guess you could say he coerced that roll."

The jury and the few spectators in the courtroom laughed. The judge banged his gavel and restored order.

Justus then asked Crabtree if he had been charged with illegal gambling for participating in the game.

"Why no," he said. "They said I wouldn't face no charges."

That prompted Justus to go into a legal tirade about uneven enforcement, pointing out that Guthrie was being accused of playing an illegal game while the other player was escaping any legal jeopardy whatsoever.

The defense attorney then went after Crabtree's assertion that Kelley Guthrie would have beat him with the bat had he refused to pay.

"Did he hit you with the bat?" Justus asked.

"No sir," said Crabtree.

"Why did you think he would have hit you with the bat?" asked Justus.

"The way he was swinging it," he said.

"Ladies and gentlemen of the jury, the Atlanta Crackers swing a bat around a lot themselves," said Justus. "There's no assurance when they go to the plate that they will hit anything."

Again, the jury laughed.

"But there is more of an assurance that they will hit something, presumably a baseball," said Justus. "There's evidence they've actually done it on rare occasion. But there is no evidence whatsoever that's been presented here today that this man -- this Northern man, this man from York, Pennsylvania -- was ever hit – much less threatened, with a baseball bat."

The other two Dazzle losers took the stand and told similarly convincing stories, all picked at here and there by Justus, but in Bocock's mind, never picked apart. Neither of the others had been threatened by the younger Guthrie, and Bocock regretted for at least the tenth time that he had not been able to persuade any of the tourists who had been beaten to return to Astoria.

Who could blame them? Those he had talked to said they felt lucky to escape with their lives and they wouldn't trust Bocock, the GBI, the State Patrol or all of the above to protect them. Clearly, losing the beating victims hurt his case, and Justus had reduced the beating threats against Crabtree to disputed allegations.

Still, when Kilgallon rested his case, the young GBI agent was confident that Guthrie would be convicted.

Kilgallon was noticeably surprised when Justus started his case by calling Melvin Guthrie to the stand.

Guthrie was suddenly the downtrodden businessman who barely made ends meet. "The only way I can make a decent living on that roadside is to be imaginative, to be a showman of sorts. I try to entertain some of those who stop by occasionally playing a game of cards with them."

"So, Mr. Guthrie, are you saying there is no Razzle Dazzle played in your store?"

"No sir," he said. "We occasionally play a game of cards with our guests if they want to."

"These people say you have a board and have them throw dice," said Justus.

"These people are lying," said Guthrie. "We play cards on occasion. Sometimes, some of them lose money. Sometimes I lose money. That's the way it goes."

Kilgallon looked at Bocock and shook his head. "I can't believe he's reversing his field like this," he whispered.

"Is this going to work?" asked Bocock.

"It depends on who they believe," said the veteran attorney. "I doubt I am going to be able to move him an inch."

Bocock returned his attention to the witness.

"Mr. Guthrie, do you have a Razzle Dazzle board on the premises?"

"No sir," said Guthrie. "I've heard of that game, but I've never seen it actually played."

"Did they confiscate such a board from your store?"

"They searched it from stem to stern, but all they took was my playing cards, which are all we have ever used to play with," said Guthrie. "Where I was raised, it was OK to play a little poker with your friends. These people that stop, some of them become my friends. Ever now and then, we play some cards."

Guthrie proceeded to tell about how he sometimes felt sorry for those who lost at cards. So sorry, in fact, that sometimes he gave them their money back."

Then, Justus played what Kilgallon immediately recognized as his trump card.

"Mr. Guthrie, you said you sometimes felt sorry for those who lost at cards. Did you sometimes not feel sorry for them?"

"Some of them are rich beyond belief," said Guthrie. "They drive fancy Cadillacs and Lincoln Continentals up to my store and then they argue about the price of peanuts I sell them. If I chat with such people and we decide to play a hand or two of cards, you damn right I don't feel sorry for them if I win.

"I consider myself the Robin Hood of the South," said Melvin Guthrie. "I look at it as recovering some of what they stole from us during the Civil War. I take from the rich and I give some of it to our poor. Our God-fearing, Southern poor."

Bocock could not believe what he was hearing.

As Justus had warned, despite vigorous and lengthy cross examination, he couldn't budge Guthrie from his story nor poke many holes in it. And during closing arguments, Justus hammered on the fact that the state had produced no Razzle Dazzle board, no dice and no baseball bat. Nor had any cash been recovered.

"This is all the state's game of chance, and they are losing big time," said Boss Griffin's son-in-law. "This is their trumped up case, but their target is not the man they really want, but this poor businessman who is known in the community for having a big heart and taking care of others who are less fortunate."

It took the jury less than 30 minutes to acquit Melvin Guthrie of all charges. Cal Bocock's case was back to square one.

Guthrie came up to Cal as he made his way out of the courtroom a free man.

"You know, Mr. Bocock, you think you are slicker than snot on a glass door knob," said Guthrie. "But you ain't got shit, not on me, not on Boss, not on anybody in this whole damn county.

"I suggest you get your sorry ass back to Atlanta where it belongs," he continued. "This is God's country and the good people of Hyde County just stuck it right up your self-righteous ass."

Bocock had been told by many that Boss' candidates had never lost an election. But what he had not considered is that a jury trial can be a much easier election to win – there are only 12 votes and Boss needed only one.

Chapter Thirty-Three

The acquittal of Melvin Guthrie was the lowest of the lows for Cal Bocock. With Fancy in Savannah, and being able to visit her only rarely when he deemed himself worthy of a day off, his life seemed more and more lonely. There were times when he wondered how he could go on. In his head and in his heart of hearts, he kept hearing a constant refrain: He wasn't smart enough, nor strong enough, to beat these bastards. It didn't matter how often he dismissed these thoughts as irrational fears because they kept coming back to haunt him, especially during his increasingly sleepless nights.

He used Fancy as a defense. She had become his strength.

They were not lovers, but that had been Cal's choice, and it had not been an easy one. Fancy was ready to accept Cal as her one and only, but his old fashioned ways and old time Southern religion had kept them from taking the final step. Cal longed to make love to Fancy just as he had made love earlier in his life to others who didn't mean nearly as much to him. But he refused to take their relationship to the next level, and she apparently understood.

She had insisted at one point that Cal didn't love her because of what she had been in Astoria, and Cal did his level best to dissuade her of that belief.

"Fancy, I've done everything but propose to you," he said one night in her little Savannah apartment. "If you will be patient, I feel confident that day will come. There is something about me that goes back to my childhood that makes me the way I am.

"I want to be true to my wife," he said. "And I want our first time to be as man and wife. That's very important to me. Your past is forgotten. All we have, and all we will ever have, is our future after all this is done."

Fancy accepted that. In fact, she celebrated it. It was a revelation to her and absolute proof that she had fallen in love with the perfect man. She was completely certain she loved Calvin Bocock and wanted to spend the rest of her life with him.

Her studies were going well. She was a fast learner, and she could see the day on the horizon that she could either work in a beauty shop, or in her greatest dreams, open her own. She knew, though, that it could never be in Astoria. Too many bad things had happened there and there were too many faces she had no desire to ever see again.

Cal had stopped for a beer or two at Bart's the night of Melvin's acquittal. He knew he had better stop at two or he could find himself in the lion's den of the Astoria city jail because he was depressed and wanted to tie one on. It had been an uneventful visit, with just a short conversation with Bart marking the evening. Bart seemed to have no knowledge of Mel's acquittal, and Cal wasn't about to play newsboy.

He drove into the Astoria Trailer Court and parked the Bel-Air, which had been repaired at state expense after the ambush in Bart's parking lot. He had one final beer from his fridge, and watched The Jack Paar Tonight Show before finally calling it a night. Sleep did not come easily as he replayed the trial over and over in his head.

He awoke with a start. Bright flashes of flames seemed to surround him and smoke seemed overpowering. His trailer was on fire!

Already struggling to catch his breath, Cal jumped to his feet. The fire appeared to be concentrated at the rear of the trailer, near his office. Immediately, he thought of the letters, his evidence, his notes. He started in that direction, but was quickly driven back by flames and choking smoke. The rear door was not an option.

Cal moved back, through the kitchen, only to discover that a separate fire was burning in the front of his 50-foot Palace Ranchhome.

Cal steeled with anger. This was no attempt to scare him as was the blast through his windshield. This was a determined effort to kill him. And saving himself was not going to be easy as the front door appeared to be engulfed in flames as well.

Cal, dressed only in his underwear, pulled the covers from his bed, grabbing a blanket. He rushed into the adjacent bathroom, plugged the bathtub drain and turned the water on full. He pushed the blanket into the filling tub and got it as wet as he could in just a few seconds. The smoke was so thick he knew he couldn't breathe safely much longer.

He came back through the bedroom and through the kitchen. He wrapped himself in the blanket and threw himself through the flames near the front door. He knew his life depended upon his ability to get to one of the two picture windows on either side of the Palace's living room area.

Cal knew the wet blanket was on fire and he was certain he had little time. He was also well aware that the window had metal supports throughout its frame and he would have only one chance to jump through. If he bounced off, he would surely die.

Cal Bocock made like the linebacker he had been at Dahlonega High School going through the offensive line in an attempt to get the quarterback. He threw himself shoulder first at the picture window at the best speed he could muster in such short quarters.

The window shattered upon impact and Cal felt himself flying through space. He immediately felt welcoming cool air an instant before hitting the gravel and concrete driveway near the trailer with a painful jolt. Cal instinctively went into a roll in an attempt to lessen the blow. The impact hurt like hell, but it also felt good to Cal because he knew it meant he had escaped the fire.

Once senses returned to his body, along with a rush of fresh air into his smoke-filled lungs, Cal suddenly became aware that people were all around. The residents of Astoria Trailer Park had gathered to watch the inferno that once had been his home.

They were all there, the teachers, the storekeepers, Flo's girls and all the rest, including the cops. Once Cal got a good look around, his gaze focused on Wesley Crane, who appeared to be fresh and fully dressed even though it had to be 2 a.m. Cal leaped to his feet and rushed toward Crane.

"You did this, didn't you, you son of a bitch?" Cal screamed.

Crane smiled and stood his ground, saying nothing.

Cal leveled Crane with a roundhouse right that Crane apparently never saw coming. But before he could do anything else, he was blindsided by Tony Wiggins, who brained him with a billyclub.

Cal was knocked senseless, but only briefly. But his adrenaline was flowing at a rate he had not experienced since Korea. Who in the hell brings a billyclub to a house fire in the middle of the night? He turned and plowed into Wiggins with a blind fury.

Colin Smith then jumped into the fray, as did Crane, who had recovered from Cal's furious punch. The three of them subdued the GBI agent with a series of punches and kicks. Crane spit in the face of the fallen man.

"You done it now, trooper," he said. "We're taking you in. You're in deep shit now."

Finally, the fire department arrived and began a futile effort to douse the fire, which now threatened mobile homes on either side of Cal's trailer. The crowd, however, was more focused on the three cops, who had battered the victim of the blaze senseless.

Standing in a tight huddle on the periphery of the crowd, dressed in pajamas and trying to mask sobs, were Jim Bob, Sassy and Zeke. They had gathered with all the other trailer park denizens to watch the fire, and had not liked what they had seen from the beginning. Their fathers, whom they had believed always worked tirelessly to preserve and protect, had seemed to have little concern for the man who had miraculously saved himself from this holocaust.

Jim Bob, in particular, felt like vomiting. Despite the passage of time, he had not recovered from the incident with Kimmie. What had happened that day had been wrong, and this was far worse. This was … criminal. And his dad, and the fathers of his friends, seemed to have done nothing to save this man and then they had offered little defense to his claims that they had been responsible for this terrible fire, the first they had ever seen in their young lives. Was all this really possible?

As they watched, their three dads roughly bullied the bruised and bleeding Cal Bocock into a squad car. It was like he was a common criminal, not the victim of a horrible fire. As the car pulled away, the residents of the trailer park gathered in groups and began to gossip the way neighbors do. The three friends were corralled by their mothers, the innocent bystanders in these goings on, and ordered back to bed.

But none of the Three Musketeers slept well that night.

As Cal Bocock sat in the back of the Astoria squad car, he realized his earlier feeling of hitting a low point had been a false alarm. He now fully expected that he would die in police custody, in the hands of those he had been pursuing all these months. Once again, he had let his temper and his sharp tongue get the best of him. What had he been thinking, attacking Crane in front of a league of witnesses and two of his fellow officers?

That wasn't the way a seasoned agent would act. That was the way a green rookie reacted to unexpected adversity.

Bocock quickly decided that all he could do was preserve his strength for whatever might lie ahead. He must be alert to any mistake his captors might make, because escape was his only chance. Any allies he had were literally counties away. That was a lonely feeling . For one of the few times in Cal Bocock's life, he felt desperation.

####

Boss Griffin was awakened by the phone. He was hung over, which was not unusual for the hour, and he was dizzy. As he had expected, it was Colanise. CeCe groaned and rolled over as Boss picked up the receiver.

"He got out? I thought you told me it was foolproof," Griffin said angrily.

"He jumped out the window," said Popsi. "Nobody I know could have done that with fires set at both doors."

"Well, what happened then?"

"He attacked Wesley Crane. Nearly knocked him unconscious."

"Goddamn!" said Boss. "Who is this guy, the Lone Ranger?"

"Clearly, he is better than we anticipated," said Popsi. "We have him in custody. What do you want us to do?"

Boss gathered his addled brain. He reached for his pill bottle, popped a couple, and rubbed his bald head. He blinked his eyes, straining for clarity.

"Were there witnesses to all this?" he finally asked.

"Numerous," said Popsi. "The whole goddamn trailer park was watching."

"Son of a fucking bitch," said Boss. "OK, don't put him in jail."

"What?" The Greek was amazed.

"Put him in the Astoria Hotel. Tell him to order room service if he wants, although in that hellhole it will be peanuts and a Coke. Tell him the fire is under investigation and we understand that he attacked one of our officers due to his confused state. He is a GBI agent, you know."

"Boss, you sure about this?" asked Popsi. "I can finish this right quick in the jail."

"There are too many witnesses, Popsi. They saw what happened. Somebody will not take our side and that could be a fatal mistake. Do this my way."

"OK, Boss. I got it."

Boss hung up the phone. He and CeCe groaned almost simultaneously as she rolled over and he turned off the bedside lamp.

He tossed and turned the rest of the night.

Less than a mile away, Cal Bocock could not believe his good fortune when he was taken not to the concrete hell of the Astoria jail, but the somewhat-inviting confines of the Astoria Hotel. But even after the obviously angry cops left him alone in his room, he could not relax.

He tended to his wounds, burns, cuts and aches and pains. Apparently, their sudden hospitality did not extend to offering medical attention.

Like Boss, much of the rest of Cal's night was sleepless, but for a different reason. Despite knowing the hotel phones were likely not secure, Bocock felt he must immediately report what had happened to GBI headquarters. And so he spent much of the rest of the night briefing state authorities about his latest near death experience.

Chapter Thirty-Four

Cal Bocock was amazed at the state response to the arson fire at his trailer. Within hours, GBI officials arrived and brought him clothes and other essentials. Despite his protests, he was taken to a hospital in Moxley and treated for his injuries, which luckily, were not severe.

Other state agents converged on the trailer park and roped off the crime scene. A second lot was quickly rented from the trailer park, and Bocock was surprised to hear that a nearly identical trailer was in en route from Atlanta to replace his home base. The governor's office went to work copying their copies of all of the Astoria complaint letters. They obviously could not replace Cal's case notes, but his memory was good and work could always be redone.

Agents swept through the trailer park, interviewing residents about what they had seen and heard. Cal figured his attacking Crane would poison any sympathy he might have had, but only these interviews could determine that.

Cal had just come back to his hotel room from dinner with Herman Sneed and two other agents when his phone rang.

"Cal, this is Buford Dunlap."

"Yes sir! It's a pleasure to hear from you."

"Are you OK, son? How are you feeling?"

"Sir, I feel so much better than I did just 24 hours ago."

"Do you feel like going to church?"

"Huh … I mean… what do you mean, sir?"

"Don't worry. You don't have to do nothing but dress nice – go buy you a fine suit and charge it to Herman – nod a lot and be there to observe what happens."

"Governor, I still don't understand."

"We, or perhaps I should say I, plan to attend the Sunday services at the Astoria Baptist Church. I'm going to barge in there and put the fear of God himself into that squirrelly little reptile."

And so it came to pass that Sunday that as the deacons were passing the offering plate, the back doors of the sanctuary flew open and in trooped a 10-man delegation of dark-suited representatives of the state of Georgia, led by none other than the Honorable Buford Dunlap.

There was an audible gasp as the assembled body turned and recognized the familiar face. From his typical post on the second row, Earl Griffin stood, and in a most untypical Sunday go to meeting reaction, called out, "What in the hell are you doing here?"

Dunlap paused, but he did not react in any way to Griffin's outburst. Instead, he grabbed the arm of a shrinking deacon still holding the collection plate. He reached into his wallet, pulled out a $50 bill, and placed it into the startled deacon's plate.

"This is for the House of God, not the vipers that currently inhabit it," he said with a smile.

The Rev. Thomas Griffin was standing at the pulpit, and for one of the few times in his life, was speechless. Dunlap continued to stride toward the front of the church. His delegation followed him at a respectful distance. Dunlap strode to the podium, shook the reverend's hand, and announced, "I do apologize for interrupting your worship service, pastor, and may God forgive me for this breech in holy protocol. But I got some things to say, and I figure most of the folks who need to hear them are within earshot."

Almost to the second, the door flew open again. Everyone but Dunlap turned to look. This time, the new visitors were known to almost no one except some of the governor's people, who had alerted them in advance of the governor's appearance. The new arrivals were Wilmer Montgomery of the Atlanta Journal, Lewis Rome of United Press International and Cliff Cannon of WWGS radio.

Dunlap paid them no mind and instead addressed the congregation. Boss Griffin, obviously not used to being ignored, sat back down but was clearly fuming. The governor had no prepared text or notes, but clearly knew exactly what he was going to say.

"Ladies and gentlemen, many of you may not be aware of the horrendous criminal activities that have recently taken place in this community near your homes, notorious acts that not only endanger you and your families, but also threaten the core of civilized society as we know it.

"There have been two attempts in recent weeks on the life of Special Agent Calvin Bocock of the Georgia Bureau of Investigation, who is here with me this morning. Many of you know Cal."

Thus prompted, Cal, who was facing the throng from below the pulpit, nodded, and noted looks of sympathy he had not expected to see. Facing the crowd, Bocock felt a bit like he was trapped in an episode of Ralph Edwards' "This Is Your Life," Astoria edition. Patsy Griffin was focused on Dunlap, a look of hate on her pretty face, until she saw Bocock look at her. Then she gave him a smile and a sly wink. Bart Taggart gave him an unabashed thumbs up. Melvin Guthrie threw him a middle finger, right there in the House of God. Cal also saw Sassy Smith, the little girl he'd met in the trailer park, dressed in her Sunday best, and she looked at him with wide eyes. Boss Griffin was focused on Dunlap with a murderous glare. Meanwhile, the governor continued his unlikely sermon.

"The people who run this town want Cal Bocock dead because he knows the truth and is working to expose it!" Dunlap thundered. "On September Fourth, he was nearly shot dead in his car. Last Wednesday night, as he slept among you in the heavily populated Astoria Trailer Court, arsonists set his mobile home ablaze."

The congregation was totally enthralled. Thomas Griffin had nearly put some of them to sleep only moments earlier preaching about Jesus' disciple, the Apostle Paul, and some of his letters to somebody about something. All of that was quickly forgotten, because now, suddenly, church had gotten unexpectedly exciting.

"This fire was deviously planned and executed so as to immobilize both exit routes. Bocock, who is a decorated veteran of the Korean War, outsmarted these weasels. He soaked a blanket with water from his bathtub, wrapped himself in it, galloped through the flames and threw himself out a picture window."

Those who had not heard the details stirred and reacted with gasps of surprise.

"Bocock proceeded to confront one of your local law enforcement officers, who should have been working to save him, but instead was standing by not doing jacksquat with his fingers up his ass! Reverend, I apologize for that."

The congregation laughed. "Buford's just being Buford," one elderly man said audibly, prompting more laughter.

Dunlap continued. "Bocock questioned this officer because his investigatory work to that point had given him reasons to doubt the integrity of the Astoria Police Department and those who direct its activities."

Dunlap paused to survey the congregation, and looked for the first time at Boss Griffin. His lips were pursed, his face beet red. His eyes projected pure hatred toward his rival.

"Thus confronted, this officer declined to deny that he was involved in this capital crime. Now recognize that Bocock had just flown out the window of a burning house trailer. The blanket he had wrapped himself in was still on fire. He was burned, cut and aching from going through a glass window and making a hard landing on gravel and concrete.

"Bocock was not offered aid, nor was he comforted, as police officers are sworn to do to the victims of such crimes. Instead, he got a smirk and a wisecrack.

"So Bocock decked him," said the governor. The crowd roared.

"That might have been out of line, I don't know. I probably would have done the same thing myself," Dunlap chuckled. "Anyway, two other police officers – and I use that term loosely – then came up and the three of them proceeded to beat the hell out of Calvin Bocock, our state's special agent investigating the corruption in their own department.

"Was Bocock then taken to the hospital for treatment? No. The poor man was in his skivvies. Was he given clothes? Hell no. Sorry again, pastor!

"At some point, some authority figure, someone with a modicum of good sense, must have intervened, because Bocock was not then taken to jail for assaulting an officer who had declined to offer him help, but instead was taken to the local hotel where he was checked into a private room at the expense of the city.

"At that point, we came to his aid ourselves because obviously nobody in Astoria was going to, except maybe the desk clerk at the hotel."

The crowd twittered again.

"We have focused the entire resources of the state's crime fighting agencies on this unspeakable crime," Dunlap said. "Bocock won't be alone here in Astoria any more. Apparently, some people want him dead and I won't have it. No siree.

"I am here to announce that there are additional resources that will be focused on this case. As you all may know, I am no fan of the federal government. In fact, getting in bed with them is the last thing I want to do. But on this occasion, I must. The federal boys offer us certain powers and abilities that we as a state do not have.

"I have asked the United States Attorney General to join our investigation into the corruption in Astoria and Hyde County. And he has agreed."

Boss Griffin looked at Melvin Justus, and Justus looked back. Those who knew the men closely might have picked up tension and concern in their eyes.

"The United States Government can and does investigate criminal activity through laws and statutes unavailable to us here in the fine state of Georgia," Dunlap droned on. "Among these powers is the ability to investigate whether people pay their taxes. People who skim money from places and other people tend to not report all this extra income. These kind of people would steal the nickels off a dead man's eyes in the middle of the funeral."

Again, Dunlap paused to acknowledge laughter.

"The Justice Department and the Internal Revenue Service are going to be on these guys like a pack of hounds on a running 'coon. I will remind y'all that this is what the feds used to get Al Capone. If they can nail a professional mobster like Al Capone, they can get the rank amateurs that run this place."

Now Dunlap added some comments especially requested by Bocock.

"It has come to my attention that most of you who have been approached by Mr. Bocock have declined to give him any useful information. Hell, many of you won't give him the time of day, and not only is that unfortunate, that is dead wrong. Don't you people care that your county is a notorious crime center? Don't you care that you are negatively perceived by people all over this nation? I know I would care if I lived in Astoria. Hell, I care because Astoria is *in* Georgia and I'm the governor of Georgia! Pastor, I'm sorry, sometimes when I get going I can't control myself!

"If you have information that would advance this investigation, please, for God sakes, share it with Mr. Bocock and the other agents who will be joining him here in your community. You should not fear any retribution or threats from these people for doing your civic duty to restore lawful life hereabouts. I know there has been such retribution in the past, and I'm standing here today swearing on the pastor's good book that we will prosecute anybody who theatens, coerces, hurts, shoots at, sets fires, steals horses, whatever."

Again, Dunlap got a big laugh from the congregation.

"Thank you, ladies and gentleman. I again apologize for this interruption. You can go back to "Doxology," or whatever comes next.

"Oh, I'd also like to welcome the gentlemen of the Third Estate. I'll be available outside for any questions you might have."

With that, Dunlap turned, shook Thomas Griffin's hand, and stepped down from the pulpit. Again, his delegation followed him, single file. Dunlap shook every hand that was extended his way as he strode down the aisle, and they were numerous.

At the door, he turned and motioned to Bocock. "I think that went rather well. What do you think?"

"Governor, it blew me away," said Bocock.

"Good. Now let's make sure the boys in the press get all the pithy comments they want. Floyd, you got those handouts from the U.S. Attorney's Office confirming all this, right?"

"Yes sir," replied the governor's chief of staff.

"Good, now let's start part two."

"Mr. Montgomery, how are you today? How's you wife? And the boys over at the fishwrapper?

"Lewis, haven't they made you bureau chief yet?"

"Mr. Cannon, I got to say I have heard your newscast during my travels south and I thoroughly enjoy it."

"Gentlemen, do you have any questions?"

####

The governor had pegged it. The congregation was about to sing the doxology, and as soon as it was over, Boss Griffin turned to Marvin Justus.

"Do we have problems, Marvin?"

"Boss, I never anticipated any federal tax audits," the attorney replied nervously. "There could be problems going all the way back to the early '40s."

"Holy Jesus, Good God, Mary and Moses," said Boss Griffin. "Get to work immediately and get all this fixed."

"Boss, I don't think you understand," Justus whispered. "You can't just fix unreported income. You can't make it go away. Cash is not a problem. It's the land."

Boss wiped sweat from his brow. He wished he'd brought his pocket flask, but CeCe had laid down the law on drinking in church. Instead, he dry swallowed several pills and waited impatiently for his long-winded nephew to wrap up the service so he could go home and start drinking and worrying in earnest.

Chapter Thirty-Five

In south Georgia, warm weather usually hangs on long after the boys of summer wrap it up and football becomes the local pastime. And that was the case this particular fall as the October nights still felt like summer even though some of the leaves on the hardwoods were starting to show their first signs of seasonal change.

It was late on such a fall evening that a familiar scene repeated itself on U.S. 55. The blue light of a rapidly pursuing Astoria Police Department cruiser were turned on, and a similarly blue 1954 Buick Roadmaster, thus prompted, pulled over on the right of way near the Altamaha River.

At the wheel was a 28 year old man from Columbia, South Carolina named Jerome Whitley. In the passenger seat was his 23 year old fiancé, Jenny Faye Washington. They were on the way home to Columbia after visiting Washington's folks near Jacksonville, Florida. Whitley had asked Jenny's father for the hand of the beautiful model in marriage, and Mr. Washington had consented.

So the couple was blissfully happy and full of talk about their future plans. Whitley had not been paying attention to his speed, and that is understandable, because U.S. 55 near the river is ruler straight, level and otherwise unremarkable.

A big patrolman came to the driver's window. Jerome had only opened it a crack.

"Boy, open this window right now!" demanded the officer.

"Who are you calling boy?" retorted Whitley, who just happened to be black.

"Out of the car, right now!"

"Hey, I done nothing wrong. Why don't we start this over again?"

"This is already started, and I'm going to finish it," said the officer, his hands visibly shaking in anger.

"Please, officer, I apologize! I didn't mean nothin.'" Jerome had opened the door and had started to climb out.

Before he could raise to his full height of more than six feet and two inches, Whitley had been hit square on the head with a billy club. The blow was a hard one and blood spurted from the contact point above Whitley's left eye. Jenny Washington screamed.

For the first time, the cop eyed Jenny and his eyes bulged in obvious interest. But for now his focus was on Jerome Whitley.

Whitley staggered and grabbed the side of the car to maintain his balance. But as soon as he had steadied himself, a second blow came to the other side of his head. And then there was a third, and finally, a fourth. Jenny continued to scream. There was no one there to hear her except her fiancé's assailant as the road was dark and deserted. And Whitley was now lying by the car, bleeding and unconscious.

The officer turned his attention to Jenny, who was now off her seat and huddled in the floorboard of the Roadmaster. She was in tears and looked up at the big officer in utter terror.

"We're going to get married," she said. "We're not bad folks. My daddy's a preacher."

"I don't give a shit if your daddy is, what's his name, Martin Luther King himself," said the officer. "What kind of name is that, anyway?"

The officer grabbed the keys out of the Roadmaster's ignition. He walked to the back of the car and opened its trunk. Jenny was too terrified to do anything but shiver in fright in the floorboard.

She felt the car shake and heard a big thump. She realized that the cop must have put Jerome in the trunk! Why would he do such a thing?

The officer slammed the trunk and then returned to the open driver's side door and got into the car. He reached across behind Jenny and locked her door. Then, as she watched his every move, he put the keys into the ignition and started the car.

"Where are you taking me? Where is Jerome? What did we do, anyway?"

"Jerome is on ice, sweetcakes. And you and me are going on a little ride."

"Where to?" She thought about unlocking the door, jumping out and making a run for it, but where would she go? And how could she help Jerome?

"A place I know," said the now-leering cop.

"Why?"

"Oh, you'll see."

Less than 200 yards down the road was the once graveled river road that led down to The Pit. The cop pulled the car off the roadway and the Roadmaster rolled down the little trail until it reached its closest point to the river bank. He stopped right at the curve at the very spot where Astoria's kids had used a tire swing to propel themselves into the deep and cooling waters of The Pit for years.

Overhead, the bridge over the river loomed, and a car thumped over it as the officer put the Roadmaster into park and cut off the engine.

Jenny Faye Washington was hysterical with fright. Suddenly, she made her desperate bid for freedom, getting her hand onto the door lock. But the cop grabbed her before she could open the door. He pushed her head into the passenger side window so hard that Jenny nearly passed out. She immediately realized her head was bleeding.

"Please don't hurt me! Please! I'll do anything you want."

"Don't worry," he said. "You're going to do just that. You are one pretty little nigger girl."

The cop got out and looked around. He wanted to make sure no teenagers were swimming nearby or even hanging out. Seeing and hearing no one, he quickly came back to the passenger side of the Roadmaster and violently pulled Jenny out of the car.

Pleading for mercy and screaming, Jenny had trouble keeping her feet. The big cop pulled a handkerchief from his pocket and stuffed most of it in her mouth. He took a pair of handcuffs and cuffed both her hands together, managing to keep one cuff loose enough to hang it on the Roadmaster's passenger door handle before closing them with a click.

"I don't know that I ever saw such a good-looking colored girl as you," said the grinning cop as he proceeded to grope the shivering woman. Without another word, he ripped off her clothes and proceeded to rape her.

Jenny could not even plead for mercy, being that she could hardly breathe with the gag stuffed into her mouth. She struggled against the handcuffs, but could do nothing as she was firmly attached to the car.

The patrolman completed his evil deed, and with no regard for his victim, proceeded to pick up her ripped up clothes and return to the driver's side door. He got into the car, tossing the clothing into the empty passenger seat.   Jenny continued to struggle and thrash, but there was nothing she could do.

The cop put the car in neutral, rolled up the windows and aimed the wheels toward the river. He then got out of the car and moved to its rear. With one determined push, the Roadmaster was moving and within seconds, it was at the edge of the cliff over the river. Jenny was pulled alongside – she tried planting her feet, but the momentum of the car could not be slowed.

The Roadmaster toppled down the cliff, Jenny Washington attached by the hands, her unconscious fiancé helpless in the trunk. It gained more momentum down the cliff and plunged hoodfirst into The Pit.

The cop watched to make sure the car was fully submerged. Bubbles rose in the water as the air inside the car escaped. The cop had grown up swimming in those waters and knew the Roadmaster would settle into very deep water.

Gagged, Jenny Washington could not even scream. Nor could she do anything in the waters of the Altamaha but be pulled under by the weight of the big car.

The cop, fully satisfied that he had left no visible evidence on the road or in the water, turned and walked back up toward U.S. 55 to his squad car. He would resume his patrol and ticket several more motorists before ending his shift that night. No others, however, would face the grim fate of Jerome Whitley and Jenny Faye Washington.

Earlier that same evening, Jim Bob, Sassy and Zeke had decided to enjoy the warm night by hanging out together. School had been going as well as could be expected, and their common experiences there dominated their conversation more so than the still stark reminders of the trailer fire that nearly killed the young GBI agent.

They could have walked to the store for a cold drink. They could have hung out in the trailer park playground. But Sassy had suggested they relive their summer routine and go to their private lair under the bridge, overlooking the slow-moving river. So by chance, they were there when they saw a blue Buick come slowly down the trail toward the water, their bicycles lying in the high grass a safe distance off the trail.

The three could hardly believe their eyes when a police officer got out of the car. In the dusk, and the distance, the three squinted to try and determine who it was. Whispers confirmed that none of the three knew who it was.

The scene turned to one of horror when they saw the muscular cop pull the young woman from the automobile. Jim Bob had to put his hand over Sassy's mouth to keep her from crying out as they saw the cop brutally disrobe the young black woman.

"Oh no," Sassy sobbed quietly. "No God, please!"

Sassy could not watch. Zeke and Jim Bob, now crying themselves, surrounded the girl and the three of them huddled in anguished silence.

Jim Bob knew what was going to happen when the officer – and he still could not get a clear look at his face because of the difference in elevation – went to the back of the car.

"God, don't let him kill her!" he whispered.

When the car toppled down the cliff into the water, causing a loud splash, all three put their hands over their mouths to muffle the sounds they could not help making.

How could this have happened? One of their fathers – and honestly, none of them knew which one as all three were working this Friday night – had just raped and murdered a young woman. They continued to watch in silent grief as the cop surveyed the crime scene and then calmly turned to walk back up the path toward the highway.

"Should we try and find out whether that was my daddy, or yours, or Zeke's?" asked Jim Bob.

"There's just no time, Jim Bob," said Zeke. "If we go back up to the road, and he sees us, he'll probably figure that we saw everything."

"And no telling what he would do then," said Sassy. "Any man who could do what we just saw could do anything."

All three had been launched into a mutual, yet private hell. Each had been angered by the banishment of Kimmie – and Jim Bob's dad had ensured that all three were punished for befriending the little black boy.

All three had been horrified by the beating of Cal Bocock, though they had initially justified it with the knowledge that Bocock had thrown the first punch.

Sassy had sat in church and listened to the Governor of Georgia belittle the police department and the city fathers, stopping just short of calling the officers criminals.

And now, all three knew that one of their fathers was a rapist and a murderer.

"Guys, I really hate to say this," said Jim Bob. "But it might not really matter which one did it. They all do the same job and they all have the same way of doing things."

"Yeah," said Zeke. "They never disagree about anything."

"How do we know that all three of them aren't rapers and killers?" asked Sassy, her pretty face red with tears.

"I guess we don't," said Jim Bob.

Jim Bob sat his friends down. "We got to figure out what to do, but not tonight," he said. "For now, keep your eyes open and watch for signs, anything that might tell us something. It's Friday, so since there's no school tomorrow, let's get together in the morning and maybe then we can figure out what we ought to do."

"Good idea," said Zeke. "Let's sleep on it."

"I'm not sure I want to go home," said Sassy.

"Sassy, you gotta," said Jim Bob, pulling her close and looking her directly in the eye. "And you gotta act like nothing happened. If you can't do that, go home and go straight to bed."

That is exactly what all three did. Their mothers considered it strange behavior, since most Friday nights they had to be ordered to bed, but they attributed it to weariness caused by a long week of school.

And in a sense, that's what it was. It was world weariness for three kids who shouldn't have had to see what they had witnessed from their favorite perch on earth.

Chapter Thirty-Six

Fancy Fontaine had come to love her new life. Beauty school wasn't that difficult – she'd always had a good eye for how to do hair – and graduation was only two weeks away. Her Savannah apartment was modest, but comfortable. She had found a place in what was being called a "public housing complex," a new concept.

Populated by working class people, the almost new Hatch Village had the look of what some might describe as row houses. They were closely packed together, but the residents were fairly well behaved, so the area was usually pretty quiet, except sometimes on weekends. Fancy's place was an easy walk to the riverfront, and she liked to go down there sometimes and sit by the Savannah River and reflect.

Cal came to visit her on the weekends when he felt he could take a day off. He usually arrived in late morning and spent the day with Fancy. She would typically fix him lunch, but he always insisted he take her to dinner, and there were several restaurants within walking distance.

Their relationship was still hanging in the area between a steady couple and being officially engaged. Cal had made reference to marriage a time or two, but he had never really asked, and Fancy never pushed him. Likewise, their physical relationship was similar to that of many dating couples in those days – sex had been postponed, at least for now.

This Saturday night had been fun and relaxed for the young couple. They had watched a very funny new film, "Some Like it Hot," with Marilyn Monroe and Jack Lemmon, and then they had dinner at a new riverfront restaurant. Cal had never spent much time in a city before, and appreciated the fact they could walk from Fancy's apartment to the theatre, restaurants and the riverfront.

After they returned from dinner, the pair shared a soft drink – Fancy had a glass of wine at dinner, but Cal had abstained, citing the long drive back to Astoria. When he made comments about leaving, Fancy was as forward as she had ever been with her beau.

"Cal, you can stay if you like," she said, looking him in the eye.

"Fancy, don't make this difficult. You know I want to. Forgive me for being old fashioned."

He had used the line repeatedly, so much so that it annoyed Fancy a bit. But she wasn't about to jeopardize the first true relationship she'd had in years.

"Cal, you do know I love you, right?"

Cal smiled, and pulled her tight. "And you must believe me that I love you, too."

There was a long pause, then Cal moved toward the door. "I'll do my best to come back next week. I have some help now, you know, and that gives me a little more freedom."

She worried about him constantly. She had not known about either the ambush or the fire until she read about it in the Savannah newspaper, which had published the UPI story on Dunlap's appearance at Astoria Baptist Church. They had almost had a fight over Cal's silence on the issue, but he had convinced her he kept it to himself because he didn't want her to worry. Like that would help! She knew those people and she knew what they were capable of doing. And her greatest fear was that Cal wouldn't be as lucky the next time.

Finally, Cal pulled Fancy close for a long good night kiss. Before he could reconsider her offer, he pulled the door shut behind him and headed for the BelAir. His mind was so scrambled with conflicting thoughts, including sadness at leaving her behind, that he did not see the dark shadow of a man who watched him closely as he got into the Chevy and drove away.

####

Fancy had changed into her gown and robe and was preparing for bed when she heard someone fumbling at her door. Startled, she had begun to move toward it when it opened a couple of inches. She had latched it with a chain, and it caught, preventing a larger opening. But then she heard the heavy crash of a big foot on the door, which broke the chain and caused the door to slam back against the adjacent wall.

"What are you doing here?" she cried in fright. It was a familiar face from Astoria, one that always caused her alarm.

"I am here to administer your punishment," said the man, who was dressed in black and wore a hat pulled over his eyebrows.

"Get out of my house. Now!" she cried.

She was in the kitchen, and she quickly opened a drawer and pulled out a butcher knife and waved it toward the intruder.

He laughed. From his pants pocket, he pulled a small handgun, specifically a Colt Model 1908 .25 automatic. Fancy knew she had no chance with her three-inch kitchen blade.

"What did I do to you?" she said tearfully.

"You talked, you bitch. You talked way too much. You talked yourself ... to death."

He fired a single shot that struck Fancy in the chest. She grabbed a kitchen chair, but both she and the chair fell to the floor with a crash.

The man was nervous, out of his element. He walked to his victim, checking to see where the shot had entered her body. She seemed barely conscious, and her attacker was quickly satisfied that his work was done.

He turned and rushed from the apartment, closing the door behind him. There was activity on the street, and that worried him. But he saw no reaction to his appearance outside the apartment. He rushed to his dark sedan, which was parked about two blocks away.

There was a damn parking ticket on the car! Irritated, the man reacted just as Boss Griffin had several months ago in Atlanta. He pulled the yellow card from under his windshield wiper, tore the ticket in two and threw it onto the pavement. Then he got into the car and drove away without incident or alerting suspicion, which had been his goal.

Inside the apartment, Fancy slipped into and out of consciousness. She could feel her life hanging in the balance, but her overriding thought was, "I must help Cal."

She looked around her. There was no way she could crawl or get to her feet. There were two things near her as she lay in a puddle of her own blood – her bag of beauty school supplies that she had dropped in the floor near the table and a wooden soft drink carton containing two empty bottles – the drinks the couple had shared less than an hour before. She struggled to reach the bag, and with painful effort, managed to leave her lover a message before she felt everything go black.

####

It was the wee hours of Sunday morning when the phone rang in Cal Bocock's new trailer. Jerked from deep sleep, he picked it up.

It was the Savannah Police Department.

"Agent Bocock, I regret to inform you there has been a shooting here," said the female caller, apparently a dispatcher.

Cal's heart skipped several beats. "Fancy? Is she all right?"

"Agent, the homicide squad is at her apartment. They found a document in her purse that you were to be notified in the event of an emergency. "

"Where is she?"

"Agent, all I know is an ambulance was called along with homicide. I can see that here on the dispatch log. Homicide has requested your presence at the crime scene."

"I'm a couple of hours away. I'll get there as quickly as I can."

Cal threw his clothes on, emotions swirling within him. Had he stayed as she had asked, he could have protected her. Why had he let his silly childhood upbringing keep him from embracing – and protecting – the woman he loved?

As he drove, he tried to figure out what could have happened. It was probably a street thug who had seen them out together and had seen him leave. Had she locked the door when he left? He couldn't remember, and he knew he had not asked her to lock it. Yet another reason to feel guilty, and Cal already had a gutful of guilt.

Sunlight was starting to creep into the cityscape when Cal once again pulled up at Fancy's apartment. Four Savannah police cruisers were parked at various angles near her building. Neighbors who had been watching the cops come and go were milling about on the sidewalk. Cal pushed through them, but was stopped at the door by a plainclothes detective.

"And you are?"

Cal flashed his badge and GBI identification. The detective nodded and let him into the apartment.

"Detective Alex Barlow," said a middle-aged man with bloodshot eyes. He was dressed in a rumpled suit, his narrow black tie loosened, a fedora propped on his head.

Cal Bocock tried to maintain his professionalism. But it was damned difficult.

He introduced himself, but then stepped a bit out of line.

"Detective, I'm not objective here because I was going to marry this woman," he said. "Can you tell me where she is?"

"Son, I'm sorry, they took her away several hours ago. My understanding was that it was a fatal shooting. That's really all I know. We asked you to come here because of what we found near the body. We don't know if it's related to the murder or your case work up in Hyde County."

Cal felt his eyes well with tears, but he fought for and regained his composure. "Show me, detective," he said.

"She apparently pulled some lipstick from this bag," Barlow said, pointing to what Cal recognized as Fancy's beauty school supplies. "And then there's this."

Barlow put on a glove and reached for a paper bag. With gloved hands, he pulled out a soft drink bottle and set it on the table.

"Don't touch it," he said. "We haven't looked for prints yet."

Cal was initially puzzled, but quickly he understood everything. Fancy had drawn a circle in red lipstick around the label on the soft drink bottle. She had circled the word "Pepsi."

"Of course!" Bocock said loudly, causing the weary detective to pull back a bit. "She told me all about this guy. Our shooter is Popsi Colanise. He works for Earl Griffin, the so-called Boss of Astoria."

"Would he have a motive to kill Miss Fontaine?" asked Barlow.

"You damn right he would," said Bocock. "She was a confidential informant who gave me a significant amount of information about criminal activities in Astoria. I already had reason to believe that Colanise was in the middle of it. Now I have evidence tying him to a murder."

"In that case, we'll prepare a warrant," said Barlow. "Oh, and we also have a neighbor who thinks she saw the shooter leave the apartment and walk away. I can get her for you and see if her description matches this Colanise."

Within an hour, Cal was introduced to the woman next door. She had not only seen a man leave the apartment, but she had also heard the gunshot. After a brief interview, Cal was convinced the woman had seen Popsi Colanise leave the scene of the crime just minutes after she heard what she believed was a gunshot.

The woman, Sally Tucker, told Cal that she and Fancy had become acquaintances when their paths crossed near their doorways.

"I went inside and found her," Tucker said. "It was awful."

"Nobody has told me where they took her," said Cal. "Do you know, perchance?"

"They rushed her to St. Joseph's Hospital," said Tucker.

"Hospital?" Cal asked eagerly. "She was still alive?"

"Yes, didn't they tell you? They said her vital signs were faint and she had lost a lot of blood, but she was alive. I was going to go see her, but they told me I needed to talk to you instead."

"Let's go together," said Cal with urgency. "Now!"

####

The hospital was not far from the waterfront, and Cal was quickly ushered in to see Fancy's physician, Dr. Ross Bentley.

"The fact that Miss Tucker found her quickly, and they got her to us as soon as they did likely saved her life," he said. "Luckily, the bullet missed all her major organs, but she was close to bleeding out."

"Can I see her?"

"I don't see why not. Don't let her move around, though. The next day or two will be crucial."

Sally Tucker was pretty astute, and she had concluded that Cal and Fancy were an item. She kindly consented to wait in the hall so Cal could visit Fancy alone. "It's the least I can do," she said with a smile.

"You have already done so much you will never know," said Bocock.

Fancy seemed to be asleep when Cal entered the room, but she opened her eyes when she saw her visitor.

"Cal! I was so afraid I would never see you again!"

"You don't know the half of it," said Bocock, who kissed Fancy on the cheek and clutched her hand.

"You're going to make it," he said. "And as soon as you're able, we're going to be married."

"Well, Mr. Bocock, aren't you getting a little ahead of yourself?"

"What do you mean?"

"You haven't asked me yet," she said.

They both laughed, but Fancy's was short.

"Ouch, that hurt," she said.

"No more laughing," Cal said, wiping tears from his face. "And lady, that was some kind of clue you left me."

"I guess since I lived, you really didn't need it," said Fancy. "In a way, that's a little disappointing."

"Fancy Fontaine, I'm going to …" He stopped and laughed again, and then cried a bit as well. "Love you with all my heart for the rest of my life."

Chapter Thirty-Seven

The next afternoon, Cal was catching up on a big pile of paperwork when he heard a tentative knock on the front door of his trailer. That was a bit unusual, because he rarely got visitors. Despite the governor's admonitions, Astoria's collective attitude about talking to state authorities had not changed.

Until now.

Bocock opened the door and saw three kids -- two boys, and the girl he had met, Sarah "Sassy" Smith.

"Cal, can we talk to you?" asked Sassy. "It's kinda important."

"You bet, come on in quickly before … somebody sees," said Bocock. The three kids were on foot, and Bocock realized it was the first time he'd not seen them on bicycles.

Sassy looked tentatively at the other two, and they gave her helpful nods. Bocock noticed tears were forming in her blue eyes.

"We didn't know what to do," she said. "I heard what the governor said, and I have met you and I like you, so we decided to talk to you despite what it will mean for all of us."

Bocock decided to give her a minute to let her compose herself. "You guys want a Co-Cola?" he asked. "I'm pretty sure I got some."

They did, so he pulled three six and a half ounce bottles out of his refrigerator. He had a sudden thought of Fancy – he wondered what she would have done had they drunk Cokes that night instead of Pepsis. He took a few more minutes introducing himself to Jim Bob and Zeke, but his main intention was giving Sassy time to calm down.

"You guys just relax," he said. "I promise you we will do the right thing with whatever you have to tell me."

"It was awful," said Sassy. "He killed her while we watched."

"After he … raped her," added Jim Bob.

"Who?" asked Cal.

Again, the three looked at each other, as if they gathered strength from their unity.

"One of our dads," said Zeke, who promptly burst into tears.

Bocock was flabbergasted by these three remarkable kids and their determination to do the right thing. He initially found it difficult to believe they didn't know who had been the killer, but he had seen the three cops together often enough to understand. They could easily pass for brothers, and at a distance, in bad light, elevated as they had been under the bridge, it made perfect sense.

"So this is a true crap shoot for all of you, if you excuse the expression," Bocock said candidly. "One man did this, and none of you know if you are actually turning in your father."

Sassy pursued her lips and her head sagged as she looked down at her feet. "Cal, we've all come to understand that all three of them are bad. They beat our mommas. They get drunk and yell and hit us. We still … love them, I guess, but if they are hurting and killing people, and it's obvious they are, somebody had to do something."

"Yeah, I guess it's us," said Jim Bob.

The agent got all the information he could from the kids – the time of day, exactly where the car had been parked and their best estimate of where it hit the water. The fact there were three of them, and their story did not waver, convinced him it was rock solid information.

Bocock looked at the three as they sat at his metal dinette set. "I want the three of you to tell nobody you came here and talked to me. In fact, we're going to be very careful that nobody sees you leave this trailer. You're going to leave one at a time and only when I tell you the coast is clear.

"At home, act like nothing is different. And for a little while, nothing will be. But pretty soon, change is coming, big time."

They nodded. Bocock was touched that when they all stood to say their farewells, each of them came up and hugged him tightly. All three were crying.

"When I have kids, if I am lucky enough, I pray to God they are as brave and honest and as pure of heart as you three," he said through his own tears.

When they were gone, Bocock returned to his table and sat down to think. His plan had been to immediately arrest Colanise, but now everything had changed and he decided that could wait. With some luck, he could wrap this thing up in a hurry.

Even though there was a hint of a chill in the air, Bocock got a towel and some warm clothes. He was going swimming.

He knew the correct protocol was to immediately call in state divers to search for the woman and her car. But the hubbub of all that activity would certainly get the attention of his friends at the APD. He knew Boss had somebody watching his car, and since the river was within hiking distance, he figured he could sneak down to The Pit without anyone seeing him, or figuring out what he was up to.

He left the trailer, carrying his extra clothes and his sidearm, wrapped up in a towel and out of sight. He made it appear he was heading to the community laundry. But instead of going in there to wash clothes, he zipped behind the building, through the playground and into the woods. He knew of a trail that would lead him to The Pit.

Cal was a strong swimmer, and he steeled himself for a plunge into deep and cold water. He saw some indications along the bank that the falling car could have caused, so with that information and the kids' account, he was able to determine about where it would have entered the water.

He dived in and the water was so cold it took his breath away. So he made sure his lungs were as full of air as he could get them before he made a surface dive and started down. And down. And even further down. He was amazed at the depth and realized what a perfect place it was to hide evidence of such a dirty deed.

It was almost completely dark at the depth when he finally saw the outline of the Buick Roadmaster, which had returned to all four wheels on the sandy bottom. Sure enough, a young black woman was handcuffed to the passenger side door handle, just as the kids had said. The handcuffs would not give, but Bocock saw what he wanted to see – they were standard police issue.

As he began to labor for air, he realized there were other dark shapes in the water. A quick look confirmed it. There were other cars nearby in the river! Apparently, other unlucky motorists – or at least their cars -- had met their demise in the murky waters of the Altamaha.

Bocock surfaced and gasped for air. And immediately, he recognized a new hazard. He saw the unmistakable form of an alligator not 50 yards away. It had seen him surface and was headed his way.

The young agent made like an aquatic sprinter, but a quick glance confirmed his fears - the alligator was gaining ground!

Bocock found purchase near the shore about where Zeke Wiggins had landed the day Sassy almost drowned. He quickly made his way out of the water and made a beeline for his handgun, pulling it from the holster and preparing to fire.

But the gator had no interest in pursuing his prey on dry land. He eyed Bocock, turned around and headed for the other side of the river and the adjacent swamp.

Cal dried off, put on his dry clothes and hot-footed it back to the trailer park. Within seconds of hitting his front door, he was on the phone to Atlanta, barking orders to GBI headquarters. All of which, admittedly, was a bit out of protocol, since he was dictating instructions to his boss, Herman Sneed.

"We need a search warrant for the Astoria Police Department – specifically their equipment records," said Bocock. "I guarantee you, our killer has claimed very recently that he lost his handcuffs and has requisitioned a new pair. While we're at it, we might as well hit their arrest files, their financial records and their ticket books.

"And if you think we can get it, let's also get into Boss Griffin's office. No telling what we might find in his files. I suspect he's too cautious to leave anything interesting lying around, but you never know.

"The timing has to be perfect – we pounce, and hopefully we can arrest Colanise at the same time. And as soon as we're doing that, I want divers in the river. There are at least three cars there and at least one victim.

"Oh, by the way, I want an agent with a high-powered rifle guarding the divers," said Bocock. "There are hungry gators in that river."

Sneed was impressed. "This is a great plan, Bocock," he said. "We have a friendly judge who will most likely give us the warrant we need by tonight. I'll go ahead and get the people moving – but we'll make sure they don't hit town until we are ready to roll in the morning.

"By the way, Bocock, I was wondering when you were finally going to pull the trigger on something," Sneed said. "I mean, something other than that petty gambling case. They kicked your ass on that one."

Bocock laughed at his boss' obvious sarcasm. "We're not there yet, but we're on our way," he said. "You can tell the governor that his speech at church brought at least three new converts to Jesus."

"Bocock, I'm going to pretend you didn't say that," chuckled the veteran GBI boss.

####

The next morning, most of it went off just as Bocock had planned. A virtual army of armed GBI agents and state troopers barged into the courthouse just as it was opening for business. Carole Friedlander jumped on the phone to warn someone, but she hadn't gotten more than four words out of her mouth before Bocock himself pulled the phone out of her hand and returned it to its cradle.

"Sorry, talking's not allowed," he said with a smile.

Agents combed the building looking for the big prey – Boss Griffin and Popsi Colanise. Neither could be found. In fact, the only APD personnel present were Friedlander and the jailer, Curly Walton. Both were cuffed and taken away for questioning.

Bocock found what he was looking for in the records within a few minutes. The fact he was a cop and knew how cops organized things made it relatively easy. Not only did he know which patrolman had requisitioned for cuffs in the last week, he also had the serial numbers that had been imprinted on the "lost" pair.

The patrolman had obviously believed the deep waters of the Altamaha would protect his secret forever. He had been very wrong. It was a secret for less than a week.

As GBI agents carted away filing cabinets of records from the police department, Boss Griffin's office and the county property assessor's office, Bocock decided to take leave of the raid and head to the river.

Not only were three state divers already in the water, but a wrecker with a winch capable of pulling cars out of deep water was making its way down the steep trail toward the bank. Bocock pulled in behind it, and got out as soon as it was close to the curve where the Roadmaster had made its plunge.

One of the divers was emerging from the water, and Bocock noticed his billboard-guarding buddy, Trooper Oscar Sloan, on duty on the bank with a high-powered rifle.

"Hi Cal," said Sloan. "Hope I get one," he added, motioning toward the water and referring to the alligators. "They say they taste like chicken."

Bocock smiled and walked up to the diver, who was removing his mask and pulling off his heavy tank of oxygen.

"You missed one, agent," he said. "There are four cars in the water. There are three women in the other cars."

Bocock shook his head in amazement. "I thought I was trying to bust up a speed trap and now it looks like we're going to catch a serial killer."

Chapter Thirty-Eight

At the river, the divers were hard at work attaching cables to the deeply submerged cars so they could be winched to the surface. The first order of business had been to free the body of the woman who had been handcuffed to the Buick Roadmaster. The divers ended up taking the door handle off the car and bringing the woman's body out of the depths before beginning the process of raising the car. It was a time-consuming job, but it would have been inhumane to drag the car out of the river with the victim still bound to the passenger door.

Meanwhile, Cal had discovered the home address of Buck "Popsi" Colanise in the confiscated Astoria Police Department records. He decided it would be worth his time to go there to see if he could find and arrest the man who had shot and nearly killed Fancy. Meanwhile, Fancy was still in the hospital in Savannah, under a 24-hour guard courtesy of the Savannah Police Department.

Cal was accompanied by Trooper Wayne Pickens, who had been guarding the governor's billboards along with Sloan the day

Cal first drove into Astoria. Sloan, meanwhile, remained occupied on alligator guard duty at the river, protecting the team of GBI divers.

Cal and Pickens pulled up to a dirt and gravel driveway about four miles from town. There was a rusty metal mailbox there with a number that matched Colanise's address. The driveway – if indeed it was one -- led into the woods.

"Wayne, let's do our best to sneak up on him," said Bocock. "Let's go in on foot."

Sidearms drawn and at the ready, the two state officers walked up the trail. In the distance after about a quarter-mile walk, they saw a tin-roofed, tar paper shack. It wasn't much of a residence for the man they now knew was the acting chief of police for Astoria, succeeding the late Carl Griffin. A dark Plymouth was parked out front, and Cal immediately suspected it was the car he'd seen following him on more than one occasion. And a quick check of its tag indicated it was the very Hyde County-owned car that had gotten a parking ticket in Savannah not far from Fancy's apartment the night she'd been shot.

Cal nodded to Pickens and gave him a thumbs up when he confirmed the tag number from a note he had in his pocket. This was a final piece of corroborating evidence that Cal felt would definitely nail Colanise. They had been amazed that the Savannah PD had been able to advise them so quickly that a car from Astoria had been illegally parked near Fancy's home. That was top-notch police work, tediously going through stacks of paper, and Cal realized he owed a debt of gratitude to Detective Barlow, who had birddogged the case from its onset.

"Wayne, this guy is going to run," said Cal. "He won't turn and fight until he's cornered. "I want you to barge through the front door, and I'm going to cover the back." Bocock pointed to a second door around the corner that appeared to lead into a kitchen.

"I got it, Cal," said Pickens.

"I don't have to tell you this guy is dangerous," Cal whispered. "If he appears and he's armed or he goes for a weapon, don't be a hero."

"Cal, you don't have to tell me this stuff," Pickens deadpanned. "I knew once you got on the Bureau you'd turn into a pointy head and think you know so much more about fighting crime than your old trooper buddies."

"OK, you're right," Bocock chuckled. "I just want this to go down the right way."

"Give me a thumbs up when you're ready. I go in at the count of five," said the trooper.

Bocock placed himself right beside the back door and then slipped around the corner to give Pickens a thumbs up. There had been no signs of activity in the house, nor any noise, and anything even resembling a window was blocked by blinds, or in a couple of cases, tacked up plywood.

After about five seconds, Bocock heard Pickens announce, "We're state officers, and we're coming in! Drop any weapons and lay on the floor! Now!"

The door was unlocked, but the trooper, his weapon raised in protective mode, pushed it open with a loud crash and entered what appeared to be a totally dark living room area. All he could see was a pot-bellied stove and a couple of pieces of rough-looking furniture. He immediately heard a rustle in the next room.

"Don't move! Stay right where you are!"

Pickens quickly moved into the next room, which appeared to be a bedroom. A middle-aged, olive skinned woman was in bed, apparently naked. She screamed and pulled the covers up around her breasts.

A man grabbed something off a table and jumped right through a hastily opened window just as Pickens barged in. The man was now on foot, outside the house, not far from where Bocock was waiting.

"Ma'am, show me your hands, now!" demanded Pickens. "Heads up, Cal, suspect escaped through a window!"

Bocock saw Colanise jump out the bedroom window not 15 feet from where he was waiting outside the back door. "Stop! State officers!" challenged Bocock.

Colanise looked toward Bocock, snarled, and dashed toward the woods. He appeared to be barefooted and dressed only in a pair of briefs.

"Stop, or I'll shoot!" said Bocock, but Colanise continued to run.

"Pursuing suspect on foot!" he screamed towards Pickens and proceeded to do just that.

Colanise was at a disadvantage with no shoes on, and both men knew it. Bocock closed quickly and soon was close enough to consider tackling the fleeing suspect.

But suddenly, Colanise stopped and turned and Bocock realized for the first time he was holding a blade, probably six inches long. Cal backed off to a comfortable distance.

"Come and get me, motherfucker!" said Colanise. "I don't think you're man enough."

"Oh, I'm going to get you, all right," Bocock said calmly. "The question is, do you want to be healthy at the end of this?"

Colanise laughed, then charged directly at the young agent, preparing to slash him with the long knife.

Bocock raised his sidearm and shot Colanise in the right knee. The big man, obviously surprised, screamed and stumbled, but did not fall.

Bocock advanced, and using a Taekwondo technique he'd learned in Korea, knocked the knife from Colanise's right hand with a lightning quick kick.

Then he broke the big Greek's nose with a right hand lead. Colanise screamed in pain once again and went sprawling into the pine straw at his feet. Bocock was immediately on top of him and within seconds, Buck "Popsi" Colanise was cuffed and immobilized.

"That one was for Fancy," said Bocock of his roundhouse right. "You are under arrest. It's all over for you."

Colinese was bleeding from the knee and the nose, and for once he had nothing to say. He groaned, but then immediately began to loudly complain.

"Fucking fire ants!" he said. "Let me up!"

"In time, Colanise. In time."

The ants were all over him now, and Bocock did get him off the fire ant mound in a fairly reasonably amount of time. But he didn't do anything to brush off the ants that were still feasting on Boss' leader's quickly reddening body. Colanise proceeded to do a strange and almost comical dance as he tried with cuffed hands to knock the stinging, burning insects off his bare legs, feet, arms, chest and face. The way he was squirming, Bocock figured they'd also gotten into his shorts.

Sloan came up behind Bocock. "I see you need no help," he laughed.

"What'd you find in the house?" asked Cal.

"A naked woman, maybe his wife, maybe his mistress. It appears we caught old Popsi with his pants down," said Sloan.

Colanise cursed as the two state officers shared a laugh at his expense. "Mr. Colanise, come with us," said Cal. "You're on your way to state custody on a number of charges, including attempted first-degree murder, resisting arrest, assaulting a state officer, and whatever else I can think of on the way."

#####

With Popsi on ice, so to speak, Cal and Pickens made their way back to The Pit to see what the divers had found. The last of the four vehicles was being dragged from the water as the two law enforcement officers drove up in Cal's Chevy BelAir.

Herman Sneed himself greeted the pair. He had already heard about Colanise's arrest on the radio and smiled at Bocock despite the grim nature of the crime scene.

"We now have five victims," he told Bocock.

"Five? I'm no math major, but I just see four cars."

"There was a dead man in the trunk of the first car," said Sneed. "In fact, we've identified the couple. They were reported missing when the young woman's parents couldn't reach them on the phone and when they didn't go to work last Monday."

"The others are more of a mystery, though we've got some indications of their identities from the contents of their soggy purses, which contained no money, by the way," said Sneed. "Not only were these cops rapists and cold-blooded killers, they were also armed robbers."

"Cops?" said Bocock. "I've only implicated one so far, through the serial number on the handcuffs."

"We got two now," said Sneed. "Look what one of the agents found in that car over there," pointing to a mud-covered 1953 Chevy sedan.

"He handed Bocock a plastic evidence bag. It contained a police officer's name tag. It had most likely been ripped from his uniform shirt by his soon-to-be-drowned victim, who, like Fancy Fontaine, had managed to leave a telling clue to identify her assailant.

"Unbelievable," said Bocock. "I bet he worried about having left this near his victim when he realized it was lost."

"I'd say he thought he'd never be caught," said Sneed. "Just like his buddy, who was cavalier enough to leave his police-issued handcuffs on his victim."

Sneed proceeded to tell Bocock and Pickens that each of the three women had been found bound in their cars. One was horse-tied to her steering wheel. Trapped in their cars, they had drowned when the vehicles filled with water.

"What gets me is that you guys say kids swim here all the time," said Sneed. "Didn't they think anybody'd ever find any of them?"

Bocock told his boss he had never been so deep in a body of water in his life. "It was not really safe, it was so deep," he said. "These guys grew up here and I expect they didn't know anybody who'd ever been brave or stupid enough to find the bottom of this hole."

"Then there are the alligators," added Sneed.

"Don't I know that," said Bocock. "I'm glad the one that chased me wasn't waiting for me when I came up or when I went down. He would have had me for lunch."

The talk quickly turned to the uncaptured suspects, the uniformed officers of Astoria.

"We need to get these guys, and quick," said Bocock. "They have to know by now we're in the water and surely they are smart enough to know they've left evidence."

Sneed reminded Bocock he'd left a unit on the river bridge who had watched closely for any Astoria police activity along 55 since the divers had arrived. He'd seen none, said the veteran GBI boss.

"I think they've laid low ever since they got word of the raid," said Sneed. "I doubt they've laid as low as your friend Colaise, however."

Bocock laughed.

"We need to get to the trailer park. That's where all three of these guys live," he said.

"Oh yeah," said Sneed. "That's where they stood around hoping to watch you burn up a while back."

"But now they're the ones with the hot feet," said Cal. "It's a question of how much they think we know."

He pulled Sneed aside for a private chat, and the GBI's top man quickly agreed, if possible, to take the three families into protective custody if there was an opportunity. "These are the kind of guys who would not hesitate to take their family members hostage if they thought they could use them as bargaining chips," he said, and Bocock nodded.

"C'mon Wayne," Cal said to the waiting Pickens as he and Sneed moved toward waiting vehicles.

"Hey guys, how about me?" called out Sloan. "The divers are done and I didn't even get to shoot this baby." The trooper patted his high-powered rifle. The rogue alligator that had made a run at Bocock had not shown himself again.

Sneed laughed and motioned for Sloan to join the group. "Let's go get these guys," he said.

Chapter Thirty-Nine

Herman Sneed was already thinking strategically by the time he and Bocock had pulled up the river road from The Pit to U.S. 55. He got on the radio to the unmarked unit he had stationed on the bridge as well as to Sloan in the patrol car behind him. He instructed both men to keep watch on the bridge.

"Be ready to act quickly," he said.

Bocock and Sneed, with Pickens in the back seat, drove back up 55 toward the trailer park and saw no squad cars parked at any of the officers' three trailers. "We need to work fast," Sneed said. "Each of us needs to knock on a door, see who's there, and if it's just family, as I suspect, let's gather them someplace safe – I'd suggest Cal's trailer."

The kids were all in school, and only two of the three wives were at home. Pickens was assigned to brief Charlotte Smith and Beverly Wiggins on the situation and keep them safe for the time being in Bocock's home. Not knowing the whereabouts of Dorothy Crane, there was nothing the officers could do to protect her.

In quick order, Pickens once again, a bit sadly, found himself pulling guard duty. Sneed and Bocock planned to go into town to see if the three officers were possibly at the courthouse. There had been no immediate reason to hold Dispatcher Carole Friedlander or the jailer, Curly Walton, so the GBI head assumed the office was back open for business and was a possible haven for the missing cops.

Sneed knew Pickens had a lot of explaining to do, as clearly, both wives were totally in the dark. The most telling comment had come from Charlotte Smith.

"He's been acting weird, but he's always weird," she said of her husband, Colin. "He packed some stuff this morning and put it in his car, and I asked him what he was doing. All he said was, 'Police Business.' It's always Police Business and to tell you the truth, I get damn sick of it."

Sneed and Bocock took their leave from Pickens and the two women, and Sneed instructed Cal to head toward town, with the GBI director riding shotgun. Two blocks from the courthouse and APD headquarters, they saw an Astoria patrol car coming in the other direction. Two cops were in the car – an unusual sight for Astoria.

"Those are the two we want!" said Bocock, who had gotten a quick look at the officers' scowling faces. He did a quick U-turn and began a pursuit, his BelAir's portable siren blaring and blue light blazing.

The fleeing Astoria cops hit the gas, and their powerful eight-cylinder engine jumped into passing gear. Ironically, the cops ran the most famous red light in Georgia on their way out of town.

Sneed got on the radio immediately, using a channel he knew the city cops could not access. "All units, this is Sneed. Set up a roadblock immediately on the 55 bridge. Subjects are headed your way in a marked APD unit. Over."

He got two confirmations, the unit already on the bridge, and another GBI unit that had been in town working on the raid.

"Two cars don't give us a great roadblock, but it will have to be enough," he said to Bocock.

Cal had floored the BelAir, which was no slouch itself when it came to high-speed pursuit. One of the officers leaned out the window, and Bocock quickly warned his boss.

"Incoming fire!" he said. The shot missed.

Then he noticed even the driver was turning to aim out the window. "Both of them are firing at us!" he told Sneed.

The GBI head rolled his window down and aimed his sidearm at the fleeing patrol car. He squeezed off a shot, and then a second, aiming for the squad car's tires.

One of the Astoria cops' rounds found its target, and Cal's Bel Air once again had a pierced windshield, though this one didn't do as much damage as the ambush blast.

"You OK, boss?" asked Bocock. Sneed answered by firing another shot. "I think I got a rear tire!" Sneed exclaimed.

By this time, the bridge was looming in the distance. Bocock was already starting to slow because he saw the two state units had the far end of the two-lane bridge completely blocked.

But the Astoria car continued to approach the bridge at full speed.

"He's so busy shooting at us, I don't think he sees the roadblock," shouted Bocock.

Sneed was quickly on the radio. "Units alert! Suspects appear likely to ram the roadblock. Take cover!"

At the last possible moment, Officer Colin Smith saw what was in his path. There was no way he could stop, so he aimed the big Ford at the small gap between one of the cars and right-side guard rail of the 55 bridge.

He screamed, and for the first time, a moment before impact, passenger Wesley Crane also became aware of the danger.

The impact was violent, sounding like an explosion. The squad car was going about 85 miles an hour when it hit the unmarked GBI unit blocking the right lane and shoulder of U.S. 55.

The officers' car was launched into the air by the violent crash. Smith's last second steering had aimed it right, and that was exactly where it went. It went airborne, and smacked the guard rail. The metal rail was ripped away by the impact. With nothing else to stop it, the Astoria patrol car plunged toward the Altamaha River.

Smith, thrown forward by the tremendous impact, hit the steering wheel hard and was knocked senseless. Crane was thrown into the metal dashboard and his head crashed through the windshield.

As Bocock and Sneed stopped on the other end of the bridge, they heard the squad car hit the water below. Cal executed another quick U-turn and hit the gravel and dirt river road with as much speed as he dared.

Smith regained consciousness to discover the car was sinking fast into the murky river. He was groggy and it seemed every part of his body hurt. He looked over at Crane, and screamed when he realized his partner had been decapitated.

Finally, the squad car hit the sandy bottom of the Altamaha with a thud. Water had been rushing into the car since impact, and there was very little air left. Smith struggled against the door, which was so badly damaged in the crash that it would not budge.

Then he saw ghostly figures outside the car. He screamed in mortal terror. It was the black couple! They were going to kill him! A partially decomposed man leered at him and it stuck its horrible skeleton hand through the broken windshield, reaching for him. The woman was at his car door, scratching it, trying to get inside.

Smith was mortified. With his next scream, he took a big gulp of water that promptly caused him to empty his lungs of all his remaining air. Now he was struggling to escape the car and the two dark figures, and with no air, he had no chance. Colin Smith drowned behind the wheel of his squad car, beside his headless colleague, Wesley Crane.

By the time Bocock reached The Pit, there was nothing visible but air bubbles. For the second time in two days, he stripped to his skivvies and prepared to dive into the chilly waters.

"Chief, do me a favor and watch for that gator," he said. Sneed almost told him not to bother getting into the water, but instead just nodded. If I was his age and as full of piss and vinegar as he is, I'd try to save them myself, he thought.

Cal gathered himself and once again dived into the dark depths of The Pit. Once again, he was amazed by its depth – it seemed even deeper today than it had the day he'd found the Roadmaster, if that was even possible.

He found the squad car and quickly realized there was no movement within and the battered car was already filled with water. Quickly running out of breath, he swam for the surface.

Finally, his head popped out the water and he gasped for air. He turned toward Sneed and shook his head. The GBI chief had already called for the divers and the wrecker with its winch to return to The Pit.

He had also confirmed that neither of the state officers on the bridge had been hurt in the collision. They were already in the throes of investigating a double-fatal crash.

####

Cal Bocock had hurt a lot inside when he realized from the serial numbers of the handcuffs found on Jenny Faye Washington that her killer was the father of the little girl who had befriended him on his first day in Astoria. Jim Bob Crane's father was the second rapist and murderer, implicated by the discovery of his own nametag in the car of his victim.

Cal realized he would probably never know who raped and killed the other two women, and he couldn't help but wonder if Tony Wiggins was somehow slipping from his grasp. How could two of these cops be dirty and one clean? After all, he thought, they are all cut from the same murderous mold.

####

The next few hours passed in a blur. The officers' three kids were brought home from school, and Cal himself delivered the terrible news to Sassy and Jim Bob. It turned out that Dorothy Crane had been grocery shopping, and she saw the crash's aftermath through tied-up traffic on 55 as she returned. That required another tough briefing, this one handled by Sneed.

Meanwhile, Sneed surprised Bocock by giving him the assignment of informing Gov. Buford Dunlap of the day's developments by phone. He was put through to the governor within moments.

"Son, I can't tell you how proud I am of you and what a service you have done for the state of Georgia," he said. "You've wiped two killer cops off our roadways, and you pulled a third killer out of his filthy bed and brought him to justice. That is service, son, fucking service!"

Bocock acknowledged the praise, knowing even as he spoke what the governor's next comment would be.

"Now how about that murderous bastard who put all these guys up to this?" asked Dunlap. "What about Griffin himself?"

Bocock explained that they had found nothing to date that linked Griffin to any of the crimes. His records from his courthouse office were as clean as the dining room table in the Governor's Mansion. Cal said it was possible he didn't even know that his renegade cops were rapists and murderers.

"Maybe he doesn't know," mused the governor. "He does have a streak of dumb ass. I seen that myself.

"I suspect it's time for you and Herman to drag him in for questioning," said the governor. "That is, if Herman thinks that's the proper move at this time."

Dunlap always went out of the way to avoid any suggestion that he directed the activities of his law enforcement agencies. Wasn't that the way of all chief executives, controlling, yet appearing to only be supervising and offering suggestions?

"There's one thing I'd almost bet the Gold Dome itself on," said Dunlap. "When you guys go get him – if you do, of course, if that's the proper next step in this here investigation – he's gonna be so drunk he'll have to hang on to the grass to keep from falling off the earth."

Dunlap gave that a second to sink in.

"And in that state, he might tell you something. You never know."

Bocock reported the governor's comments to Sneed, who had finished his talk with Mrs. Crane.

"I hate to say it, but Buford's right," said Sneed. "We got only two big loose ends left, Wiggins, and the biggest of them all, Boss Griffin."

"We have lots of small loose ends," Bocock pointed out. "Don't forget the cathouses and the clip joints."

Sneed nodded. "Don't worry, son," he said, sounding almost like the governor. "I'm working on a plan to nip all that in the bud."

"Boss," quipped Bocock. "Have you been watching Andy Griffith?"

"Always," said Sneed. "It's just the best show on television."

"If only law enforcement was that easy," said Bocock.

"Astoria is no Mayberry," said Sneed. "You knew that from day one. And by the way, quit calling me Boss. Boss is the guy in town pulling all the strings."

SPEED TRAP

Chapter Forty

After the action-packed developments at the courthouse, in the woods near Popsi's house and at the river, the ensuing days seemed slow in comparison. The Powers That Be decided they would need to go back before a judge before Boss Griffin could be officially questioned. And the feds should be involved since it appeared the best case to be made against him would be for tax evasion.

So without immediate urgency, the wheels of justice slowed to a relative snail's pace. But finally, a subpoena was drawn up and served on Griffin. CeCe answered the door the day it was served, and her husband was angry that she had called him to the door.

Marvin Justus wisely counseled Boss that he could not ignore a federal subpoena, so after some back and forth with federal prosecutors he made arrangements for the two of them to appear in Savannah at the federal courthouse in a week's time.

Meanwhile, Bocock was briefed on Herman Sneed's plan to attack the cathouses and clip joints, which had continued operations even without the clandestine protection from the Astoria Police Department. Cal had not been able to go in undercover at any of the illicit establishments because his face was too quickly known to everyone in town. But GBI agents who were now assisting in the investigation weren't known to anyone in Astoria, and Sneed had them disguised as truck drivers, traveling salesmen and even a chicken farmer. They were all assigned cars with out-of-state plates, which, in the minds of the Astoria entrepreneurs, made them free game.

Two GBI agents successfully stung Flo Riley and her new No. 1 girl on the very same day. Riley cursed and made quite a scene, and Cal Bocock arrived in time to see part of it.

"You are the bastard that did all this!" she screamed when she saw him arrive. "I knew your word was shit when Fancy Fontaine told me."

Bocock calmly approached the red-headed madam, who was dressed in a lacy, black negligee.

"Any protection you might have had went out the window when you gave up Fancy to Boss Griffin," Bocock said softly so only Riley could hear. "You nearly got her killed. You deserve jail just for that."

Flo's house of ill repute, office and cabins, was shuttered, never to open again. A similar scene played out at Dolly's, the cathouse that catered to African American customers.

Melvin Guthrie faced a different kind of legal peril when he made the mistake of scheming a state agent in a spirited round of Razzle Dazzle. This agent, a slow-talking country boy from McCaysville, Georgia, had convinced Mel he was a chicken farmer from North Carolina on his way to Florida for a once in a lifetime vacation.

Guthrie went red with rage when the officer showed his badge and placed the life-long con man under arrest seconds after being informed that he owed the establishment $1,473.

"I beat you sumbitches once in court, and I will beat you again," he said.

"You'll be testifying against yourself this time," said the agent, displaying the primitive, but effective taping device hidden in his bulky overalls. Guthrie cursed again, but did not resist when the agent handcuffed him.

A similar fate was suffered by the operators of Astoria's other clip joints. It took some time, but one by one they were taken down thanks to clever undercover work by Cal's GBI brethren.

Bocock himself took a state search warrant to the Astoria Hotel to look for the device that flipped Astoria's lone traffic signal from green directly to red. He had it on good authority that the city of Astoria regularly booked room number 16, which was right down the hall from the room he was given the night of the fire. Hotel owner-operator Biff Carlyle basically confirmed the city regularly paid the bill for the room, but denied any knowledge of what went on inside.

He personally let Cal into the room and stood by while the young agent searched every nook and cranny. Bocock observed that the sight lines through the windows were absolutely perfect for such an operation. He saw places where wires could have been run, but there was no device nor any other evidence that Room 16 was anything but a haven for a weary traveler eager to escape the road.

Cal suspected that the red light operation had been shut down almost immediately upon his arrival in Astoria and had never been used again.

Meanwhile, the case against Buck "Popsi" Colanise improved considerably once authorities got a hit on the big Greek's fingerprints. It turned out that Popsi was really a man named Petra Papantonio. Papantonio was a known mobster in Jersey City who had faced a score of charges when he mysteriously disappeared in 1955.

New Jersey authorities had assumed Papantonio was murdered by a rival mob. Instead, he had reinvented himself, moved South and began working shrimp boats on the Georgia coast until he happened into the employ of Boss Griffin. Now it appeared that with any luck at all, the man Astoria had known as Popsi Colanise would be behind bars for the rest of his life.

Finally the day arrived for Boss Griffin to appear before federal and state authorities. He and Marvin Justus arrived at the federal courthouse in Savannah 15 minutes late. As usual, Justus was dressed to the nines, and Griffin was in his standard, rumpled faded black suit, his white shirt brown with age and tobacco stains, his black tie poorly tied. His breath smelled of alcohol despite Justus' futile attempts to keep him sober.

Bocock sat at a big round wooden table with a host of state and federal representatives, including Richard Kilgallon, the state's attorney who had failed to convict Melvin Guthrie; Herman Sneed, Silvester Conrad, an attorney for the Internal Revenue Service; and Peter Presley, the agent in charge of the Savannah FBI office.

In a corner of the room sat a court reporter who would take down every word that was spoken.

Conrad opened the meeting, and recognized Sneed, who wanted to question Griffin about Cal's investigation.

"Mr. Griffin, as you well know, Astoria has justifiably earned a reputation as the home base of a corrupt criminal enterprise. It is well known that you run the entire county. How could these activities take place in Hyde County without your knowledge or consent?"

Griffin looked at Justus, who nodded, prompting Griffin to launch into his prepared spiel.

"These officers were notorious for doing what they wanted, when they wanted," he said. "All I have ever done is unofficially administer the local government to bring as much prosperity as possible to the good citizens of Hyde County."

"How do you define prosperity?" asked Sneed.

"We instructed the police to aggressively and fairly enforce traffic laws to maximize our local revenues," he said. "That, along with wise fiscal management, allowed us to have excellent schools, much better than those of the counties surrounding us. Our businesses prospered because we were wise enough to serve the tourists who drive through on 55 and 42."

"Serve them?" Sneed interrupted. "They were endlessly harassed by overzealous law enforcement officers, sometimes imprisoned, sometimes beaten, unfairly scammed for their money, and sometimes, we have learned of late, they were raped and murdered and thrown into the Altamaha River."

Boss Griffin began to reply, but Justus silenced him with a stern look.

"My client has no knowledge of any illegal activity by any police officers in Astoria, living or deceased," said Justus. "He was as shocked as anyone when he learned about the cars and bodies found in the river."

"What about the activities of Petra Papantonio, alias Buck "Popsi" Colanise? We have it on good authority that this Colanise answered only to Mr. Griffin, doing his bidding. This bidding included the attempted murder of one Fancy Fontaine, a state informant. He is also suspected of a number of other crimes in Astoria that we won't detail now."

Justus let Boss handle that one.

"Colanise was a freelancer," said Griffin. "He ran the police force after the death of my cousin. Anything he might have done was without my knowledge."

"Why was a felon with no police training and no professional certification picked to run your city police department?" Bocock asked.

"I had no knowledge he lacked any qualifications," said Griffin.

The interrogation continued for hours, with neither Griffin nor Justus yielding an inch. Bocock felt at times that he had accomplished nothing in his quest to end Griffin's rule.

But then Silvester Conrad of the IRS took over the role of questioner.

"Mr. Griffin, our investigation has concluded that in the last 26 or so years, you have efficiently and very quietly emerged as one of the largest landowners in the state of Georgia. You have vast tracts of forest land worth millions. You own land that likely is worth millions in mineral rights. You own long stretches of coastline that are likely to be developed in the years to come, which could earn additional millions of dollars.

"Many of these holdings were bought by dummy corporations that we have been able to trace either to you or your family members, including Mr. Justus here. Property records appear to indicate that most, if not all of these transactions were conducted in cash.

"Mr. Griffin, how could it be that we find no traces of any of these transactions on your federal income tax returns, going all the way back to before World War II?"

For the first time, Griffin appeared uncomfortable. He reached to loosen his tie. He took a long drink of water from the glass that had been placed for him on the table. Then he looked to Justus for help.

"Mr. Conrad, my client invokes his Fifth Amendment rights against self-incrimination," said Justus.

Conrad proceeded to ask a series of similar, but more probing specific questions about the Griffin property portfolio.

Each and every time, Justus spoke the same sentence in response.

Sneed turned toward Bocock, and with his face concealed from the two Astorians, he winked at his special agent in charge.

It was a matter of time, but Sneed knew in his heart the feds would get Boss Griffin. He was the south Georgia version of Al

Capone, the Chicago mobster who never bothered to pay his taxes.

Chapter Forty-One

Cal Bocock was doing his best to finish up his Astoria investigation. There was little he could do to assist the feds who were combing the tax and property records in their dogged pursuit of Boss Griffin. He was actually thinking more about his upcoming wedding to Fancy Fontaine than the case, which was rapidly winding down.

But then the phone rang. GBI headquarters in Atlanta had a lead for him to follow up. They had gotten a call from a young woman in Tampa, Florida, who said she had been raped near a little south Georgia town and it must have been Astoria.

Cal had traced such leads before, but virtually all of them had been related to the clip joints or beatings or imprisonment for failure to pay a speeding ticket on demand. A rape allegation was a first and definitely heightened his interest.

It took several calls to get the woman on the line, but that evening, he succeeded. She identified herself as Carly Sue Jennings, and said she was a restaurant cook in Tampa.

"Agent Bocock, it took a lot of courage for me to leave my abusive husband up in Albany," she told Cal. "But then the same thing happened to me, a rape at the hands of a brutal cop up there in Georgia. I was going to let it go, like I always had with my husband.

"But then I realized that to start a new life is to say no to such things," she said, her voice strong with conviction. "I left my husband, pregnant with a child, because I wasn't going to take it anymore.

"And I'm not going to accept the fact that this police officer raped me and just sent me on my way," she said.

Carly Sue said she had come to her decision slowly after seeing a UPI story in the newspaper on the death of the two Astoria cops. The story had included their pictures, and details about the bodies in the river.

"I realized two things very quickly," she said. "Neither of those cops was the one who raped me. I never forget a face and I'll certainly never forget his. The second thing was that I was just lucky I wasn't in the river and I'd better step forward in case this cop is still out there before some other innocent woman ends up dead."

Bocock was excited. It had never made sense to him that Tony Wiggins had avoided any repercussions from his longtime involvement in Boss Griffin's criminal scheme. With no reason to charge him, Cal and Herman Sneed had concluded they could not remove him from duty. Therefore, he currently remained on the force – the only active patrolman left in Astoria.

Cal told the woman there was indeed a possible suspect and he greatly appreciated her willingness to come forward. He advised her to visit the Tampa Police Department within the next few hours. He would telecopy pictures of several men to the department and if she saw the man who had raped her among the photographs, please let him know immediately.

Cal had a number of pictures from the Astoria police files. He made contact with a detective in Tampa, and then proceeded to telecopy photos of Wiggins, Carl Griffin, Popsi Colanise and Curly Walton to Florida. He had created what was in effect a long-distance photo lineup, and a proper ID would ensure that Jennings wasn't just another victim of Crane or Smith who had been lucky enough to escape with her life.

Several hours later, Jennings called Cal from the Tampa police headquarters. She had picked Wiggins without hesitation, a fact confirmed by a Tampa detective. Cal had his case. And it was yet another family tragedy, this one hitting Beverly Wiggins and her son, Zeke, who had slowly come to accept that Wiggins had not been a party to the heinous activities along the Astoria roadsides.

Cal went to the Wiggins family trailer himself to make the arrest. The cop, who offered no resistance, didn't seem surprised.

Frankly, his wife didn't either. But Zeke was clearly devastated. He had so wanted to believe his father was better than the others.

Boss Griffin had slipped deeper and deeper into a self-imposed funk in the days and weeks after giving his deposition to state and federal agents in Savannah. He was angry at his family, he was angry at his associates, he was angry at the world.

He blamed Marvin Justus for not solving his tax problems. He blamed CeCe for not being supportive of his plight. He had lost all patience with Patsy, considering her a partying slut. His daily drunken stupor and pill-induced paranoia had driven CeCe to the edge.

Without discussing it with anyone, and why should she because she had to live with the man? (Patsy and Marvin could, after all, escape to their own home) she decided to throw him out of the house. CeCe waited until a Monday morning when Griffin was sober – badly hung over, but at least sober – to break the news.

"Earl, it has become impossible to live with you," she said. "You are making my life a living hell. I am honestly sorry you've gotten yourself in trouble, but it sure as hell isn't my fault. I didn't ask you to do anything other than provide me a home and be a husband for me and a father to Patsy.

"I want you gone. Pack a bag and go."

Griffin got this news in his bathrobe while drinking his first cup of coffee – spiced with a shot of bourbon. And once again, he exploded.

"You are a sorry bitch and you never loved me," he said. "I worked my ass off to give you all you wanted. I lied and cheated and yes, stole, to make your damn schools the best they could be.

"You have been a positively shitty wife and a horrendous mother," he said. "Why do you think Patsy is the whoring slut that she is? She takes after her mama."

CeCe slapped Earl in the face, hard. The old man hadn't been hit since Buford Dunlap punched him in the governor's office many months ago.

"Fuck yes, I'm out of here. I ought to fucking kill you, but you ain't worth the trouble."

"You don't have the courage to kill me," said CeCe. "All your puppets who do all your dirty work are either dead or in prison. Call me all the filthy names you want. But you are, without any doubt, a stinking, worthless, unfaithful ... *homosexual*!"

It was the first time Griffin's secret sin had been brought out into the open. He was left speechless by his wife's outburst.

Griffin stormed out of the kitchen, and in the living room he stopped to totally trash a table of glass figurines CeCe especially treasured, collected with care during the couple's infrequent

373

international travels. She did not even come into the room to see what he had broken. She had known he would find some form of senseless revenge.

Griffin proceeded to pack a bag, but it was not the typical suitcase of clothing. He cleaned out his liquor cabinet, and his medicine cabinet. He did take a few items of clothing, but he had decided he wouldn't need much.

So at midday that Monday, Boss Griffin, with no other place to go that immediately came to mind, found himself in Room 16 of the Astoria Hotel. Innkeeper Biff Carlyle had been amazed to see Griffin, who, to his knowledge, had never sat foot in the hotel before, unless it was some civic affair in its undersized ballroom. He gave him Room 16 because he knew, at least indirectly, who paid the bill each and every week.

Griffin looked out the windows and wept as he surveyed his former kingdom. He gazed up and down the streets, watching the noon day activities. Some of the locals were on their way to lunch and a few travelers were making their way – without incident – through the red light that had been an excellent profit center for his longstanding enterprise.

He realized he had not brought a glass, and none were in Room 16, so for the first time in his life, he drank directly from the fifth of bourbon. He had always considered such behavior boorish and unbecoming a cultured man of the South. But now it didn't matter.

Boss took several pills, not even noting what kind they were. He mused about the past. He thought about his father and how he would be so ashamed that the family legacy had come to this. All these years of Griffin family rule, ended by scandal and ruin. Ended by the incompetence of police officers who could not accept the good things they had going for them. Cash cuts from every ticket! Free booze at the local bar! Hell, free lays at the cathouse! None of that was enough for them. They resorted to raping and killing innocent women they had pulled over to ticket. It was true, he thought. Absolute power corrupts, absolutely.

It was nothing but disgusting, the misbehavior that had occurred because of the failures of those under him. And it weighed on Griffin's conscious. Yes, he had ordered people killed, but those were the people who deserved it: the idiot Sullivan who started all this trouble by blabbing about the traffic light. Then there was his totally incompetent cousin Carl who mismanaged the police department, including his inexcusable hiring of old high school buddy Sullivan. There were others, several actually, but these seemed the most important, because they had directly led to this. This emptiness. This despair. This uncontrollable sense of inexcusable failure.

Even his most trusted confident, Popsi Colanise, had turned out to be unbelievably incompetent. How could he have not finished off the whore in Savannah? How could he leave clues all over the place, even a parking ticket two blocks from the crime scene? And how could he have been at home in bed fucking some slut when he needed to be in charge, saving the day from fucking Bocock and that despicable Dunlap, that two-bit tinhorn up in Atlanta?

Everyone has failed me, he thought. All of them. I couldn't count on a single one of 'em, not even my wife. She kicks me out of my own fucking house.

Griffin felt pain building in his chest. Stabbing pain, like a knife. He had been drinking and popping pills for hours. Midday had turned into dusk, then darkness.

He threw water on his face. He took another long slug from the bottle, but it was empty. He slung it against the bathroom mirror, and both shattered.

He pulled a snub-nosed revolver from his bag. He put it in his mouth. Pain welled in his chest; Boss Griffin was nearly certain he was having a heart attack. This needs to end, now. Nobody on earth could make it through such pain, such utter failure.

He pulled the trigger.

####

Carole Friedlander called Cal Bocock with the news and he rushed to the Astoria Hotel. He used the phone in Room 16 to advise Herman Sneed, who quickly called Buford Dunlap.

Boss Griffin was gone. An era had passed in Georgia.

It had been just a matter of time as the new decade slowly began to bring change to Georgia. Dunlap moved into retirement, replaced by another kind of populist with even bigger ambitions. Change was even more dramatic in Astoria. For the first time in generations, there were free elections that weren't controlled by one man. New leaders meant a new beginning, an end of the old ways, and finally, the death of the culture of corruption.

Along the coast, a brand new superhighway, Interstate 95, was being completed. No longer would thousands of Florida-bound or northbound tourists ply U.S. 55 or State Route 42. The tourist trade dried up as quickly as a puddle in the south Georgia summer sun. Astoria soon became a backwater afterthought.

####

With Boss Griffin out of the way and a new governor in Atlanta, and eventually a new attorney general in Washington, interest in pursuing the complicated tax case waned. As a native Georgian would say, there was no dog in the fight. So the Griffin family managed to hang on to its fortune. But no longer were they in power.

Marvin Justus, who might have had aspirations of following his father in law to the throne, was warned in private by both state and federal authorities – avoid politics or face the consequences.

As for Cal Bocock, he was finally given leave of Astoria. There was an old fashioned church wedding in Bocock's hometown of Dahlonega. Herman Sneed was his best man. Fancy was a beautiful bride.

The maid of honor was pretty young for the role, but she played it perfectly. It was Sassy Smith. There were two similarly young groomsmen, Jim Bob Crane and Zeke Wiggins.

Missing the wedding, but showing up in time for the reception, was an honored and unexpected guest. It was private citizen Buford Dunlap.

Dunlap had not lost his knack for stealing the show. He made a grand entrance just as Cal's father was about to toast the young couple. The elder Bocock wisely yielded to the former governor.

"I have rushed here from Atlanta, and I would have been here sooner if not for the godforsaken traffic," he said, causing the room to erupt in laughter. "I have not had the pleasure until today of meeting Mrs. Bocock, and what a pleasure it was.

"Cal, you know how to pick 'em, son. This woman is truly magnificent. I wish I was a lot younger so I could try to steal her away from you. Just kidding!

"Now for Mr. Bocock. This young man is a patriot, a warrior, a man's man, an All-American boy. I cannot even begin to describe what he has meant to me and what a tremendous asset he has been, and will be, to the state of Georgia and these United States.

"A salute, to Cal and Fancy Bocock! Toast!

"By the way, Cal, you got something a little stronger than this fruity punch? It's been a long drive from Atlanta, you know."

The entourage danced and partied their way into the wee hours. The Bococks' new life would be in Savannah, with Fancy running her own beauty shop, and Bocock settling in as the new special agent in charge of the GBI's Savannah office.

He had new fish to fry, new cases to tackle, a new life to live, a beautiful woman to love. Astoria was in his rearview mirror, and soon would be forgotten by just about everyone, except those changed forever by what had happened there.

Made in the USA
Lexington, KY
09 July 2017